MW01109537

PICTURE OF GUILT

Mary Roberts

PRAISE FOR PICTURE OF GUILT

Winner—Best Single Title Award
Orange Rose Contest!

Winner—Favorite Mystery
Sime~Gen Reviewers Choice Award!

Winner—Favorite Mystery Author
Sime~Gen Reviewers Choice Award!

Finalist—Best Romantic Suspense
Golden Quill Awards 2002!

"5 Roses!...This book is truly a winner...Ms. Haddad is a wonderful writer who will rank with authors such as Kay Hooper and Kathy Reichs...If you love a good whodunit that will keep you mesmerized from first page to last, I suggest you grab this one fast."

—Deborah Baker
Escape to Romance Reviews

"5 Stars!...How can a woman fall in love with a suspected murderer? Read *Picture of Guilt* to find out how."

—Linda Nelson
Sime~Gen Reviews

"4½ Daggers!...An engrossing romantic suspenseful four-star mystery...*Picture Of Guilt* combines a double homicide, jealousy, vulnerability, arrogance, protectiveness, weakness, greed, and unspeakable evil. Through the whole tale are two threads: manipulation and unquenchable desire. Ms. Haddad reveals manipulation in its most inhibitive, controlling and destructive ways and, using that same sleight of phrase, she turns lust into a beautiful coming together of a man and a woman who can't stay apart. This is one of those suspenseful tales that has you trying to talk to the characters, 'Why can't you see that?!' 'Forget that; investigate this!'"

—Evelyn Gale
All About Murder Reviews

"4 Stars! Excellent…Helen Haddad leaves a trail of love as well as leaving readers guessing the killer's identity up to last few pages."

—*Romantic Times Magazine*

"4&1/2 Stars! Though more of a police procedural then a romantic suspense novel, fans of both sub-genres will fully enjoy this strong tale."

—*Affaire de Couer*

"5 Stars! Helen Haddad has set her star high with *Picture of Guilt*, her first book."

—Cathy Gladstone
Sime~Gen Reviews

"Ms. Haddad's first novel is an excellently written and plotted romantic-suspense. Her main characters, Maureen and Brody, come alive under her skilled touch. Each supporting character is fully developed and highly enjoyable, as is the balance of action and narrative during the course of the book. If you're in the mood for a fast-paced action story and enjoy riveting and spontaneous combustion between the leads, *Picture of Guilt* is for you."

—Denise Clark
Road to Romance Reviews

PICTURE OF GUILT

BY

HELEN HADDAD

AMBER QUILL PRESS, LLC
http://www.amberquill.com

PICTURE OF GUILT
AN AMBER QUILL PRESS BOOK

This book is a work of fiction. All names, characters,
locations, and incidents are products of the author's imagination,
or have been used fictitiously. Any resemblance to actual persons
living or dead, locales, or events is entirely coincidental.

Amber Quill Press, LLC
P.O. Box 50251
Bellevue, Washington 98015

Rating: PG

Layout and Formatting provided by: ElementalAlchemy.com

PUBLISHED IN THE UNITED STATES OF AMERICA

*This is for Henry
and all the rest of the True Believers
and Gentle Persuaders.
You know who you are.*

The spirit that I have seen may be the devil, and the devil hath the power to assume a pleasing shape.

—*William Shakespeare*

PROLOGUE

I must look like somethin' the cat dragged in. I haven't been able to close my eyes since it happened, and that was like, twenty-four hours ago. So don't sweat it. I know I'm a mess.

Now you? You look great. And at this time of night, too. How do you do it? Even on my best days, and believe me this isn't one of them, along about this time I get a little frayed around the edges.

But havin' great hair helps, doesn't it? Bet you hear that all the time. Jeannie is…was…a blonde, too.

Jeez. Jeannie.

No, I'm okay. Just gimme a minute.

Let's see. Where were we? Oh, yeah. Hair. Guys really get off on hair, don't they? Mine's what they call a "Cinnamon Red." Now, I'm not sayin' I don't give it a little help now and then, but hey, I read somewhere most blondes come outta a bottle. Not you though. Yours looks real natural. But I'd lose those specs if I were you.

Listen, if it's okay with you, I'm just gonna walk around while we talk. I dunno what's the matter with me. I just gotta keep movin'. Gotta work out the kinks.

Yeah, kinks. Being stuck in that closet so long is what did it. All cramped up, too scared to breathe. If it hadn't been for that little crack between the door and the jamb, I probably wouldda suffocated.

You know, I didn't wanna watch, but it was like I couldn't help myself. Like when you're a kid and you cover your eyes with your hands so you won't see somethin' gross? But you always leave that one

1

little space between your fingers so you can peek out? And believe me, it was gross. Everywhere he stuck the knife, the blood just sorta...bubbled outta her. Lemme tell you, you never saw nothin' like it on TV. I mean, all that blood, just bubblin' outta a person.

But if you ask me, I think it was the neck that finished her. 'Cause she didn't make any more noise after that. Just sorta hung there in his arms, while he kept whackin' away with the knife. The only thing I heard was the sound of it goin' in, like he was slicin' open a melon or somethin'. Like, you know, pop, and then the blood, just bubblin'...

Jeez, I feel like I'm gonna be sick. And I'm bouncin' around this room like a pinball. I could sure use a cigarette or some coffee. Just somethin' to steady me, you know, till I get past it.

But you're a good listener. I really appreciate that. Last night, that Chief Marsh and Lieutenant Stanton? It was just one question after another. Non-stop. They never gave me a chance to get my thoughts together and make any sense of it.

And they didn't fool me. Not for a minute. I knew what they were thinkin'. That I shouldda done somethin' more. Shouldda helped Jeannie. But there was so much blood and I was so scared. When he broke into the apartment, it was Jeannie he was after. Not me. He'd forgotten all about me. Forgotten there were two of us at the Crocodile Grill.

Don'cha see? That's why I was able to hide. But if I tried to help, if I'd come outta the closet, he would have killed me too, wouldn't he? It wouldda been my blood all over the place. My blood bubblin' out...

Take a look at me, will you? I'm five-four, maybe a hundred pounds soakin' wet. What chance would I have against him and his knife? Lemme me tell you, I stayed in that closet a long time, even after he'd left. My legs were like paralyzed, like I was in a coma or somethin'.

It was the smell finally brought me out of it. Like a sewer, that's how it smelled. Like a rusty old sewer after it rains. Back in L. A., it doesn't rain much. Not like here. But when it does, like in February, it really comes down, and then the sewers back up, and you can...

Jeez, there I go again. Rattlin' on about somethin' that has nothin' to do with what we're talkin' about. It's just nerves, you know. Just nerves.

Hey, lookit here! They found us some java. I knew there hadda be coffee around here somewhere. Where there's cops, there's coffee. That's a no-brainer. Did Stanton tell you I'm a waitress? Waitresses and cops live on this stuff. I take mine straight. Black, without nothin' in it to muddy it up.

Mind you, it wasn't coffee Jeannie and I were drinkin' last night at the Crocodile Grill. Not that we were loaded or anythin'. I wouldn't want you to think that. We weren't there long enough to get really tanked. The minute Jeannie saw that dude watchin' her we were outta there.

Don't ask me why. She'd get like that sometimes. Just clam up and then there was no gettin' anythin' outta her. We've been roomies for a couple a months, but never got, you know, really close. In fact, last night was the first time we went anywhere together.

First and last time, huh?

But I gotta tell you, if it was me that guy was givin' the eye, we wouldda stayed. I mean, you shouldda seen him. He was hot. Just the kind you're hopin' to meet when you go to a place like the Grill.

Who knows? Maybe if we'd stayed and had some fun, the three of us, none of this wouldda happened. Maybe Jeannie givin' him the cold shoulder is what set him off. You never can tell. You could see just by lookin' at him that he wasn't used to gettin' that kinda treatment. Not him.

Yeah, yeah. I know how it sounds, me talkin' this way about the guy who killed Jeannie. Like I'm a weirdo. Like I'm some kinda head case. Maybe I shouldn't be talkin' to you. Maybe I should be talkin' to a shrink.

'Cause you know what? When I saw his face there at the Crocodile Grill, and then later, through that crack in the door? There just wasn't that much difference. Do you hear me? He didn't look mad, or excited, or…anythin'. Just takin' care of business. That's how he looked.

Now, that's scary.

You know, this place really had me fooled. After L. A., I thought, wow, lookit here. No drugs, no gang-bangers, no drive-byes. Everything so green, and clean smellin'. So what if the townies are stuck on themselves. It's the same all over. Just keep thinkin' about those pretty old houses, and those big leafy trees with the birds chirpin' their heads off, and the crickets doing' their thing.

And that sweet little river.

If you're not safe here, I said to myself, you're not safe anywhere.

Yeah. Right.

Lookit me, will you? I'm sweatin' and shiverin' at the same time. But lemme tell you, I'm not the only one should be lookin' over her shoulder. Not by a long shot. Every woman in Granite Run oughtta be watchin' her back.

'Cause he's out there and he's crazy.

And he doesn't look like a murderer.

CHAPTER 1

Maureen Lowe wasn't sure which interviews were harder to handle. Victims or witnesses.

Victims were often struck dumb by what they'd endured. They were like zombies. The living dead. She had to draw them out, to carefully wring every bit of painful information from them like they were so much dirty laundry.

Witnesses could go one way or another. They could be as leaden as victims, or they could be hyper, adrenaline charged, spewing out more details than were necessary, or even, at times, bearable. With them, Maureen served as a filter, catching what was important, and letting the rest drain away.

With both she was attentive, sympathetic. Kept her voice low and encouraging, so as not to spook one of them at the wrong moment. And all the while, like cops and emergency room personnel everywhere, maintaining that necessary wall, that objective distance between herself and them.

Otherwise, years ago, she would have drowned in all the tears and blood. And sooner or later, if she were patient, they almost all got around to one version or another of that all too familiar refrain. The one that had begun to echo through Maureen's dreams.

He didn't look like a murderer, a rapist, a...whatever.

That was Maureen's signal to pick up her pencil and go to work.

She took a deep breath, and forced herself to focus on the woman who had just flung herself into a chair on the other side of the table.

Dreams weren't Lisa Adams' problem. Reality was. Her nightmares were still ahead of her.

Lisa shuddered and the manic energy that had driven her around the room went out of her like a sigh. "He doesn't look like a murderer," she repeated dully. Minus the panic her voice was like the rest of her. Pinched and undernourished.

Maureen reached across the table and put her hand on the other woman's arm. "It would be great if criminals had capital C's tattooed on their foreheads, Lisa. But they don't. That's why we're here. To turn your memories into something concrete. Something that'll help the police catch the man who killed your friend."

Lisa tugged on a strand of "Cinnamon Red" hair. She darted a glance at Maureen's face, then looked quickly away. "Lieutenant Stanton said you're a foren—a foren—?"

"A forensic artist." Maureen frowned. "That's just an uptown way of saying police sketch artist."

"Yeah, forensic artist. That was it. He said your drawings have led to lots of arrests."

"Witness descriptions led to the arrests. I'm just a tool. Think of me as your hands, Lisa. Together, you and I are going to make this man pay for what he did. If you can describe him, I can draw him. If I can draw him, the police can catch him. Then you and everybody else in Granite Run will be safe. That's what you want, isn't it?"

Lisa fingered the blank pad on the table between them. "I thought you would have books full of noses and eyes to show me, and then I would pick out the ones that looked most like…him."

Maureen groaned. Cop shows! Television had produced more law enforcement experts than police academies had. "Some departments rely on identification kits or computers to crank out composite images. Others believe the sketch method produces more realistic results. Why don't we give it a try? You describe him as best you can, and I'll do the rest. Okay?"

"Yeah, well, I already told you he was good lookin'. Had this interestin' voice too. When we first sat down I heard him order a drink and…" Lisa's voice trailed off. Her hands dropped into her lap and the tension in her face eased. Maureen was willing to bet Lisa was no longer in a police interview room. She was in a dimly lit bar, and there was a man sitting across from her.

"His voice was kinda husky," Lisa said softly. "Like sandpaper. Kinda sexy."

6

Maureen hardly dared breathe. She hadn't seen this sort of trance-like, self-hypnotized recall often, but it happened, and when it did it was much more valuable than hysteria and often produced dramatic results.

Unfortunately, she couldn't draw a voice.

"Lisa, when you first noticed him, what was your general impression? Was he a big man? Thin or heavyset?"

Lisa squinted, and for a moment, Maureen felt as if she were right there with the other woman, trying to see through a smoky haze.

"Hmmm. Taller than six feet, I guess. And thin, but hard lookin'. Like he pumps iron or somethin'."

"Are you sure? Fear often makes the person you're afraid of seem larger than he or she really is."

"Afraid?" Lisa's head jerked and suddenly it was a police interview room again. "I told you I was afraid, hidin' in that closet." She choked on a sob. "I know I shouldda tried to help Jeannie. I know…"

Damn! "Fear" wasn't a productive word. Using it had just thrown Lisa back into the middle of the murder scene. Back into that closet. Which was not where Maureen wanted her to be. They'd been there once tonight, and the memory of what Lisa had described came rushing back at Maureen, in all its coarse, chilling clarity.

She leaned forward, talking low and fast, almost as much to herself as to the other woman. "Listen, Lisa. Take it easy. No one blames you for hiding. Your staying alive is what will lead to his arrest. But right now, I need you to forget the murder itself and concentrate on the man who so impressed you at the Crocodile Grill."

Lisa began to rock back and forth in her chair. "I'm tryin'," she moaned. "I'm really tryin'."

And she was. Maureen couldn't help but admire the poor woman's desperate need to communicate, despite the terror. She deserved a break from all the horror, all the blood.

God, they both did.

"How about some more coffee, Lisa? There's still some left in the thermos Lieutenant Stanton brought us."

"Brought you, you mean. There wasn't any coffee around here last night."

Maureen poured, and Lisa wrapped both hands around a mug and raised it gingerly to her lips. After a swallow or two she sat back in her chair. For the first time that night she looked directly into Maureen's eyes and attempted a shaky smile.

"You know, it really helps, you being a woman. Those other cops, Marsh and Stanton? Someone oughta smack them upside their heads."

Maureen bit back a grin. She'd heard similar complaints before, but that was an observation she'd keep to herself. "Actually, I'm not a cop. I'm a civilian. I freelance. When the police need the services of a sketch artist they get in touch with me."

"Is that right? Jeez, I haven't lived in Granite Run long, but up until last night it seemed like a low-key kinda place. Is there enough forensic stuff goin' on around here to keep you busy?"

Maureen glanced around the interview room, with its institutional gray walls and the stale odors of cigarette smoke and strong coffee emanating from every corner. Forensic stuff. Here? The idea was almost laughable. The worst crimes described or confessed to at this battered old table had probably been those of petty vandalism and joyriding.

Up until tonight. Now there was a murderer loose in Granite Run, moving over the same tranquil, tree-lined streets where Maureen had played as a child. No. This wasn't where she usually practiced her craft. It wasn't New York, or Los Angeles, or New Orleans. But then violence didn't necessarily have a big city address anymore.

The proof of that was sitting across the table.

"I don't live in Granite Run," Maureen said. "I grew up here, but now my home is in Philadelphia."

"Philly? You came all the way down here from Philly?"

"It's only a thirty minute drive and Clay Stanton is an old friend. I couldn't turn down a call from him. He and my dad once worked together."

"Stanton and your dad? Is your dad a cop?"

"Was." Maureen felt a sudden sting of tears behind her eyelids. God, what a baby she was. Eight years, and the mere thought of their deaths could still do this to her. "My parents were—died just before I graduated art school. Clay was the one who suggested I think about Forensic Art as a career. So, you can see why…"

"Then you're an orphan." Lisa's face lit up. She looked as if she'd just discovered a long lost friend. "Me too."

Maureen frowned. A twenty-eight year old orphan? Was there such a thing? Well, considering her emotional response a second ago, maybe there was. But what was she doing sharing so much personal information with a witness? What had happened to distance? To objectivity?

Lisa Adams was the one who should be doing the talking.

Maureen gauged Lisa's present demeanor. Steering the conversation away from the murder for a few minutes appeared to have worked. She was definitely calmer and more in control.

But Clay Stanton had cautioned Maureen that there was a deadline that had to be met. "Let's see." She picked up her pencil again, keeping the tone of her voice conversational. "You said the man you saw at the Crocodile Grill was tall and attractive."

"Yeah." Lisa shrugged. "Dark hair. But, I think, maybe, blue eyes. And, he had this…"

An hour and a half later Maureen yawned, stretched her five feet seven inches to their limit and frowned again. She concentrated all her training and experience on what the interview had produced so far. From her pad an angular, intense face stared back at her. Black, close cut hair. Deep set eyes. Prominent nose, high cheekbones. Full, sensual lips.

Maureen fingered the thin gold chain at her throat. Something was wrong with this picture, but she couldn't quite get a bead on it. And she was losing the witness. While she'd been studying the sketch, Lisa had gotten up from her chair and was once again pacing the room.

"We're almost there, Lisa. Hang with me. Take one more look at this. Is there anything I can do to improve it?"

Lisa stopped by Maureen's side and peered over her shoulder for a long moment. Suddenly, she inhaled sharply. "No, no. You got it all wrong. Jeez, weren't you listenin'?"

Maureen winced. She glanced up at the clock on the opposite wall. They'd been at it for almost three hours—a longer than usual interview. Was it possible that she'd dozed off, or been daydreaming? For how long? She turned to Lisa, who was now breathing hard, her finger pointing to the down-turned lips on the sketch.

"His mouth was wider." Lisa choked. "Much wider. And hard looking."

Luckily, charcoal pencil was a forgiving medium. With a few quick strokes, Maureen was able to incorporate the changes Lisa demanded. Yes, the wider, firmer mouth made a big difference. But there was still something about the drawing that disturbed Maureen.

She readjusted her glasses and took a closer look. Was it possible that wider and sterner also seemed more…? What was the word she was looking for? More appealing? Yes. That was it. If she hadn't known this was the face of a murderer, she might have read the challenge she saw there as confidence. The steely stare as concentration, the...

"Yeah. Now, you've got him," Lisa whispered. "That's the guy who killed Jeannie."

Maureen put down her pencil, pushed her glasses up into the blonde tangle above her forehead and massaged her temples with her fingertips. Her head was pounding, she was bone-tired and Clay was probably going out of his mind waiting for them to finish.

But she and Lisa Adams had done what they'd set out to do. They'd finished the sketch in time to get it into the morning newspaper.

Maureen got up from the table. She carried her sketchpad over to the door, opened it and leaned out into the corridor. Twenty feet away Clay Stanton was sitting at his desk in the squad room, his steel gray head bent over a stack of papers.

Maureen waved the pad. "You've got your sketch, Clay."

His big, ruddy face came up grinning. He heaved himself out of his chair and started toward her.

Maureen turned back to the witness. Lisa Adams was standing in the middle of the interview room, staring blankly into space. Used. Wrung out. Like so much dirty laundry.

For a heartbeat, Maureen was tempted to invite her out for something to eat. Then, just as quickly, she rejected the idea.

Distance. Remember?

But she went to Lisa. Patted her on the shoulder. "That was a spectacular job. This is the face we had to get down on paper. This is the murderer's public face. This is the face that's going to get him arrested."

*   *   *

After the interview with Lisa Adams, Clay offered to have the department spring for a hotel room if Maureen wanted to avoid the late night drive back to Philadelphia. But though she felt drained, even a bit spacey, she wanted to get out of Granite Run as fast as she could.

That was unusual. She'd always enjoyed her infrequent trips home before, had always jumped at the chance to spend time with Clay, exchanging cop talk and reminiscing about old times.

But tonight was different. This time she'd come on a professional call, and even the drive along the winding, unlighted road leading back to Highway One and Philadelphia unsettled her. The familiar old woods lining the road seemed denser and more shadowy than ever, the great elms and oaks looming black and huge against a sky that threatened rain.

It was well past midnight when Maureen let herself into her condominium. The storm held off until she'd stowed her portfolio in the hall closet, and made her way to the living room. Before she had a chance to hit the light switch a flash of lightning silvered the room's bare hardwood floors, its taupe painted walls and slipcovered couches.

Her answering machine blinked red in the darkness. She walked over to it and stared down at the display. Four calls. She just couldn't face them now. Maybe later, after she'd had a couple of hours sleep.

In the bedroom she peeled off her clothes and climbed between the sheets, only vaguely aware of the rain beginning to pelt the windows. As soon as her head hit the pillow she drifted off to sleep, and sometime during the next few hours, to the accompaniment of lightning and thunder, she dreamed.

And knew she dreamed.

She saw herself as she'd been as a twelve-year old, coming downstairs on a Christmas morning. The lights on the tree were so bright it hurt her eyes to look at them. But to her delight, beneath the tree's branches she found a stack of brand new sketchpads and a sealed box of rainbow colored pastels.

Gifts from her parents. Best of all, they were both suddenly beside her, and for the first time ever appeared ready to pose for her. She was so pleased. Always before they had her sent off to the Brandywine Museum to copy the paintings there, or suggested she choose a subject from nature, like the river or the picturesque, dilapidated old buildings that dotted the landscape around Granite Run and Chadds Ford.

But this time her father sat down opposite her, smiling encouragement. She tore open the box of chalk and went to work. Her hand flew across the page and in what seemed like seconds she'd managed an amazing likeness of him, capturing not only his features, but his intelligence, his humor.

When the sketch was finished she continued to draw. In fact, couldn't stop herself, and under her hand the lines on the page began to change, to squirm and writhe as if they were alive. Before long her father's image grew bloated and hideous, his neat brows turning into a bristling black line, his smile transformed into a shocking leer.

She started to cry and raised her eyes to where her father was sitting, only to find him gone, replaced by her mother. Maureen tore off the offending page, threw it aside and started to draw again, and the whole, ugly process repeated itself. A perfect rendering of her mother's gentle, loving expression wavered and morphed until the eyes bulged and seethed with inexpressible fury.

Tears poured down Maureen's cheeks as she drew. She squeezed her eyes shut and when she opened them, her mother had vanished. Clay Stanton had taken her place. The twelve-year old's fingers cramped around the chalk and once again, her hand began to move of its own volition. This time, when the bizarre, frightening changes began, she screamed.

Terrified, Maureen clawed her way back to consciousness, dragging herself free of the damp, tangled bed sheets, pushing herself upright, trying to slow the desperate pounding of her heart.

Mother of God, she'd had nightmares before, but nothing like this. She reached for the robe at the foot of the bed, pulled it around her shoulders and staggered across the room to the window, cranking it open and gasping for a breath of rain-fresh air.

The storm outside had passed. The first light of morning streaked the April sky with pale pinks and blues. There was just a hint of clouds off in the distance, somewhere in the direction of Granite Run.

Maureen sighed. The details of her dream were still with her. They hadn't faded as most did upon waking. They were as clear and sharp as crystal cutting into her brain, and it wouldn't take a genius to interpret them. Anyone who'd sat through Psych 101 could figure them out.

She'd come home from her first case in Granite Run, and dreamed about people from there. People she loved. People she knew were as good as gold. And she'd turned them into monsters.

While earlier tonight she'd listened to Lisa Adams describe a murderer, and the face Maureen had drawn was appealing, for God's sake. Talk about incongruity.

Maureen lay her forehead against the cool glass of the window. Where had Lisa Adams slept tonight? Not in the apartment she and Jeannie Starbuck had shared. That was a crime scene now, sealed off by off by the police. They'd most likely stashed Lisa away in some cheap hotel room, with a grim-faced guard stationed outside the door.

Poor kid. Had she gotten any rest at all?

Had she dreamed?

CHAPTER 2

When the telephone rang for the first time Brody Parrish was on the flagstone terrace at Riverbend, the sprawling Parrish estate on the southern bank of the Brandywine River. He had just seated himself at the outdoor table and was gazing longingly down a grassy incline to where a fiberglass, flat bottom canoe bobbed cheerfully next to the family pier.

Once again the cordless phone he'd brought out to the terrace with his coffee and the morning paper rent the silken springtime air. Two rings. If he let it go to four the answer machine would take over and he could be gone, flying along the river in the canoe, slicing a paddle into the current's shimmering depths.

But someone in the house would most likely pick it up before he had a chance to make his escape, and come find him.

Resigned, he punched the talk button. "Parrish here," he said into the receiver, his eyes still on the beckoning river.

"Brody, this is Chief Marsh. Have you seen today's paper?"

Chief Marsh? When the hell did Paul get so formal? This must be serious. Brody's hopes for the morning, and freedom, faded.

"Good morning, Paul. No, I haven't gotten around to it yet. But by the sound of your voice, I imagine this has something to do with one of your investments. What's the problem?"

"I'm as happy as a clam with my investments, Brody, thanks to you. This is a police matter. Is the *Chronicle* handy?"

"Right here."

"You better take a look at the front page."

Brody picked up the folded newspaper, flipped it open and spread it out on the glass tabletop. Its white surface blazed in the sunlight, the black print standing out in stark relief. Suddenly, the gentle morning breeze took on an ominous chill.

After a long moment he said, in a voice as controlled as he could keep it, "What is this all about, Paul?"

"You heard that Jeannie Starbuck was murdered over at the Kennecott Square Apartments Saturday night, didn't you?"

"I heard."

"Well, there was a witness, and—"

"A witness? That, I hadn't heard."

"We kept it quiet. We didn't want anything to happen to her."

Her, Brody thought. A woman. Without taking his eyes from the paper he picked up his cup. The coffee was no longer as hot as he would have liked, but the caffeine helped steady his nerves.

Marsh's voice sputtered in Brody's ear. "Are you still there, Brody?"

"Go on, Paul."

"Listen, it's some kind of crazy mistake, and if I hadn't had a speaking engagement last night none of it would have happened. The *Chronicle* never would have gotten its hands on the sketch and—"

"Where did this picture come from?"

"Clay Stanton's butt is on the line for this one. His nose is still out of joint because he didn't get the chief's badge. Yesterday, while I was gone, he decided to play big shot. Called in a forensic artist he knows to interview the witness. I'd be willing to bet he even hand delivered the damn sketch to the *Chronicle* and—"

"You mean this witness described me? That's why my face is splashed across the front page under the headline 'Suspect sought in Kennecott Square Murder'?"

"Listen, if I'd seen the sketch last night it wouldn't have been released to the press. We'd have dealt with this mess before there had been any publicity. But now, well, the department's already received some calls this morning mentioning your resemblance to...the picture in the paper."

Up until this moment Brody had managed to sound merely annoyed. Reasonably annoyed. But now, through tightly clenched teeth he heard himself hiss, "Do you have any idea what this could do to my business, Paul? Not to mention how it will affect my mother. Damn it!

You tell Clay Stanton I'll kill him if this nonsense interferes with her recovery."

"Now, you watch your mouth Brody. If we weren't friends you wouldn't be getting this...courtesy call. You get in touch with that slick Philadelphia lawyer of yours, and the two of you haul your asses down here to the station house. We can set this right in a matter of minutes. By this time tomorrow you, your clients and your mother will all be laughing up your sleeves about it. And thanks to Stanton, the joke will be on me."

"We'll be there in an hour." Brody switched off the receiver, punched in the telephone code for Richard Bailey and quickly made the necessary arrangements with his lawyer. Then he stood, refolded the newspaper and stuck it under his arm. With one last glance over his shoulder he turned his back on the river and walked through the open French doors into the house, across its Persian carpeted floors, up its curved wooden staircase to his bedroom.

Brody had closed up his apartment in town after his mother's stroke. It had taken a while to get used to being back in his boyhood home, fussed over by his mother and her housekeeper. But Victoria was almost her old, hard-to-live-with self again. Which meant he could soon be back on his own. Back in town, where he belonged.

In his room he tossed the paper onto the bed, stripped off his jeans and sweater and changed into the uniform of his chosen profession: a gray, lightweight wool suit, narrowly striped white shirt and a bright but discreetly patterned silk tie. Before leaving he stopped and checked his reflection in the mirror above the bureau. The face on the front page of the newspaper glared back at him.

"Damn sketch," he muttered under his breath. By now everyone in Granite Run, if not the whole state, had probably seen it. What were his clients thinking? People liked their investment advisors to look prosperous and conservative. They didn't like them to look like murderers.

"Brody? Brody?"

His mother! What was she doing wandering around without Mrs.Hartman? He'd better get downstairs before she tried to get up here all by herself.

On the way out the door he retrieved the paper, stuffed it into his briefcase and snapped it shut. From the top of the stairs he could see his mother waiting for him below, looking peeved and formidable despite her cane and the almost imperceptible trembling of her left hand. She was over sixty, and despite her recent illness, still beautiful. Except for her smooth coil of silver hair she looked much like her son. But in her face, his chiseled features were rounded and softened, and she lacked the slight Native American cast that had distinguished the Parrish bloodline since the first of them had come to the New World with William Penn and married an Algonquin woman.

"Brody," Victoria called up to him, "Margaret and I can't seem to find the morning newspaper."

Brody took the stairs fast, anxious to be gone. He gestured with his briefcase. "I'm taking it with me to the office. There are some important stock quotes I need to check on. Tell Mrs. Hartman I'll try to make it home for dinner."

"Dear, you know I like to read the paper while having breakfast. Just take the financial section and leave the rest."

He brushed a hurried kiss across her forehead and turned toward the front door. "Mother, I'm in too much of a hurry to stop and sort through…"

Her fingers closed over his arm. Tremor or not, her grip was as strong as ever. "Is there something in the *Chronicle* that I'm not supposed to see, Dear?"

What was the use of trying to delay the inevitable? He shook his head and sighed. "I should have known I wasn't going to get away with that one." He put his hand under her elbow and steered her down the hall. "Come into the library and I'll explain. But you have to promise not to get upset. There's been some kind of stupid mix-up in town…"

*   *   *

Over the last few years Maureen Lowe's travels had taken her into police stations all over the country. Most of them had erected bulletproof plexi-glass walls between their personnel and the citizenry they'd vowed to protect and serve. They communicated with each other through stainless steel grates set in the plastic, or black telephone speakers.

Just like prison inmates and their visitors.

Granite Run's lobby, Maureen had noticed last night, was still a hold out to gentler times. It was open, welcoming, its walls painted in clear shades of blue and gray and displaying smiling photographs of former chiefs dressed in civilian clothes. Except for the presence of the uniformed officer behind the front desk it might have been the reception area of a prosperous doctor's office.

This morning Maureen again followed Clay Stanton through the lobby, past the closed door of the Chief's office, down a corridor to the much more utilitarian detective's area and interview rooms. Here, the gray prevailed. Here, as in most squad rooms, scratched metal desks, bent folding chairs and overflowing file cabinets made up the decor. Here, there were wanted posters and statistical crime charts thumb tacked to the walls.

Before dropping into the chair beside Stanton's desk Maureen glanced around the room. It was one o'clock in the afternoon, three hours until the next shift change. The town must have seen some population growth since she'd left, but she imagined it could still only afford a force of about thirty officers. Almost all of them seemed to be here now, either taking calls or milling around in varying degrees of agitation.

Something was definitely up.

A uniformed female officer approached and handed Stanton a note. He read it, nodded and the officer turned on her heel and left.

Maureen felt the hairs on the back of her neck come to attention. "Don't tell me you're getting feedback on the sketch already?"

Clay's pepper and salt mustache twitched over a Cheshire Cat smile. He winked. "Better than that. We have a suspect. He and his mouthpiece are back there with the Chief right now."

"But the public only got to see it this morning, and then, only in the local newspaper. Who turned him in? He isn't from around here, is he?"

"Oh, there have been plenty of calls mentioning his name, but he turned himself in. Arrived here about ten o'clock with his lawyer in tow. Seeing his face in the paper must have been quite a shock." Stanton chuckled. "I know it gave Chief Marsh some gray hairs."

"Does the suspect resemble the sketch?"

"A dead ringer. You were right on the money, as usual. The guy could have posed for it."

Maureen shivered. She had to confide in someone or she would go out of her mind. "Clay, about that sketch...it...wasn't the first one I drew last night."

"You had an earlier job? No wonder you were so tired. You should've said something."

She shook her head. "No. That's not what I meant. I was tired, but Granite Run had been my only call."

"Then I don't get it. What's this about another sketch?"

"What I gave you last night was a corrected sketch. When Lisa

Adams saw what I originally drew she went ballistic. Said it wasn't the murderer. That I hadn't been listening. Of course, I made the changes she wanted. They were few, but significant enough that when I corrected the sketch it was a different face. A different man."

Clay sat back in his chair, clasped his hands on top of his head and stared at Maureen for a long moment. Then he shrugged. "So, you dozed off and made a mistake. It happens."

"It doesn't happen to me."

"Whoa! Don't tell me you're beginning to believe those press notices of yours. That one hundred percent arrest and conviction record must mean more to you than you've let on."

Trust Clay to go for the jugular. Maybe she had gotten overconfident and forgotten who was responsible for her sketches. Didn't she tell people she was only a tool? Perhaps the problem was the tool.

"You know Clay, I've been thinking about taking a break, maybe even getting out completely. It's been eight years since my parents' murder. Back then, I had this crazy idea that one day I might be able to assist the police in finding the person who was responsible for their deaths. That one day I would be interviewing a witness and suddenly know…know that…" She couldn't go on.

He dropped his arms and leaned forward, reaching for her hand. "And now you know that that was a dream. A fantasy." His shrugged. "You aren't the first person who had to give up a dream. But you're overreacting to that, and what happened last night. Sure, take a vacation. A nice long one. Go to Europe. Do the museums. But promise me you won't make any major decisions until we've talked again. I'd hate to see you throw in the towel. What you do is important."

She looked down at his hand. Had his knuckles always been this gnarled and knotted? Arthritis? Clay? He'd only been a little younger than her dad, and a cop for more than half his life. Not making chief last year had to have been a terrible disappointment. The end of a dream. Compared to his problems what did she have to complain about? Eight years on the job. Her first professional mistake? A couple of bad dreams?

She smiled at him. "I promise. Now, let's talk about something else. For instance, why I'm here. I'd just gotten back to sleep this morning when the dispatcher called with your message. If you've got your suspect why am I needed?"

"Because Lisa Adams won't go through with a lineup unless you're there holding her hand."

"What?"

"You heard me. Seems you made quite an impression on her last night. She told the Chief she can't handle the process alone, and there's no one else in Granite Run she trusts. Marsh argued with her for over an hour, but finally gave in. Against his lawyer's advice our man's demanding an immediate lineup, and unfortunately he's used to getting what he wants, when he wants it."

A lineup! Maureen's pulse began to race. "But Lisa won't be alone. You'll be there, and the Chief. She'll be looking at the suspect through a one-way mirror. There's no reason for me to be here, Clay. My only connection to the case is over."

He examined her as if she were a valuable piece of evidence. "You're perfectly within your rights to refuse."

Maureen frowned. "No. No. I was just caught off guard by the idea. You must admit it's an unusual request. But if that poor woman needs some emotional support to get through this I'd be an awful snake to refuse."

"Marsh said to tell you that you'll receive your usual hourly fee for whatever time you spend with Ms. Adams."

"Tell him to forget it. Last night I was employed by the Granite Run Police Department. Today I'm here because Lisa Adams needs a friend. My friendship, in case you haven't noticed, doesn't require a fee."

"Okay. Okay." With his forefinger Clay tapped the note the officer had left. "They've finally been able to pull together a passable lineup. It wasn't easy rounding up four guys that looked enough like the suspect that he wouldn't stand out like a sore thumb, and at the same time different enough not to confuse the witness."

"Where is Lisa?" Maureen stood. "I should speak to her before…"

Stanton heaved himself up out of his chair. He cocked his head to the right. "She's in Interview Room A. You won't have much time to gab. In a couple of minutes Marsh is going to herd our cast of suspects into the next room. Then, he and I and Parrish's lawyer will join you and…"

Maureen heard raised voices and heavy footsteps behind her. She turned just in time to see Chief of Police Paul Marsh plow into the squad room at the head of a jostling line of men. One of them stood head and shoulders above the others, with darker hair and an easy, confident swagger that would set him apart in any group. As he filed past Maureen he came to an abrupt stop. Their glances met and held, and for the flash of a second, his wide, firm mouth softened into an almost smile, and his cobalt blue eyes ignighted with obvious interest.

For a heartbeat, the air that inhabited the space that separated them seemed to sizzle and snap dangerously, like a power cable crackling in a windstorm, like kindling about to catch fire. Then the man behind him put a hand on his shoulder and they moved on. Before Maureen could catch her breath he and the others had disappeared down the corridor and into Interview Room B.

But already memories that had slumbered in her subconscious for fifteen years were struggling to the surface. "Parrish! My God, Lisa described Brody Parrish last night. Brody Parrish. When I was a kid I saw him save a girl's life out on the Brandywine River. Her boat overturned and everybody just stood there, and then this gawky Ichabod Crane type came loping out of nowhere and—"

"Yeah, I figured you'd recognize him sooner or later." Stanton took her arm. "Come on, Maureen, the lineup is about to start."

As he propelled her down the corridor, Maureen clutched his sleeve. "You must remember, Clay. Didn't the town give him some kind of award for heroism?"

"The only thing I remember is that no one could explain how the damn boat happened to capsize in the first place. But we have more important things to worry about now. Here we are."

Stanton pulled open a door and all but shoved Maureen into the same room she and Lisa had used the night before. Only now, the lights had been turned down and the table they'd talked across was pushed up against the back wall. Two rows of folding chairs filled the table's former space.

Lisa Adams sat hunched in the first of them.

At the sound of their entrance she turned in their direction. In the half-light her heavily made up skin appeared pale and pasty, and there were purple shadows under her eyes. She made a tentative move to get up, then sank back in her chair, her hands fluttering uselessly in her lap.

As if she been holding her breath she took in a great gulp of air. "Chief Marsh warned me you might not come but I told him what you said. I knew you wouldn't let me down."

Maureen put her hand on the other woman's shoulder. "What I said?"

"You know, about our being in this thing together."

Together?

Think of me as your hands Lisa. Together you and I are going to make this man pay for what he did.

But Maureen had said that or something like it, hundreds of times. It was part of her spiel, her way of getting victims and witnesses to open up, to deliver the goods. It meant don't be afraid to remember. I'm here to help. You're not alone.

You're not alone.

Maureen looked down into Lisa's upturned face. Her little speech had never been taken so literally before. But had any of the others she'd interviewed been as needy as this woman? A newcomer to Granite Run? No family to turn to, no friends except for the one that had been murdered before her very eyes?

Behind them the door opened again and Chief Marsh barged into the room, followed by a heavyset, well-dressed man Maureen assumed was Brody Parrish's attorney. Correctly assumed, it turned out. Marsh jerked his head in the man's direction. "This is Richard Bailey. He wants it known that his client is taking part in the lineup against his advice. Bailey, you've met Lieutenant Stanton before. The young lady next to him is here at the request of the witness." The chief sat down next to Lisa, but he continued to stare pointedly at Maureen.

He didn't appear to be in a particularly good mood. Maureen vaguely remembered when he'd joined the Granite Run police force ten years before. The young officer's experience and educational background had impressed her father. She was surprised to find that in the ensuing years he'd matured into a mildly attractive, middle-aged man who wore his tailored uniform with more than a little panache.

What she knew about his personality was hearsay, and not particularly flattering. Clay Stanton considered him a "climber," an ambitious politician for whom the police department was just a stepping stone to bigger and better things.

"Ms. Lowe," Marsh said, "I would like you to stand behind, and to the left of this second row of chairs." He indicated the large tinted window in the opposite wall, through which Maureen could see the movements of several shadowy figures. "Once the lights go on in the next room, you are not to touch or communicate with Ms. Adams in any way."

Next he rested his arm along the back of Lisa's chair. "Ms. Adams, we'll be able to see the men behind the window but they won't be able to see us. You should know that just because these particular men are taking part in the lineup doesn't mean any one of them is a suspect. We don't expect you to pick out someone if you're not absolutely certain he is the man we're looking for. Please don't say 'I think such and such is the man.' I want you to be as sure of your identification as you are of your own name."

Lisa swallowed and nodded, for all the world like a dashboard doll. But Marsh's instructions had impressed Maureen as more limiting than she'd expected, and curiously, directed as much to her, Clay and Bailey, as to Lisa.

Without another word Marsh stood, walked to the wall separating the two rooms and rapped on the window. Interview Room B exploded with light. Maureen felt her heart thud against her ribs.

A tableau of five men had been arranged behind the window. Brody Parrish was seated second from the left. Like the others he wore a shirt open at the collar and a tie loosely knotted below the first button. But with that, and the color of their hair and eyes, all similarities ended. The set of Parrish's shoulders, the confident tilt of his head, his cool expression, all but screamed for attention.

Gone was the gangly, self-conscious teenager of Maureen's memory. This whip-lean, self-assured man had replaced him. Almost as if he could feel her eyes on him, he leaned forward, away from the others, his hands clasped loosely between his knees, and stared straight into the glass, eyes icy with challenge.

Maureen was transfixed. Inexorably, her gaze was drawn from that implacable, arresting face to the hands that had supposedly wielded a knife a mere forty-eight hours before. To the elegant bones of his wrists where they emerged from his rolled back sleeves. To the fine, black hairs visible on either side of his gold watchband. To his long, powerful looking fingers.

Lisa's soft, quaking voice dissipated the electric stillness that had fallen like a net over everyone in the room. "Aren't they going to stand?"

For several seconds there was silence. Then Marsh shrugged and answered. "This is a small town, Ms. Adams. We may do things a little less formally here than they do in the big city."

Maureen slid her eyes his way. There were measurement markings on the wall behind the lineup's participants. What was Marsh up to? Was their being seated just a way to disguise Parrish's height? Was the Chief of Police having the same problem she was? Was he finding it difficult to believe that any of the men in the next room was a murderer?

Maureen heard metal chair legs scrape against the wooden floor.

She turned her head, just in time to see Lisa, on her feet, rushing toward the window, pointing a trembling finger in Brody Parrish's direction.

"Him! That's him," she cried. "He did it. He stabbed Jeannie Starbuck to death."

CHAPTER 3

"He's not going to be arrested," Clay said.

He, Maureen and Lisa were still in Interview Room A. Chief Marsh and Richard Bailey had stormed out immediately after Lisa's identification of Brody Parrish.

Maureen's mind still reeled from what had just happened. She couldn't tear her eyes away from the window into the next room. The lights had gone off but she could hear the lineup participants filing out into the adjacent corridor.

She turned and stared at Clay. "Not arrested? Why not?"

"He claims to have an alibi."

Maureen felt a fleeting moment of elation, and then she heard Lisa Adams' horrified gasp. Lisa, who had seen Brody Parrish murder Jeannie Starbuck. Who had described him. Who had picked him out of the lineup.

She looked to Maureen for support. "That's crazy! It's him. I know it is. You know it is!"

"Clay, if the man has an alibi why did we just go through this charade?" Maureen demanded.

"It was Parrish's idea. His supposed alibi involves one of his investment clients. He didn't want us to get in touch with the client unless it was absolutely necessary. He figured a lineup was the quickest way to clear his name. Guess he was counting on Ms. Adams here not being able to identify him."

Moaning, Lisa began to pace the room.

Maureen lowered her voice. "How long will it take to check out his story?"

Stanton shrugged. "Who knows? Could be an hour, could be a couple of days."

"And until then, he walks?"

"Yup. Marsh isn't going to put a member of one of Granite Run's most prominent families behind bars until he has an open and shut case and no other options."

Lisa stopped her frantic pacing and wailed. "I heard that. That murderer's lawyer was in here with us. He'll tell Parrish who I am. He'll come after me, I know it. I'm going to end up just like Jeannie."

Stanton held up his hand. "Ms. Adams, Parrish has a legal right to know who his accuser is, but believe me the department will provide you with round the clock protection. He won't get anywhere near you."

"Oh, sure. I'm supposed to depend on a police force whose chief is chummy with a murderer. I'm suppose to stay in a town where I'm a nobody, a waitress, and the killer is some kind of big shot." With a gut-wrenching sob Lisa turned to Maureen. "What am I going to do?"

Maureen watched Lisa drag her hands through her hair. She was working herself into a state of near hysteria. Logic and promises weren't getting through to her now. Clay ought to see that. The poor thing was going to pieces while they just stood there, watching, doing nothing.

Maureen was sick to death of watching. Of doing nothing.

Together, you and I are going to make this man pay.

She stepped between Clay and Lisa. "Listen, both of you, I have an idea," she blurted out before her better judgement got the upper hand. "Until Brody Parrish is safely behind bars, Lisa can come home to Philadelphia with me."

*   *   *

Maureen unlocked the door to her condo. She forced a smile, hoping it didn't look as insincere as she was beginning to feel. "Welcome to Chez Lowe, Lisa."

Lisa glanced up and down the corridor. "Maybe I shouldn't have come."

Maureen juggled her purse, the mail, her door key and the bag of groceries they'd purchased on the drive into Philadelphia. She tried not to sound impatient. "Why on earth not?'

"If Parrish finds out I'm here you'll be in trouble too."

Maureen dropped the mail on the console in the condo's entry. Lisa wasn't the only one having second thoughts about this arrangement but Maureen was determined to make the best of the situation. "Brody Parrish doesn't know I exist, much less where I live." Doesn't now and never did, she thought, remembering her long-ago, from-a-distance hero worship of him. Well, today's lineup had certainly put an end to that pretty little girlhood foolishness. With a vengeance.

She started down the hall to the living room. "Lisa, please come inside and lock the door after you." She was relieved to hear the door swing shut, the dead bolt slide into place and Lisa's tentative footsteps behind her.

"Oh, wow! This place is gorgeous."

Her spontaneous response charmed Maureen. She allowed herself a quick proprietary glance around the room. "Thanks. It still needs a lot of work but you should have seen it when I moved in. If it hadn't been for the complex's great location I might never have made an offer on it."

"You mean you own this? It isn't a rental? Boy, forensic art must pay better than I thought."

"Better than illustrating children's books anyway. Why don't you put your things in the guest room down the hall, and then check out the rest of the condo while I fix supper?"

In the tiny kitchen Maureen emptied the grocery sacks, turned on the oven and tied an apron around her waist. The demands of her job didn't allow time for gourmet cooking, but take-out and frozen meals had begun to bore her. She couldn't avoid them when traveling, but when she was home she made it a point to cook. Had, in fact, developed fast and fresh food preparation into something of an art.

With the aid of a supermarket crust, some vegetables and a chunk of Parmesan cheese she was able to slide a fairly interesting looking pizza into the oven in a matter of minutes. A head of romaine lettuce, a splash of rice vinegar and a few black olives became a salad before the cheese on the pizza had begun to melt.

By the time Lisa had finished her tour of the condo and rejoined Maureen she was setting the table in the dining alcove.

Lisa pulled out a chair and sat down. "I saw those paintings in that back room. You know, the messy one."

Maureen smiled. "My studio."

"Whatever." Lisa twisted the cap off the bottle of pop Maureen had set down in front of her and poured some into a glass. "The paintings are cute but kind of scary."

"Fairy tales can be pretty frightening. There's a cautionary aspect to most of them. But it was probably the size of the paintings you found overwhelming. In a book they'll be smaller. Less intimidating."

Lisa watched as Maureen took the pizza out of the oven. The odors of sweet basil, roasted garlic and melting Parmesan filled the room. "Let me get this straight," Lisa said. "You'd rather paint pictures for kid's books than do what you're doing now?"

"Don't get me wrong. I'm proud of my work. But it does involve a lot of travel. I get calls from all over the country. Last month I was gone three weeks out of four." Maureen slid generous slices of pizza onto plates, added mounds of salad and carried them to the table. She sat down. "It's exciting but draining, and it doesn't leave much time for a personal life."

Lisa nodded knowingly. "I get it. No guys."

"Oh, there have been a couple. But when push came to shove neither relationship seemed worth making any grand sacrifices or lifestyle changes for. On anybody's part."

"Men are just bastards."

Maureen looked down at her plate. "No. The truth is I'm to blame. I'm never in one place long enough to get anything meaningful going. And I'm good at what I do. But when I was in art school my first love was children's book illustration. Recently I've given some thought to returning to it. This condo and the paintings in the studio are steps in that direction. It's my first commission. If and when I'm ready to make the change perhaps there'll be enough of them so that I can stay in Philadelphia and still support myself."

"That's one good thing about being a waitress," Lisa said, pushing away from the table and standing. "The pay is lousy but at least you never have to worry about finding a job."

After cleaning up the kitchen the two women went back to the living room and settled themselves in front of the television set with a bowl of popcorn between them. During commercial breaks they turned down the volume and talked about their respective pasts. The contrast between Maureen's loving, secure upbringing in Granite Run and Lisa's description of a hand-to-mouth existence in a densely populated, blue-collar suburb of Los Angeles couldn't have been more dramatic.

"How old were you when your parents died?" Maureen asked.

"They didn't die. They took off. They left me in a bus station when I was four."

"Oh Lisa, how awful for you. Did you have grandparents?

Relatives?"

"None that anyone knew about."

"Who raised you?"

"Who do you think? I got sucked into the system. You know, foster parents. Different ones every couple of months. It wasn't a walk in the park, I'll tell you that. But the last few years weren't so bad. I spent them with good old Lucy and Chuck Gance. They were...okay," Lisa said wistfully. Then her tone abruptly hardened. "But the state paid them. They did it for the money. It wasn't like having a real mom and dad." She eyed Maureen enviously. "If your parents were alive I bet they'd be proud of what you do."

"The forensic art?" Maureen bit her lip. "I think so. Though sometimes I wonder if they didn't want something else for their only child. Remember, I grew up in Granite Run. There's quite an artist's colony in the Brandywine Valley. You may have heard of one of them. Andrew Wyeth? His work is on display in the museum over in Chadds Ford. My parents sacrificed to send me to a prestigious art school. They might have hoped I'd follow in Wyeth's footsteps."

Lisa grinned. "You know what a shrink would say, don't you?"

Maureen nodded. "That the paintings in my studio have more to do with what I just told you than any desire on my part to change careers and settle down. Could be. Popcorn and pop-psychology certainly make for interesting conversation, don't they?"

They turned up the volume on the TV again, retreating into the safety of the impersonal. A couple of situation comedies later Lisa snuggled down into the sofa cushions with a contented sigh. "This is nice. Cozy."

It was nice, Maureen decided. About five seconds after she'd invited Lisa to stay with her she'd had second thoughts. What had possessed her to let a total stranger into her home? Especially one connected to a case she'd worked on. That was a career no-no. Maybe she was even more burned out than she realized. Until today she'd made a fetish of keeping her professional and private lives separate.

Private life? What private life? Since she and Pete called it quits she'd kept busy working, fixing up the condo, painting. But tonight she'd enjoyed showing off her home, cooking for someone other than herself, sharing confidences.

All of a sudden Lisa sat up and pointed at the TV. "Hey Maureen, look at that! Isn't that you?"

Sure enough, the entire television screen was taken up by a candid still shot of her face, blonde hair blowing across her cheeks, eyes framed by her huge, purposely unfashionable glasses.

"You ought to lose the specs," Lisa offered.

Maureen grabbed the remote control and punched the volume up even louder. The voice of the local TV anchorman filled the room.

"Channel Nine News learned today that a recent kidnapping case in Larkland, Missouri was solved with the help of a Philadelphia artist named Maureen Lowe. After spending little more than an hour with a witness to the abduction Ms. Lowe was able to produce the sketch seen here."

On a split screen a photograph of a very ordinary looking man, juxtaposed with a black and white sketch of his face, replaced Maureen's image. Her initial surprise gave way to a moment of professional pride. That particular rendering had turned out to be a very good likeness and seemed to have achieved the desired result.

"Which led to the arrest last week of Arthur Walsh after a routine traffic stop. Noting Walsh's resemblance to Ms. Lowe's sketch police took him in for questioning. A short time later he led officers to a motel room where they found his victim bound and gagged but in otherwise good condition.

"This is only the latest in a series of high profile crimes that have been solved with this artist's expert assistance. Police departments from Seattle to Miami are clamoring for her services. Channel Nine News is confident this won't be the last time we'll be reporting on the exploits of the lovely Ms. Lowe."

"Now, up next with the business report is our own..."

Maureen sank back against the arm of the sofa. Oh, great. The exploits of the lovely Ms. Lowe. So professional. They'd made her sound like a comic book character. Wonder Woman, ready at a moment's notice to fly anywhere and do battle with the forces of evil. With a pencil.

She sighed and switched off the TV. At least there'd been a silver lining to the report, no matter how overblown it had been. The Larkland case had had a happy ending.

"That was exciting. Did you know you were going to be on TV?"

"No. Channel Nine must have gotten its information from the Larkland authorities. I wish the station had checked with me before airing it. I'm getting too much publicity lately. It's making me jumpy."

"You know, last night when you first walked into that interview room I thought you looked familiar. I bet I saw your picture somewhere." Lisa narrowed her eyes. "Hey, you aren't the one Chatter Magazine said can read people's minds?"

"I'm the one, minus the psychic powers." Maureen laughed uneasily. "After the mess I made of that first sketch last night you shouldn't have any doubts about that."

"Yeah. Yeah. I guess so. I mean, I wouldn't want to get mixed up in anything weird. I have enough to worry about with that creep Parrish being on the loose." Lisa continued to study Maureen with a wary eye. "As long as Channel Nine was doing a story on you I'm surprised they didn't mention Jeannie's murder and the drawing you made of him."

"Well, he isn't actually under arrest yet and maybe the station manager doesn't consider Granite Run important enough to make the Philadelphia news."

But that didn't make sense, even to Maureen. Granite Run was small but the Brandywine Valley was a popular tourist destination, and the state of Pennsylvania and the Parrish name had been linked since colonial times. If the Philadelphia media had had the story they would have run with it. If they'd had it.

So the Granite Run Police Department was keeping the Parrish connection under wraps. Maureen had thought there'd been something peculiar about the way the investigation had been handled from the start. For example, Clay's actions last night. Once he'd seen her sketch he must have known it was Brody that Lisa had described. Why had he given the sketch to the *Chronicle*? Why didn't he just go out and bring Brody in for questioning?

And this afternoon hadn't Paul Marsh done everything but turn somersaults to keep Lisa from picking anyone out of the lineup?

Across the cushions Lisa stretched and yawned.

"This has been a long and difficult day, Lisa. Why don't we both turn in and get up bright and early tomorrow morning? You might want to join me for a jog around the neighborhood. Historic Philadelphia is only a couple of blocks away, and it's well worth exploring."

With drooping eyelids Lisa dragged herself to her feet. "I don't know about that bright and early stuff. I'm kind of a late sleeper."

"Then I'll try not to wake you when I leave." Maureen stood and started for her room, but halfway there she stopped and turned back to her guest. "Lisa, can I ask you a question?"

"Sure. Ask away, girlfriend."

"Are you certain you never ran into Brody Parrish before the night of the murder?"

Lisa's eyes flew open. "Yeah, I'm certain. I told you, I'm new in town. What made you think...?"

"Well, you saw that sketch of the kidnapper on TV a few minutes ago. It reminded me of my interview with the witness. Her description of the kidnapper wasn't as precise as yours of Jeannie's killer. Most witnesses aren't able to dredge up the amount of detail you did. I just wondered if you'd met Parrish before and had perhaps forgotten."

"I never laid eyes on him until Saturday night at the Crocodile Grill." Lisa's voice had a little catch in it. "You believe me, don't you Maureen?"

Maureen tried to make her smile reassuring. "Please don't get upset Lisa. Your seeing him before wouldn't have been a problem. It might just have been important to the investigation. That's all. But if you say you didn't, then of course I believe you. What reason would you have to lie?"

*   *   *

He climbed into the canoe and lay down on his back, eyes closed and hands loosely clasped on his chest. The boat rocked gently with the rhythm of the current and every so often it bumped against the wooden piling to which it was tied. The resulting sound reminded him of a heartbeat.

This is what it must feel like in the womb, he thought. How appropriate. He laughed softly to himself and remained perfectly still for a time, savoring the idea and the sensations that accompanied it.

Finally he grew restless and opened his eyes. Above him the moon was a silver dagger in the midnight sky. Wreathed in misty clouds, the cool white gold of it put him in mind of Maureen Lowe as he'd seen her on TV earlier tonight, her hair a pale froth around her lovely face, her green eyes magnified by the glasses she wore. She was a moonlight blonde. An artist. Not brassy and common like Jeannie Starbuck.

He turned and raised himself up on one elbow and let his gaze climb the gray-green slope to the house. Riverbend would be a fine setting for a jewel like Maureen, and she was a worthy successor to Victoria Parrish. Yes, he could imagine Maureen gliding gracefully through the rooms, arranging flowers in the Baccarat vase in the parlor, straightening the Gresham painting in the entry.

But now that he knew she existed imagining her was not enough. He needed to feel her pulse beating under his hands, needed to hear her speak his name. And he could make it happen, because now he knew where to find her.

*   *   *

Maureen saw him before he saw her.

Still panting from her morning run and weighed down by perspiration drenched sweats she stopped and simply stared, her pulse pounding in her ears.

In front of her building, Brody Parrish was closing the door to the luggage compartment of a gunmetal gray sports car. His back was to her but she knew who it was. There was no mistaking that neat head of black hair, the powerful width of those shoulders. Even dressed in washed-out jeans and a tired tweed sweater he looked like a million dollars in cool, hard cash.

Denim, tweed and a Jaguar. If that wasn't casual chic, what was?

Maureen shivered inside her sweats. Here she was, checking out a murderer while his accuser slept five stories above their heads. What was he doing here? What if Lisa were to wake up and look out the window? Or if she decided to take a stroll around the complex? If she saw him she'd freak out. And if he saw her...?

Maureen darted a quick glance up and down the concrete sidewalk. It was eight o'clock. The street should have been full of people leaving for work. Where was everybody? Except for an elderly man peering under the hood of his car in front of the building next door she and Parrish appeared to be the only two people in the vicinity.

Without warning he straightened and started to turn in her direction. Maureen took a deep breath, ducked her head and made a beeline for the safety of her building's glass enclosed lobby. If she could just get past him before he recognized her...

But he saw her and his long legs carried him to the entrance before she could get there. "Well," he said coldly, "If it isn't the lovely Ms. Lowe."

Cold or not, it was a great voice. Like sandpaper, Lisa had said. No, more like gravel-laced cream. A voice any male radio or TV personality would kill for.

She glared at the outstretched arm that blocked her way and clenched her teeth to keep them from chattering. "Please let me by."

"Which is your place?" he demanded. "We need to talk."

If Maureen weren't so terrified she would have laughed out loud. Instead she stepped back and dug her fists into her hips. "We need to talk? Does that line get you into many women's apartments?"

Had it gotten him into Jeannie Starbuck's?

"But we're not total strangers, are we, Ms. Lowe? You've known my name since yesterday afternoon, and now thanks to the miracle of television and my contacts here in Philadelphia I not only know your name, but where you live."

"Channel Nine shouldn't have run that piece without letting me have a crack at editing it."

"That's an interesting remark coming from someone who provides the media with portraits of people who haven't been charged with any crime, much less convicted. People who are supposedly innocent until proven guilty. They might like a chance to edit the news too."

Bulls-eye! And on his first shot too. How had he managed to hit on the one the aspect of her work that worried Maureen most? The public's tendency to draw conclusions from little, if any, evidence. To take accusation and arrest as proof of guilt.

But she had no intention of sharing that concern with a murder suspect. She made another move toward the door. "I don't provide the media with anything," she snapped. "I'm employed by the police. What they do with my sketches is up to them."

"So your hands are clean, are they? Do you know anything about me or my family, Ms. Lowe? Do you have any idea what business I'm in? What kind of reputation I need to maintain?"

She knew he'd once pulled a drowning girl out of a river. That for years he'd been the yardstick against which she measured all her high school beaus. Wasn't that a hoot? She raised her chin. "None of that has anything to do with my work."

"Comfortable position, that. It allows you to distance yourself from any damage you do."

Damage. Maureen winced. "Mr. Parrish, why are you here? You're smart enough to realize your quarrel isn't with me. I'm an artist. I just put down on paper what's described to me."

The second the words were out of her mouth Maureen wanted to snatch them back. The last thing she needed to do was remind him that there had been a witness to Jeannie Starbuck's murder. Especially when that witness was asleep five stories up from where they were standing.

But she was totally unprepared for what happened next. In an instant the fire in his eyes died. He sagged back against the concrete arch that framed the doorway and dropped his arm, and Maureen thought she glimpsed in his contorted features an echo of the teenage boy he'd once been.

"You're right. My beef is with your mistaken witness, and the system, and the newspaper, and..." He plunged his hands into the pockets of his jeans and shook his head. "Look, when I saw your face on the television screen last night I guess you just became the most accessible target for all my frustration."

Target? Had he meant that to sound threatening? Maureen pushed hard against the heavy glass door that led into the outer lobby.

He leaned toward her. Something about him, the soap he used, his aftershave, maybe just the lingering scent of the Jaguar's leather interior, smelled good. Dark. Rich. Subtle. Like him.

"Wait, don't run away. Let me explain. When I saw the TV spot I wasn't simply angry. I was surprised. The minute I heard your name I realized you were Barney Lowe's daughter. Maybe that explains what happened in the squad room yesterday, before the lineup. Maybe I remembered you from…"

All the sarcasm was gone from his voice. It had become softer, edged with intimacy. More disturbing, if that was possible. The door finally gave way and Maureen was almost safely inside. Almost, but not quite.

"I thought we made a pretty powerful connection there. One well worth exploring. Was I wrong?"

No, he wasn't wrong. She remembered that moment, that jolt, that connection shared with a murder suspect. Just the fact that it had happened at all was a sure sign she needed a vacation. Maybe more than a vacation.

She refused to look at him, unwilling to let him see his effect on her. But she could make out his reflection in the glass door. He was so close. Too close. What was the old bromide? The best defense was a good offense. It was worth a try.

"Am I reading this right, Mr. Parrish? Are you hitting on me? Don't you think your timing is a little off?"

"Hitting on you!" He laughed. A nice laugh, from somewhere deep in his chest. "You don't mince words, do you? I guess it's the business you're in. What I had in mind was dinner. As for the timing, if it's the murder charge you're hung up on, you can forget it. By this time tomorrow it'll be water under the bridge."

His confidence was unnerving. But then he figured he had a police chief in his pocket, didn't he? And he thought all he had to do was crook his little finger and she'd jump right in there too.

"Listen, I apologize for being so hard on you about the sketch. It's going to take some explaining to my clients but I'll handle it. That leaves us with only the question of dinner to settle. How about it,

Maureen?"

Maureen? When had she stopped being the lovely Ms. Lowe? Oh, he was smooth. He'd find a way to handle his clients all right. Just the way he thought he was handling her.

Well, he had another think coming. Maybe he'd forgotten about Lisa, but Maureen hadn't. If ever there was a time and place for a lie this was it. "I can only speak for myself Mr. Parrish, but what you saw in that squad room yesterday was professional interest, not personal."

She heard him suck in a breath. He stepped back, held up his palms as if warding off a blow. He wasn't laughing now. "Professional, not personal," he repeated stiffly. "Yes, of course. Thanks for setting me straight. I won't bother you again."

Don't look back, she warned herself as the door hissed closed behind her. You'll be turned into a pillar of salt, or worse. That's a dangerous man. He doesn't look or sound like a murderer does he?

She raced across the lobby and punched in the security code for the elevator. When it arrived she got in, braced her back against the rear wall and rode to the fifth floor, fighting a sense of loss all the way.

Loss? What had she lost? Nothing, except maybe her sanity. She shouldn't have spent a single second with him. She should have turned around when she first spotted him and found a place to call the police. If the old man who'd been fixing his car wasn't there through it all who knew what Parrish might have tried.

She inhaled, long and hard. Time for a reality check. Brody Parrish, this Brody Parrish, wasn't the shy, self-conscious boy she remembered. He had become a monster. A clever, seductive monster.

The elevator came to a stop, the door slid open and she stepped out into the corridor. At the door to her own condo she bent to remove the key from the little Velcro pocket she kept laced to her running shoe. Straightening, she noticed that the door was slightly ajar.

A shiver of apprehension made her hesitate. Strange. When she'd left around six-thirty she'd been certain she heard it close and the lock catch automatically.

Maybe Lisa had gone out after all, and had forgotten to secure the door behind her. Cautiously, Maureen pushed it open and made her way down the hallway to the kitchen area. Two of the half dozen poppy seed muffins she'd made before leaving were gone from the basket on the tile countertop. And there were two stained coffee cups in the sink. Two. Two cups.

Maureen rapped on the guest room door and stuck her head inside.

35

The bed had obviously been slept in, but the room was deserted. She tried the bathroom. No Lisa.She peered into her own room, and her studio with its huge canvas of Red Riding Hood in a lush, overgrown forest, being stalked by a malevolent looking wolf. No Lisa.

No Lisa anywhere in the condo.

Maureen's stomach knotted. She took another deep breath and closed her eyes, and an image of Brody Parrish carefully shutting the Jag's luggage compartment took form inside her brain.

All that blarney about the sketch and the squad room and wanting to take her to dinner. It had all been a smoke screen. He hadn't come to see her. Somehow he'd found out where Lisa was staying.

And now she was gone.

CHAPTER 4

Ordinarily Brody treated his cars with the respect well designed and engineered machines deserved. He seldom drove them over the manufacturers' suggested speed limits and he never slammed their doors.

But today was far from ordinary. On his return from Philadelphia he pulled into Riverbend's circular driveway at a speed that sent gravel flying in all directions, switched off the ignition, jumped out and rammed the Jaguar's door closed with a force that left the poor vehicle quivering in place.

Finding a police cruiser parked in front of the house didn't do much to improve his mood. For a moment he just stood there, glaring at it, clenching and unclenching his fists, trying to calm himself down.

He needed to get control of himself. If he didn't watch out he was going to blow the reputation for good judgement he'd so carefully nurtured over the past few years. Being able to gauge investments and market conditions with a dispassionate eye had brought him success in a business he enjoyed. A business in which people's confidence, their trust, meant everything.

He'd almost thrown it all away this morning. And for what? A woman. A woman who'd told him in no uncertain terms to get lost. And what's more, had called the police after he'd left.

Well, it didn't look as if any permanent damage had been done this time. He shook his head and started for the house, having cooled off just enough to be civil. If Clay Stanton was inside and wanted a piece of him now was as good a time as any to get it over with.

In the entry hall Brody found Margaret Hartman waiting for him, her hands fluttering like a pair of panicked birds in front of her more than ample bosom.

"Thank God you're here, Mr. Parrish. Chief Marsh is in the parlor with your mother."

So it was Paul's car parked outside, not Stanton's. Brody relaxed a little more. The next few minutes should go easier than he'd originally thought. "Thank you Mrs. Hartman, the Chief is just the man I wanted to see."

The woman frowned. "Actually, I was hoping you would send him packing. I don't like the idea of his coming here and upsetting Mrs. Parrish."

Brody bit back a grim smile. If anyone in the parlor were upset he was willing to bet it wasn't his mother.

When he entered the room he found exactly what he'd expected. By the French windows overlooking the terrace, Victoria was ensconced like a queen in her favorite velvet wing chair. She looked regal, fragile and utterly serene. Seated across from her was a perspiring Paul Marsh. There was a silver coffee service and an ocean of hostility separating them.

"Ah, here's Brody now," Victoria said. "You left before breakfast again, Dear. Shall I have Margaret fix you something?"

"No thank you, Mother. I can wait until lunch."

The Chief stood and reached for Brody's hand. "Am I glad to see you. I've been trying to explain to your mother that we seem to have run into a problem regarding your alibi."

"As I see it the problem is police incompetence," Victoria commented dryly.

Brody dismissed that subject with a wave of his hand. "Before we get into all that, I think you might like to hear what happened to me this morning, Paul."

"Something to do with the case?"

"I would think so. On my way back from Philadelphia I was stopped by the State Police and my car was searched."

There was a moment of stunned silence and then Victoria returned her coffee cup to the silver tray with a sigh of imperial impatience. "Really Paul, you must put an end to this nonsense."

"What were they looking for?" Marsh stammered.

"They didn't say, but I suspect it was a body."

The blood drained from the Chief's face.

"Relax Paul, they didn't find one."

Marsh didn't appear amused. "Mrs. Parrish, may I use the telephone in the front entry."

Victoria nodded and he all but ran from the room.

Brody took a seat across from his mother. She filled a cup with coffee and handed it to him. It was a delicate white china thing covered with what looked like tiny four-leaf clovers. Brody traced one of the decorations with his thumb. He could do with a little good luck right about now. "What were you and Paul arguing about before I arrived?"

Victoria pursed her lips. "It was a discussion not an argument, and it concerned the man who came to see you last Saturday night."

"Bruce Cahill? What about him?"

"The police appear to be having trouble locating him. I told Paul I couldn't provide him with any more information, other than to corroborate the fact that he had been here."

"And how exactly were you able to do that, Mother? When Cahill arrived you and Mrs. Hartman had already retired for the evening."

"Neither Margaret nor I are so decrepit that we need to go to bed at eight o'clock, Brody. We were playing cribbage in my room when we heard a car drive up, so we stepped out into the hallway to have a little look." She smiled thinly and dabbed her at lips with a lace-edged napkin. "I confess to some curiosity as to whether your visitor was a man or woman. You'd said it was a business engagement but—"

"I don't invite women friends to Riverbend."

Victoria's smile wilted. "No, you haven't in quite a while."

In the uncomfortable silence that followed Brody wondered if Marsh would be persuaded by Victoria's assurance that she had witnessed Bruce Cahill's arrival. In the Chief's place Brody wouldn't be. He knew she was capable of lying if she thought it was in his or her best interests, and of convincing poor Mrs. Hartman to do the same.

"Mother, you may want to rethink—" he began just as Paul charged back into the room.

"Brody, you damn fool," he roared. "Can you give me one good reason why you were at Maureen Lowe's apartment this morning?"

Brody groaned. So she had called the police to complain that he'd been bothering her. But that still didn't explain why they had searched his car. He shrugged. "I admit I went there because I was angry at her at first. I wasn't thinking clearly. I held her responsible for the sketch in yesterday's paper. But after I'd let off some steam our conversation…"

The memory of her face brought a sudden smile to his lips. "Our conversation took a different turn."

"Who is this...Maureen Lowe?" Victoria inquired.

"Just a woman I thought I was interested in, until this morning when she made it clear that interest wasn't returned. Does that explain things, Paul?"

"It does if it's the truth."

"My son doesn't make a habit of lying."

"Your son has never been accused of murder before, Mrs. Parrish."

"And he never would have been if the police had done their jobs properly." Victoria shook her head. "I would hate to think the Parrishes supported the wrong man for the office of Police Chief, Paul. I would hate to think that in the next election that bigot Clay Stanton would be the only choice left us."

Marsh looked as if his blood pressure had just shot up fifty points. Brody hurried to defuse the situation. "Why did the State Troopers search my car?"

The Chief turned to him. "When they pulled you over, did they ask your permission to conduct a search?"

"Yes."

"You consented? Immediately? Without any argument?"

"Of course. I had nothing to hide."

"Okay, that's good. Remember that. You had nothing to hide."

"Was there a reason they stopped me, Paul?"

"There was a reason all right. Lisa Adams, the woman who witnessed Jeannie Starbuck's murder, the woman who picked you out of the lineup..."

Brody ground his teeth. "I know who Lisa Adams is."

"Glad to hear it. Did you also know she was staying with Maureen Lowe? Did you know she went missing sometime before you and Lowe parted company this morning? Did you know that Lowe immediately concluded that you..."

"Were responsible," Brody finished. "No wonder she was so anxious to get rid of me. You have my word, Paul, I hadn't a clue as to the witness' whereabouts. If I had I would never have gone near Maureen's place." He hesitated, remembering his visceral reaction to her in the squad room yesterday. "At least, I don't think I would have."

"Look, I have to get back to town. I have a witness to find." Marsh started for the door, stopped, turned back and took up a position directly in front of Victoria's chair. He waited until she grudgingly raised her eyes to his.

"With all due respect Mrs. Parrish, before I leave, there are some things we need to get straight. I appreciate your support during the last election but I've been a policeman for almost fifteen years. I earned this badge. I may not want to be a cop all my life but I'm a good one."

With obvious effort he lowered his voice. "Now, I don't for a minute believe Brody is guilty of murder and there are a lot of people in Granite Run who feel the same way. We'll do everything in our power to keep his involvement quiet until the real murderer is found. But I'm not the only one taking part in this investigation and it won't do any of us any good if I appear to be laying down on the job. Do I make myself clear?"

Victoria turned her head and fixed her attention on some point beyond the French doors. "Perfectly," she said coolly.

Brody stood. "I'll walk you to your car, Paul."

Outside the two men paused between the sleek sports car and the nondescript police sedan. "Thanks for the vote of confidence," Brody said.

"Yeah, well, I meant every word I said in there. To you and your mother." Marsh pulled open his car door. "Wait a minute. In all the excitement about Lisa Adams disappearance I almost forgot why I came. Do you have Bruce Cahill's business card or any notes about your meeting with him last Saturday night?"

"Of course I have."

"Can I have a look at them?"

"I took the notes to my office in town this morning. I'll drop them by the station this afternoon."

The Chief squinted up at Riverbend's exterior, its warm Pennsylvania fieldstone façade turned to gold by the midday sun. "Do you often see clients here?"

"Sometimes, since my mother's stroke, if a client requests an evening appointment."

"This place must impress the hell out of them." Marsh cocked an eyebrow. "Are evening appointments unusual?"

"Not particularly. My mother said you've been unable to locate Cahill. Did you call the hotel?"

"He's not registered. Never has been."

Brody blinked. "Huh. Perhaps I was mistaken about where he's staying. There's probably something in my notes that will clarify things. If not, we can always get in touch with the charity he represents."

"Get me those notes, Brody. With a bonafide alibi for the time of the murder you'll be out of the woods. It'll be Cahill's word against Lisa Adams'. Eyewitness testimony may be the answer to a prosecutor's prayer, but it's not always as reliable as people like to think. But dammit, it won't look good for any of us if we can't find her."

The Chief slid behind the steering wheel and pulled the car door closed. But before switching on the ignition he rolled down the window and leaned out. "One more thing. I should have mentioned this yesterday when I saw the way you looked at her in the squad room. Use your head, Brody. In the future stay away from Maureen Lowe."

Stay away from Maureen Lowe. Surprisingly Brody found himself grinning again, remembering the way she'd gone toe to toe with him this morning. He had to hand it to her, she gave as good as she got. Didn't back down, even when she must have been shaking in her running shoes, knowing Lisa Adams was upstairs. Just dug her fists into her hips and told him to scram.

Professional, not personal, huh? Maybe he'd just have to see about that.

Paul Marsh cleared his throat. "She's Barney Lowe's daughter."

"I know."

"Were you and she acquainted before Barney and his wife were, well, you know what happened to them, don't you?"

"Yeah."

Marsh shook his head. "Go figure. A cop all his life. Probably never unholstered his gun. One day heads off on a vacation with his wife to Miami where some punk breaks into their hotel and..."

"That had to have been hard on Maureen. She must have been just a kid when it happened."

"Twenty or thereabouts."

"That old? No, we never ran into each other that I recall. Just moved in different circles I guess. Worse luck."

"Barney and Clay Stanton were buddies. From what I hear she and Stanton are still pretty tight."

"Are they?" Brody mused. "She has great legs, Paul."

"The world is full of great legs, Brody. Those particular legs belong to a friend of Clay Stanton's and Lisa Adams'. Go take a cold shower. Maureen Lowe is in the enemy camp."

*   *   *

Clay Stanton allowed Maureen a few minutes of frantic pacing back and forth in front of his desk before finally calling a halt to it. "Working up a sweat isn't going to get us anywhere, kiddo. Sit down and let's go over the scenario one more time. Are you absolutely certain there'd been someone in the condo with Adams before she disappeared?"

Maureen dropped into the chair opposite his and sighed. How many times would she have to go over this? She could almost do it by rote. "The door was open and there were two unwashed coffee cups in the sink. No one can get past the outer lobby without knowing the security code or being buzzed in by someone inside. There was no sign of a struggle. She had to have let Parrish in."

Once again Maureen tried to make sense of the situation. "Why would Lisa do that, Clay? You saw her yesterday. She was a basket case. She trembled every time his name was mentioned."

Clay shrugged. "She might have unlocked to door because she thought you'd forgotten your key and were buzzing to get in. Probably didn't realize it was Parrish until it was too late."

"You think that he pushed his way in and then talked her into a cup of coffee and a friendly chat?" Maureen shook her head. "No way, Clay. You know as well as I do that wasn't the way it went down."

Stanton leaned across the desk. "You still don't get it, Maureen. Parrish is a salesman. A hustler. Charming people into parting with their money, into trusting him, is what he does for a living." He wagged an accusing finger at her. "And if what I saw happen in this squad room yesterday is any indication, his brand of blarney works with most women."

Maureen felt the blood rush to her face. "I'm sure I don't know what you're talking about."

"I'm talking about the fireworks that went off when you and Parrish first laid eyes on each other. Anyone unlucky enough to have stepped between the two of you would have been burnt to a crisp."

"Clay, it was just, all of a sudden recognizing him like that, and at the same time remembering how he'd saved that girl." Maureen's chin came up. "Anyhow, you're forgetting who called you this morning, who told you that Lisa was missing and Brody Parrish was responsible."

"Right! Because you're smart enough to realize what happened yesterday was just hormones. Rub a good-looking male and a good-looking female together and what do you get? Sparks. But does a ditz like Lisa Adams understand that? I doubt it. I think she's perfectly capable of letting an operator like Parrish in, letting him bop her over the head, drag her downstairs and…"

Maureen shuddered. "You said that the State Police stopped his car and didn't find anything."

"He could have dropped her off anywhere on the highway between Philadelphia and where they caught up with him."

"Oh God," Maureen moaned. "Poor Lisa."

"Now, don't get me wrong. I'm nor saying that he necessarily hurt her. He could have simply threatened or bribed her into changing her story. When and if she turns up alive we have to be prepared for her to renege on her identification of him. Fat lot of good it'll do him. Your sketch is a piece of evidence he can't make disappear no matter how much money he throws at it."

Clay tipped back his chair and clasped his hands behind his head. "By the way, since you brought up the subject of the rescue, do you happen to remember the name of the girl Parrish 'saved' fifteen years ago?"

Maureen could tell by the tone of Clay's voice that this wasn't a casual question. And the self-satisfied smirk he'd worn most of yesterday had returned. "No," she said and waited for the next shoe to fall.

"Would it surprise you to hear it was…" he paused for dramatic effect, "Jeannie Starbuck? Some coincidence, huh?"

Maureen's blood went cold, but for some terrible reason she wasn't as shocked as Clay obviously expected her to be. Maybe she'd remembered the girl's name along with everything else about the rescue. Maybe because, from the moment she'd recognized Brody yesterday, in her mind at least, the rescue and murder were linked. Maybe Clay had just put into words something she'd subconsciously known all along.

"You really believe he murdered that woman, don't you Clay?"

"Yup," he said. "I've always thought the guy was a three dollar bill."

She stared across the desk at him. *And what do I believe?* she asked herself. Well, for starters, she thought the Granite Run Police Department was experiencing an unusual degree of internal conflict. Clay could hardly wait to slip the noose around Brody Parrish's neck, while Paul Marsh appeared determined the accused would get every chance to clear his name. Why were these hard-line, opposing stances being taken so early in the game? Surely more evidence was being collected from the murder scene. Other witnesses were being interviewed. Brody's alibi was being checked out.

Paul Marsh's position, even if dictated by political concerns, was the more rational. Why not tie up all the loose ends before making an arrest, before presenting a case to the prosecuting attorney? What was Clay's problem? Who was he trying to convince? Her? Ridiculous. Apart from her sketch and Lisa's disappearance Maureen's connection to the case was marginal.

Himself?

"Is there any evidence against him other than Lisa's identification, Clay?" she asked. "DNA? Anything?"

Clay shrugged. "It's in the works. The lab boys are processing blood and fiber samples from Starbuck's apartment and I've got a man interviewing people who were in the Crocodile Grill Saturday night. The bartender and a couple of patrons."

Maureen bit her lip. "What's your take on those recent cases of mistaken eyewitness identification? There was one on the West Coast and another in North Carolina. A woman there identified the wrong man as her rapist. He went to prison. It was years before the truth was discovered."

Clay shook his head. "Anecdotal stuff and nonsense. Eyewitness evidence is still the best evidence there is. Direct, not circumstantial. Juries eat it up."

"Yes, but…"

Stanton glared at her. "Are you saying that you think Adams is lying?"

Maureen winced. She recalled her assurances to Lisa the night before. "Lying? Of course not. But memory is a faulty thing. It abhors a vacuum. People are tempted to fill in any empty blanks in their recollections with guesses and assumptions."

Clay narrowed his eyes, searing her with a pointed look. "You know kiddo, if I were you and I really believed that, I guess I would start looking into another line of work. Eyewitnesses are your stock in trade."

Maureen sighed. Clay really knew how to stick it to a person. Of course there were problems with eyewitness testimony. Anything involving human beings was subject to error. But what was the alternative? To discount it? That didn't make any sense either. So why was she, of all people, flailing around like this, tilting at windmills?

But she knew the answer to that, didn't she? Even if she didn't want to admit it. Didn't want to deal with it. It was that first sketch. She'd drawn a face that didn't exist and she hadn't been able to forget it.

The sound of approaching footsteps made her turn and look behind her, grateful at this point for any interruption.

Paul Marsh came to a stop beside Clay's desk. "Well, well, well, if it isn't Ms. Lowe again. You're getting to be something of a fixture around here, aren't you? This makes what? Three times in as many days? Maybe we ought to put her on the payroll, Stanton."

"She's here because she's worried about Adams," Clay snapped.

"Well she can stop worrying. I just had a call from the Philadelphia police. They've had a man watching your condo, Ms. Lowe. Lisa Adams turned up there a few minutes ago without a scratch on her, wondering what all the fuss was about."

Maureen sprang to her feet. "Thank God," she cried. Until this moment she hadn't let herself deal with how personally responsible she felt for Lisa's disappearance. If she hadn't invited Lisa to stay at the condo, if Channel Nine hadn't run that piece about her last night, if she hadn't gone running this morning, then Brody Parrish would never have been able to...to...

To what? Brody Parrish hadn't done anything to Lisa. Lisa was all right.

"Where on earth did she go?" Maureen demanded.

"To see a private investigator," Marsh replied.

Maureen blinked. "To see—who?"

Two deep, vertical lines appeared between Clay's brows. "Who was it?"

"Dave Messenger," Marsh said.

Clay rubbed his hand over his chin. "He's a good man."

The two men exchanged a long, wordless look.

Maureen spun from one to the other. "You two obviously know something I don't. Will one of you please fill me in."

"Messenger is a P. I. with a certain expertise, Maureen," Clay began. "He administers polygraph tests."

Maureen watched in speechless astonishment as Paul Marsh reached inside his jacket and pulled out a sheaf of papers. "I can understand your confusion Ms. Lowe. It's hard to believe, but this morning Lisa Adams, at her own expense, underwent a lie detector test. I've spoken with Messenger. She authorized him to fax this department the results of the test along with his evaluation. I have them here." He handed the papers to Clay. "What do you think of them, Stanton?"

With maddening deliberation Clay studied each piece of paper for what seemed like an eternity. Finally he shifted uncomfortably in his chair and glanced up at Maureen out of the corner of his eye. "Lisa passed with flying colors," he said. "According to Messenger, the polygraph needle didn't jump once."

*   *   *

Brody could see that his mother was exhausted.

Only an hour ago she'd locked horns with Paul Marsh and treated him like a recalcitrant employee, her eyes flashing even when he'd refused to let her bully him. Now she sagged back against the high, upholstered dining room chair and toyed with her napkin. She'd barely touched the savory lentil soup the housekeeper had prepared for lunch, or the crusty French bread she'd baked to accompany it.

Brody put down his spoon. "Mrs. Hartman went to a great deal of trouble to please you, Mother. Don't disappoint her. She's obviously made it her mission in life to fatten you up."

Victoria sighed. "Someone should explain to Margaret and Dr. Haslip that lack of exercise does not promote a hearty appetite. I'll be able to eat when I'm allowed out of this house once in a while." She leaned forward and placed her napkin on the table. "By the way, while that fool Marsh was here I hesitated to mention that Richard Bailey telephoned this morning while you were paying a call on that young woman. What is her name again?"

"Maureen Lowe." Brody frowned and gave himself a mental kick in the pants. Paul Marsh was no fool. He was right about Maureen. Brody had wasted valuable time and energy thinking about her, and it had gotten him into deeper water than he'd been to begin with. No woman was worth it. He needed to forget about her and concentrate on his more immediate concerns.

He raked a hand through his hair. "Is Richard still angry with me?"

"He is disappointed and worried, as I am. Really Brody, what is the sense of our having a lawyer on retainer if you are not going to take his advice." She touched Brody's arm. "Richard believes you should seek criminal counsel, Dear. His firm doesn't handle criminal cases but he highly recommends a man called Hayes Wicklow."

"No!" Brody snapped. "I haven't been charged with anything. Hiring a criminal lawyer would suggest that I expect to be arrested. I don't. And even if I did Wicklow would be the last man I'd ask to represent me. He's a foul-mouthed, self-serving..." The look on his mother's face brought Brody up short. The anger again. He had to get control of it. It was unnecessary and counterproductive.

He took a deep breath and lowered his voice. "Listen, Mother, once Paul locates Bruce Cahill the whole situation will be over and done with."

"Ah, Mr. Cahill. I had almost forgotten about him." For a moment Victoria seemed to perk up, but then she snatched the napkin from where she'd placed it on the table and began to pluck at it again. "But it is too bad the murder victim had to be that little fool, Jeannie Starbuck."

Dammit! His mother didn't know when to let go of a subject. Brody pushed back from the table and got to his feet. "You look tired, Mother. I think it's time for your nap. I'll get Mrs. Hartman to help you upstairs. I need to go into town for awhile."

"Oh, I can tell you're displeased with me, Brody. But you really shouldn't be. You of all people know what mischief Jeannie was capable of."

"The 'mischief' as you see fit to call it, wasn't all of Jeannie's making. And you know it." Brody watched his mother pale. She looked as if he'd struck her. He forced himself to reach for her hand. "I'm sorry if I was abrupt, but the last thing I want to think or talk about now is Jeannie. Alive or dead. It's important that I put all this behind me and get back to work. But you're right. Her having been the victim is a complication that makes that more difficult."

"But once Mr. Cahill is found..." Victoria began hopefully.

"Yes, Cahill's the key. Excuse me, Mother. The sooner I get the notes about my meeting with him into Paul's hands the better."

A quarter of an hour later, while Mrs. Hartman was upstairs helping Victoria into bed, the front doorbell rang. On his way out, briefcase in hand, Brody answered it.

He and his visitor stared at each other in silence for some seconds. "Well, this is a surprise," he said finally. Then smiling in spite of himself, he swung the door wide. "But I'm forgetting my manners. We've done the doorstep bit once already today, haven't we? Come in. But I think you should know that just a little while ago I was warned to stay away from you."

CHAPTER 5

She was here. Here at Riverbend, standing at the window, looking out toward the Brandywine. Just as lovely, just as perfect as he'd pictured her.

He hardly knew what to think. He was elated. Ecstatic. When she'd arrived he'd been afraid he was dreaming. That he'd conjured her up out of thin air. But she was flesh, not fantasy, and close enough to touch.

Her coming put to rest any doubts he might have had. She was the one he'd been waiting for, searching for, all along. And this is where she belonged. With him. Did she realize that? Could she feel it? Riverbend needed someone like her, someone beautiful, intelligent, full of energy and life.

Someone he could trust.

Forget the river and the trees, he wanted to tell her. I'm here. See me. See your future.

*   *   *

Maureen felt Brody Parrish's eyes boring into her back. He was waiting for her to turn around and face him. To tell him why she was here.

A reasonable expectation. Only she had to get the answer straight in her own mind before she could rationally communicate it to anyone else. Especially to him. Her cheeks still burned from their encounter at the front door and she welcomed the cool breeze coming in through his open window.

The air was sparkling, honeysuckle fresh on her skin. Let him think she was simply enjoying the view for a second or two more. She certainly wasn't the first person to be struck dumb by Riverbend's natural beauty.

Just look at the place. The word spectacular didn't do it justice. It was magnificent. Commanding. The house itself crowned a sloping, wooded property in the center of two manicured semi-circles, one a raked gravel driveway, the other a clipped green lawn that backed up to the river. From where Maureen stood she could glimpse the spot that had inspired the estate's name. Riverbend; the point at which the Brandywine funneled through a narrow gorge, made a dramatic left turn and then swept down into town.

She finally found her voice. "That painting in the front hall, the one we passed on our way in here? It must have been done from just about here."

He came closer; reached around her with the glass of water she'd asked for. "You're very observant. But then you are an artist, aren't you?" He pointed out the window. "According to family legend the painter, Stephen Gresham, and his easel were fixtures on the terrace for almost a year. He did a study of Riverbend in each of the four seasons. My great-grandfather purchased Summer. That's the one you noticed in the hall. The Brandywine Museum in Chadds Ford has Autumn." He stepped back. "I understand some gallery in Philadelphia owns Winter and Spring."

"Yes, the Hauser Gallery. I know the owner, Pete Hauser." Maureen took a sip of water and glanced at Parrish over her shoulder. "Pete's pretty high on Gresham. His illusionist style is coming back into vogue. Your painting is probably worth a great deal more that what your great-grandfather paid for it."

Parrish shrugged and she became the recipient of one of his now-you-see-it-now you-don't smiles. "My mother would know more about that than I would. She's the collector in the family. Are you here to see her?"

Maureen turned and the full impact of the room she'd hurried through a few minutes before hit her. Everything in it, the paneled walls, the ceiling high bookshelves, even the leather briefcase Parrish had tossed onto the burled wood desk, gave off a warm, coppery glow. Everything that is, except a curving, citrus yellow love seat that seemed to float in the center of the room like a crescent of lemon in a cup of freshly brewed tea.

She took another swallow of water. "No, I came to see you. But I confess to being distracted by my surroundings. They make me a little nostalgic. When I was a kid my friends and I would follow the Brandywine through those woods out there, past all the big, fancy houses. It was like something out of a book or dream. The dark forest full of quivering trees, the castles on the hill, the river."

Parrish raised an eyebrow. "Ah, a romantic. I wouldn't have guessed that about you. Sounds as if you loved Granite Run. And yet you left. Why?'

"The usual reason I suppose. I went off to college when I was eighteen. Had a taste of the big city. After my parents died there didn't seem to be any compelling reason to stay, so…"

"I remember your parents. They were good people. Their…deaths were a real tragedy. But I have only the haziest memory of you. It's a small town. Before you left, had our paths ever crossed? I doubt that I would have forgotten if they had, but…"

Once, she thought, but he'd been too busy pulling Jeannie Starbuck out of the river to notice a skinny adolescent standing at the back of the crowd with her heart on her sleeve. Maureen shook her head. "You were older, went to private schools. I knew who you were, had seen you around, but we never met."

"Until yesterday."

"Until yesterday."

They stared at each other, silently reliving more recent memories. The squad room. The lineup. Their confrontation in front of the condo. Maureen downed the last of the water, amazed that she managed to keep her hand steady. He took the empty glass from her, crossed the room and placed it on a leather coaster on the desk. Then he turned, hitched his hips onto the desk's edge, folded his arms across his chest and nailed her with his eyes again.

Maureen's pulse jumped. He'd changed out of the jeans and fisherman's sweater he'd worn earlier in the day, into a pale blue shirt and tie worn under a tan, sharkskin business suit. No uniform could have lent him more authority, or could have made him seem more intimidating.

"Now that we've had our little stroll down memory lane," he said, "I think it's time you enlightened me as to why you are here."

Maureen hesitated. What could she say? That she was troubled because a semi-hysterical woman had taken a lie detector test and the needle never jumped once? That that peculiar result was so unusual as

51

to be suspect in itself?

But was she free to divulge the information about the test? Or was it privileged? The police had only told her about the results because they thought of her as a colleague. Now, with these highly questionable findings in mind, where did her loyalties lie? With Clay Stanton and the police? With the frightened, lonely woman she'd invited into her home? Or with a man who had, perhaps purposely, perhaps cleverly, raised serious questions about her professional involvement? A man she'd helped label a murderer?

No! Not a murderer. A murder suspect. She needed to remember that. Needed to remind him.

He waited, watching her, his blue eyes as interested as they'd been yesterday in the squad room, and the same curious smile playing at the corners of his mouth.

"Today," she began cautiously, "in front of my condo…"

He held up a hand. "I did not abduct your roommate."

"I know. She's been found. Or to be more exact, she's returned." Maureen looked down at the lush oriental carpet. "I'm sorry about the police stopping your car. I was the one who called them."

"I guessed as much. And if I'd been in your shoes I might have done the same thing."

His comment surprised and encouraged her. "Then you're not angry?"

"I wouldn't go that far. Not yet. Let's just say that after giving it some thought, I understand. I was out of line this morning. Having me turn up on your doorstep must have been a shock. Is that why you came? To apologize for siccing the cops on me?"

She took a deep breath and her glasses skidded down the bridge of her nose, a sure sign of the nervousness she hoped he hadn't noticed. She pushed them back into place with the tip of her index finger. "Yes and no. You said something this morning, about my sketches being released to the public before there'd been a thorough investigation. The fact is, that's worried me in the past. Of course, it's often a necessary step. When all the police have is a description of a dangerous suspect they need to enlist the public's help as fast as they can."

"Granted. But your actions this morning only prove my point. I'd been accused of one crime, so when your friend wasn't precisely where you expected her to be you jumped to the conclusion that I was responsible. Anything that happened while I was in the vicinity would have been blamed on me." He shook his head. "That sort of evidence might not hold up in court but I'm not sure my clients are going to be any more discerning about my possible guilt than you were."

"But in most cases the reason a sketch is needed is that the suspect is not a well known member of the community, doesn't have as much to lose as someone like you."

"That's a fairly elitist thing to say," he commented dryly. "A manicurist would have as much to lose. Her clientele. Her livelihood."

"Touché. You should have been a lawyer, Mr. Parrish."

"Considering the situation I find myself in, it wouldn't have been a bad idea." He grinned. Maureen found his quicksilver changes of mood disconcerting. "Look," he went on, "I'm more philosophical about this than I was earlier. There are obviously telling arguments on both sides of the issue. I have a right to protect my reputation. The authorities have to act for the greater good of the community. Your apology, if that's what this is, is accepted. You're absolved. Go and sin no more."

His last comment sounded more like a dismissal than the acceptance of an apology, but Maureen had no intention of leaving just yet. The apology had been the easy part. The rest of what she had to say would be more difficult to explain, but she'd made up her mind on the drive to Riverbend and she was going through with this come hell or high water.

She walked over to the love seat and plopped herself down in its center. "This is a lovely room. Was it always an office?"

"No. It was, and is, a library. While I'm living here I need a place to work and see clients, so I've temporarily appropriated it." He treated her to a long, amused stare. "Come on, Ms. Lowe, you obviously have something else you want to discuss. It's time to put all your cards on the table."

Do it, Maureen thought. It's now or never. Get it over with. "Is this where you saw Bruce Cahill on the night of Jeannie Starbucks murder?"

He came away from the desk with a jerk and before she had time to catch her breath he was standing over her, his eyes blazing. Now he looked more like the man who'd first appeared on her doorstep this morning. Angry and dangerous.

"For someone who claims to be only casually connected to the case you're amazingly well informed. You didn't come here to apologize, did you, Maureen? You're Clay Stanton's stealth missile. You're his spy."

Her, a spy for Clay? Where had Parrish gotten such a crazy idea?

Nothing could be further from the truth. Clay would have apoplexy if he knew she was here. But here was Parrish, standing over her, glaring, trying to make her feel like a naughty child caught in a lie. Well, she wasn't going to let him get away with that. Not when she came here to do him a favor.

"Look Mr. Parrish, I'm getting a crick in my neck from looking up at you. If you want to continue this conversation, then sit down."

His eyes widened; then all of a sudden he began to laugh. It was an exciting sound. Deep and utterly masculine. He shook his head and settled himself next to her and she quickly realized that his nearness was going to be even harder to handle than his anger had been.

"Lady, you need to lose the attitude. Nobody talks to me that way. Not in this house. Not any more."

"Well, maybe it's time someone did."

He leaned toward her, one arm resting along the back of the love seat, his fingers only inches from her shoulder. "So my suggesting you might be a spy made you uncomfortable. That's no way to treat a guest. But if you want me to trust you and your motives you're going to have to answer my question. Did Clay Stanton send you?"

It was time to stop beating around the bush. Parrish wasn't in the mood for games. "No, Clay didn't send me, but he is a friend of mine. I've been around cops all my life. That's what you have to understand. And people with jobs like mine, forensic types, lab people, trauma teams? After a while we all begin to sound like cops. Even think like them. We can't help it."

"You mean, everyone begins to look guilty of something."

She smiled. "It happens, but that's not what I meant. I'm talking about intuition. Gut instinct. Experienced officers can look at a crime scene or a piece of evidence and think to themselves, there's something wrong here. Something's missing. Out of place. Not quite kosher."

She paused, trying to gauge his reaction, but his expression remained noncommittal.

"Go on," he said evenly. "I'm listening."

"My gut instinct tells me you're not guilty." That, and a rejected sketch, and hard to swallow polygraph results, she thought.

"Your gut instinct told you something different this morning."

"I wasn't working on instinct or intuition this morning. It was more like … surprise and fear. Whatever it was, I was wrong. You had nothing to do with Lisa Adams' disappearance."

"And you don't like being wrong, do you?" He frowned. "But that can't be all there is to it. Did anything happen between then and now to change your mind?"

Maureen hesitated again. She couldn't tell him about the polygraph test. At least, not until she confronted Lisa. But perhaps there was a way she could sidestep the issue for the time being. "Your past history and clean record should have earned you the benefit of the doubt. This morning I didn't give you that, and look what happened."

"So, you feel you owe me?" he asked, not making the slightest effort to disguise his skepticism.

"You're simply reaping the benefit of any others who might have had problems because of my sketches. Theoretical problems. No one was ever convicted on the strength of a sketch alone. There's always other evidence. But even if someone were later exonerated, the image of his or her face on a television screen or the front page of a newspaper might have lingered in the public's memory. That has troubled me from time to time."

"Ah, now I understand. This is an exercise in expiation. Apology and absolution aren't enough. You're looking to do penance, to make restitution. Am I hearing an offer of assistance here, Maureen?"

Maureen didn't particularly care for the way he put it but she found herself relaxing, satisfied to have talked her way through the polygraph minefield. "I wouldn't be a bad person to have in your corner. I'm familiar with police procedures and investigations. I could help you prove your innocence."

"If I'm innocent."

"Naturally. If you're innocent."

"And if, while helping me, you came across evidence to the contrary, you wouldn't hesitate to feed me to the wolves, would you?"

Maureen smiled. "Not for a New York minute."

"I thought as much," he said.

* * *

Brody got to his feet and crossed the room to the window, where he stood with his back to her, his hands in his pockets.

Looking at her made rational thinking difficult. She was entirely too disturbing. All during their conversation he'd been watching that soft, generous mouth, catching flashes of pink tongue behind rows of small, neat teeth.

She had everything. Looks. Intelligence. Sass.

And she was no longer afraid of him.

Why?

Dammit, he had to be careful. All that talk about hunches and gut instinct. He just didn't buy it. She was concealing something. He was tempted to go along with her, just to find out what she was up to, but he would be playing with fire in more ways than one.

Not a good idea. Still, desire as immediate and powerful as any he had ever known sucked the caution out of his bones and replaced it with heat. Without turning around he said, "I admit the thought of joining forces with you under any conditions is attractive, Maureen, but the truth is, I don't require any help."

There was a second or two of silence. Come on, Maureen, he thought. Change my mind. You'll never meet a man more eager to be convinced.

"Are you sure?" she said finally. "While I was at the police station this morning I overheard a couple of pieces of information that were, in the light of your obvious confidence, surprising. You were acquainted with the murder victim and your alibi remains unsubstantiated."

Brody kept his expression impassive. "Those may be the facts, ma'am, but when you arrived here today I was on my way into town to take care of the alibi problem. To repeat what I told you this morning, by this time tomorrow I'll be completely exonerated. So you see, I won't need your assistance. Professionally."

He turned around. As he watched, she uncrossed her legs, stood, then smoothed her skirt down over her hips and thighs. Brody inhaled, felt the hollow under his tongue fill with saliva. It was a good thing there was half the length of the room between them or he might not be able to keep his hands off her.

God, he was about to make a fool of himself. "But I would like to take you out to dinner tonight," he heard himself saying.

*   *   *

All during the drive back to Philadelphia Maureen conducted a running argument with herself.

Is it my imagination, or did you just accept a dinner invitation from a suspected murderer?

Get off my back. By this evening, or tomorrow morning at the latest, he expects to be out of the woods.

Why didn't you tell him to give you a call then?

Listen, he's not lying. I've never seen anyone more confident.

Or more incredibly attractive.

Okay, okay. What's the big deal? It's not as if I'll be in any kind of danger. Restaurante Tio Pepe is a public place.

Yeah. So was the Crocodile Grill.

The driver behind Maureen honked his horn as her Jeep Cherokee momentarily skidded across the white dividing line. Maureen gripped the steering wheel tighter and pulled the car back into her lane.

Damn it, one way or another you're going to get yourself killed, the voice inside her head sneered. *And Brody Parrish is going to be the cause.*

Maureen winced. Sometime during her visit to the Parrish estate this afternoon she had forgotten about the Crocodile Grill, about Jeannie Starbuck, even about Lisa.

Lisa, who was at this very moment waiting at the condo for Maureen to return.

She took the Philadelphia off ramp and drove through the residential streets that led to the center of the city. She had some serious thinking to do before she confronted her houseguest. How was she going to act, what was she going to say to Lisa when she got home? So much had happened since the last time they'd seen each other. Since, God, had it only been last night?

If Brody Parrish were telling the truth, if his alibi checked out, then when Lisa picked him out of the lineup yesterday she'd been either mistaken or lying.

The polygraph test she'd bought and paid for supported her story. But what most civilians didn't realize was that there were those in law enforcement who put little store in the test's credibility. It was a tool, but a suspect one. Even when administered by experts it could be manipulated. Overly excited, innocent people sometimes reacted to questions in ways that made them appear to be lying, while cool, clever sociopaths or people under the influence of mind altering drugs, passed with flying colors.

As had Lisa.

Of course, there was another way to look at it. Brody could be innocent and Lisa could still be telling the truth, as she saw it. Mistaken identifications made by well meaning eyewitnesses were part of cop folklore. Despite her denials it was possible Lisa had seen Brody around Granite Run and confused him with someone at the Crocodile Grill who resembled him. That might explain the confusion about the first sketch.

But even then, the results of Lisa's test were at odds with everything Maureen knew about her. She had been as panicky and stressed out as any witness Maureen had ever interviewed. Lisa had needed her hand held during the lineup, had looked on the verge of a breakdown when she heard Brody wasn't going to be immediately arrested.

And yet she had iced the lie detector needle. It had never jumped once. Everything came back to that.

Maureen recalled the wordless incredulity on the faces of Paul Marsh and Clay Stanton this morning when they'd read the private investigator's report. The results of the polygraph supported Clay's point of view, and yet even he hadn't been able to completely disguise his skepticism.

And her own surprise had been reason enough to send Maureen racing off to Riverbend looking for the answers to questions she wasn't even sure how to frame. So instead of demanding answers she ended up offering her services as a...a what? A companion?

She pulled up in front of the condo and eased the Cherokee into the space Brody's Jaguar had occupied this morning.

Admit the truth, at least to yourself, her conscience accused. Lisa's polygraph was an excuse to see Brody Parrish, not a reason. You've been bound and determined to worm your way into his life since that moment in the squad room yesterday. Maybe even for longer than that. Maybe since the day you saw him carry Jeannie Starbuck out of the Brandywine fifteen years ago.

For a few moments Maureen remained in the car, staring into space, thinking. Was it true? Was she behaving with all the intellectual discernment of a lovesick twelve-year-old?

She got out, locked the car and glanced up at the windows of her condo. Was it her imagination or had there been some furtive movement behind one of the blinds?

She hadn't imagined it. When Maureen got off the elevator Lisa was waiting in the open doorway of the condo.

"Hi, girlfriend," she said with a worried smile.

Maureen shook her head as she stepped past Lisa into the foyer. "Hello, Lisa. Seems like we got our wires crossed this morning, doesn't it?"

Lisa closed the door and followed Maureen into the living room. "Are you mad at me, Maureen?"

"I'm waiting to hear why you took off without telling me where you were going or when you'd be back. Are you aware that I called the police?"

"Yeah. The cops told me, and then that Chief Marsh called here an hour ago and read me the riot act. Said I'd caused you and everyone else a lot of trouble. Fat lot of nerve he has, if you ask me. I'm practically doing his job for him."

"Didn't it occur to you that I'd be worried when I found you were gone?"

Lisa averted her eyes. "I guess I just didn't stop to think. I'm not used to havin' people worry about me. And I had this great idea during the night, you know, about the lie detector test, and I just wanted to surprise you. So right after breakfast I called a taxi and—"

"How did you know where to find someone to administer a polygraph?"

"Found the name the same place I found the taxi service. In the telephone book. See, I tore out the page."

Lisa looked so pleased with herself Maureen had to smile. She took the crumpled piece of yellow paper the other woman held out to her. It was a half-page business advertisement for Messenger Private Investigations. Open seven days a week, twenty-four hours a day. Experts at finding lost relatives, delinquent fathers, natural parents. Specializing in private polygraph testing.

She sighed and handed the paper back to Lisa. This bird-like, jumpy little woman was apparently more resourceful than Maureen had given her credit for being. According to Clay Stanton and Paul Marsh, Messenger was the best. And Lisa had found him on her own.

Usually, the best didn't come cheap.

"I hope you don't mind my asking, but was the test expensive?"

Lisa shrugged. "Mr. Messenger felt sorry for me. He gave me a special price. Two hundred dollars."

"Even so, on a waitress' salary..."

"Hey, what with tips and all, waitresses don't do so bad. I worked with a girl once; she got hired on by one of the airlines as a flight attendant. Real glamour job, right? Well, a couple of months later she's back at the restaurant whinin' about how she can't make it on what they pay and can she have her old job back. Naw, don't worry about what it cost. It took a hefty bite out of the little I'd put by, but it was worth it."

"Why, Lisa?"

"Why what?"

"Why did you have the test in the first place? Why was it worth all that money?"

"Jeez, Maureen, if you really want to know, it was because of that question you asked me last night. It made me nervous." Lisa's voice began to shake. "You had, I don't know, a funny look on your face. I couldn't sleep for wonderin' what was on your mind. So this morning I took care of things. See? The lie detector test proves that everything happened Saturday night just like I said it did. Now we can be friends again." She reached out and touched Maureen's arm. "I'm sorry if I worried you. You're real important to me. If you didn't trust me I don't know what I'd do. I don't have anybody else."

How terrible for her, Maureen thought. To be so very needy, so dependent on someone she's known for a grand total of forty-eight hours. What a miserable adolescence she must have had, deserted when she was hardly more than a baby, then passed from one set of foster parents to another. No way was Maureen going to add another rejection to all the others Lisa had experienced without a more thorough investigation. Right now a confrontation was out of the question. Maureen's concerns could wait until a time Lisa seemed less vulnerable.

"Lisa, if you're happier for having had the test, then I'm glad you did it."

A look of relief washed over the other woman's face. "Oh, I am," she said brightly. "And now that the cops have seen Mr. Messenger's report, they'll finally arrest Brody Parrish. Put the guy in jail where he belongs. Then you and I can relax and enjoy ourselves for a change. Maybe even go out some night and have a little fun."

"I wouldn't count on that just yet. From what I heard at the Granite Run police station today, they're still checking out his alibi."

Lisa grimaced. "Hey, let's not talk about him anymore, okay? Just the thought of him makes me wanna' puke. And I want us to eat up a storm tonight. My treat this time. We'll order in Chinese and scarf it up like there's no tomorrow."

"Sounds wonderful, Lisa, but you'll have to give me a raincheck tonight. I have a dinner date."

Lisa eyes narrowed. "I thought you weren't seeing anyone."

If just the mention of Brody's name shook Lisa up what would knowing the identity of Maureen's date do to her? "This is someone new. Someone I just met."

"Great." Lisa grinned. "When he picks you up I'll give him the once over and let you know what I think."

"He's not coming here. I always meet first dates on neutral ground. It makes it easier to walk away if things don't pan out."

Lisa flopped down onto the sofa, picked up a throw cushion and hugged it to her chest. "So where are you and this hunk gettin' together," she asked peevishly. "Or is that none of my business."

"Don't be silly," Maureen said over her shoulder as she headed off to take a shower. "I'm meeting him at a restaurant here in Philadelphia. A place called Tio Pepe's."

* * *

He put down the phone and went into the bathroom. He would have to hurry. There wasn't much time. It was already seven-thirty and Maureen would be at the restaurant in an hour.

He peered into the mirror above the wash basin and raked his fingers through his dark hair. It was no longer the flowing, poetic length most women went for, but time would remedy that.

Tio Pepe's. He could almost see it. Lots of atmosphere. Elegant Spanish food. Tex-Mex would do a better job of firing up the old libido, but his libido didn't need any help tonight. Just the thought of being in the same room with Maureen Lowe was aphrodisiac enough.

He'd called the restaurant and requested a table in a secluded corner. The maitre d' had promised to try, but at this late hour and on such short notice, the Senor must understand...

Oh, the Senor understood all right. One of the many things this town had taught him was that a properly placed greenback went a long way toward dispelling problems of that sort.

He licked his lips in anticipation of the night ahead and likened the orgasmic shot of joy he experienced to what he'd heard TV evangelists describe as being "born again." Born again. The term impressed him as particularly fitting. Last Saturday night had been the end of his old life. He'd been in a sort of limbo since then. But tonight was the beginning of the new, and Maureen would be part of it.

Perhaps the sweetest, the most important part.

CHAPTER 6

Apart from its fabulous cuisine, Tio Pepe's appeal lay in contrast. It was a hole in the ground, lit by crystal chandeliers above tables set with gleaming china and silver, hovered over by tuxedo-clad waiters.

When Maureen got there Brody had already arrived and been seated. It was widely reported that people made reservations weeks in advance, but somehow, she decided as she followed the maitre d' to where Brody waited for her, he had managed to procure for himself the best table in the house. One nestled in a private alcove just off the main dining room, with the rest of the restaurant laid out before him like a glittering panorama, while he sat back, looking for all the world as if he owned the place, and watched her approach.

On the way to his table she noticed one of the other diners, a man sitting by himself, turn and stare in her direction. It was happening more and more often lately, ever since articles and pictures of her had begun appearing in newspapers and magazines. And after that glowing piece on Channel Nine last night she could probably expect more of the same.

Lord, she hoped the gawker wouldn't stop her and ask for an autograph or anything remotely like that. She didn't want anything to spoil tonight, didn't want Brody reminded of her part in the murder case being prepared against him.

He'd been so adamant this afternoon. *Tonight is personal, not professional. Right?*

That was fine with her.

Luckily, she made it to the table without being accosted. Brody's eyes widened with approval. He stood and pulled out a chair for her. She sat down and the maitre d' fluttered a napkin into her lap and left.

"I'm impressed," she said.

Brody resumed his seat. "Good. That was the intention." He signaled to a waiter standing just out of earshot. "I find I want very much to impress you, Maureen. I thought Tio Pepe's was a start."

Maureen smiled to herself. If he'd had any idea how good an impression he'd made fifteen years ago they'd probably have been dining under the golden arches.

The waiter produced a wine list and an appetizer menu.

She looked it over. There was a dizzying array of selections to choose from. "I suspect you've been here before," she said. "Any suggestions?"

"The sangria is the best you'll find outside Madrid. It'll go well with any of the appetizers. Especially...," he paused and glanced down at the menu, "the Mushrooms from the Caves of Segovia."

"Sounds irresistible, but I don't think my appetite is up to both an appetizer and a meal. Can we share the mushrooms?"

"That can be arranged, can't it, Raoul?" Brody said to the waiter. The man nodded his approval and then headed off in the direction of the kitchen.

In a very short time he reappeared pushing a groaning serving cart. With flourishes worthy of a symphony conductor he transferred orange and apple slices into a crazed crockery pitcher, crushed the fruit with a heavy wooden spoon, added red wine, stirred and poured the sangria into their glasses.

Next, from a silver chafing dish he ladled a bubbling sauce of white wine, cream and mushrooms onto a platter of toast points and set it in front of Maureen and Brody. Then he bowed, stepped back from the table and disappeared like a will-o'-the-wisp.

"Was that a waiter or a magician?" she inquired archly. "I'm almost too stunned to eat."

Brody leaned close. "First, the sangria."

Maureen already felt an intoxication that had nothing to do with alcohol. She raised her glass and gazed at him over its rim. "What shall we drink to?"

He lifted his own glass. "To sharing."

She took the wine into her mouth, closed her eyes and held it there for a moment, savoring it. It reminded her of his voice, warm and full of promise. When she opened her eyes the expression on his face startled her. She recognized desire when she saw it, and it emanated from him like heat from a burning match. And he was doing nothing to disguise it.

Maureen laughed, whether from nervousness or pleasure, she wasn't quite sure. "Whoa! I think we'd better get something straight right now. This is the starting gate, Brody, not the finish line. You mustn't let your imagination run away with you."

"Your call. But we're not children. If I were a betting man I'd wager that our imaginations are running along the same track, conjuring up the same images. I'll tell you mine if you'll tell me yours."

No, Maureen decided, that wouldn't be wise. For the time being their "sharing" had better stop short of fantasies. Brody didn't need any encouragement from her. He was doing fine on his own.

She picked up her fork. "Our mushrooms are getting cold."

He shook his head. "Ah, Maureen, I didn't figure you for a coward."

Thrust and parry. It went on like that for the next few minutes. He wasn't simply smooth and elegant and gorgeous. He was fun and Maureen couldn't remember the last time she'd laughed so much. They sipped sangria, chased plump little mushroom caps around the platter between them and flirted outrageously. When there was only a single mushroom left Brody speared it and held it out to her. "If you want it, come and get it."

"Sounds like an offer I can't refuse." She leaned forward and bit the mushroom off the tines of his fork, sat back and slowly, purposely devoured it.

"If you keep moving your mouth like that I won't be responsible for what happens next," he commented.

"But it's so delicious." She laughed. "Do you really think it came from the caves of Segovia?"

He looked over his shoulder. "Why don't we ask Raoul?"

Unfortunately they were interrupted by an annoying and all too familiar buzz close by. Very close by.

"Dammit," Brody growled.

Maureen rolled her eyes. "Oh, no. Don't tell me I'm out with a man who takes his cell phone on a dinner date."

He slipped his hand inside his jacket. "Do you mind? It's probably just a nervous client, but there's always a chance my mother's had some sort of relapse."

The buzzing continued.

Why on earth did people carry phones around with them? Ugly, demanding things. Deliverers of bad news. Maureen flashed back on the call she'd received one night while she was in college.

Her parents. Dead. Murdered while on vacation in Miami.

She felt Brody's curious eyes on her.

"Go right ahead," she said with false brightness. "But I warn you, while your attention is diverted I plan to finish the sangria."

"I wouldn't have it any other way." He grinned and pulled out the most compact, most efficient looking cell phone Maureen had ever seen. He flipped it open and brought the receiver close to his face. "Parrish here," he said.

Still smiling at her, he listened while the person at the other end of the line apparently identified him or herself. But as Maureen watched, Brody's expression went from relaxed to fierce. The speed of the transformation was disconcerting. The man was a chameleon Maureen thought, not for the first time.

Brody muttered, "I'm listening," and after that the conversation was brief and one-sided. He ended it with a grunt, snapped the phone closed and then tossed it onto the table between them, where it lay like a small, black, ticking bomb.

Suddenly it felt as if all the light and fun had been sucked out of the room and the evening.

Too late she wished she'd asked him not to take the call. "A problem?"

A muscle in Brody's jaw began to twitch. "You tell me," he said through clenched teeth. "I've just been informed that Lisa Adams underwent a lie detector test this morning and the results don't look good for me. Were you aware of that when you came to see me this afternoon?"

Maureen chewed the inside of her lip. "Polygraph results are inadmissible in court."

"I know that. I asked you if you knew about the test when you showed up on my doorstep."

"I knew."

"Yet you, who'd supposedly come to help me prove my innocence, didn't see fit to share that information. Didn't you think I'd be interested?"

"Brody, I just happened to be at the police station when the test results came in. Otherwise I wouldn't have known about them. It was a judgement call. Under the circumstances I didn't feel right about discussing the test until after I'd talked with Clay or Marsh."

"Or maybe you and your good friend Stanton decided to keep the results secret until you wormed your way into my confidence and came up with more admissible evidence."

The look on his face would freeze fire, but she'd be damned if she'd let him intimidate her. Especially when he was back on that ridiculous "spying" kick again.

"Is there other evidence, Brody?"

He flinched, but didn't answer. If looks could kill she'd be a dead woman.

She pushed that thought away and gestured toward the phone. "Anyway, you didn't need me to tell you. You have a direct line to the Chief of Police."

He snatched the phone from the table and waved it in front of her face. "You think the call was from Paul? Well, think again. It was from Stanton."

Maureen's jaw dropped. Clay? Not closed-mouthed, "play your cards close to your vest" Stanton? Calling up a suspect to discuss a piece of evidence? Not in this lifetime. "That's absurd," she said. "I don't believe it."

"Believe it. He wanted to be the one to tell me. To rub it in. Told me I didn't have much time left. Get a lawyer. Pack my bags. There's a cell waiting with my name on it."

"Clay," she repeated incredulously. "Why?"

Brody's scowl softened. He thrust the phone back inside his jacket. "If that's not honest surprise on your face you're the best damn actress I've ever come across."

Maureen leaned toward him. "Think for a minute, Brody. I can't explain Clay's actions, but if what you believe were true, he and I would certainly be a pair of inept conspirators. That call just now would have blown my cover sky high."

The waiter chose this moment to return for their dinner requests and with a pained expression wrote down their unenthusiastic responses. He can't believe we're the same giddy couple who ordered the mushrooms, Maureen thought glumly as he hurried away. Only a minute ago she and Brody might have been any man and woman out on a first date. A very successful first date until that stupid call.

She glanced in Brody's direction. He was staring off into space, absentmindedly playing with his dinner knife, flipping it over and over in his hand, balancing first the handle, then the blade on the crisp white tablecloth.

He looked up and caught her watching at him. "Okay. So maybe I jumped to the wrong conclusion. But we can't escape it, can we? The case. How we met. No matter where we go or how hard we try to avoid the subject."

Maureen sighed. "Well, it is sort of like being told not to think about a pink elephant."

"Say the first thing that comes into your head," he ordered.

It would be silly to pretend. Bluffing wasn't her forte. She was a lousy poker player. And if she were going to spend any more time with him, she needed to know the truth. "How's the alibi situation developing? Were you or Chief Marsh able to get in touch with the client who came to see you last Saturday night?"

"I figured it would be something like that," he muttered. "Well at least you're honest." An ironic smile pulled at one corner of his mouth. "Or is that just wishful thinking on my part?"

The waiter brought their orders to the table. Maureen looked down at her paella. Fragrant, saffron colored rice. Succulent pink shrimp. Unfortunately, she was no longer in the mood to do it justice. When poor Raoul asked if he could bring them more wine or bread, she and Brody stared at him blankly, and he walked away shaking his head.

Brody grimly attacked his *arroz con pollo*.

"You didn't answer my question," Maureen prodded. "Did you make any headway substantiating your alibi?"

"No. I'd written in my notes that Bruce Cahill could be reached at the hotel but the management claims there was never anyone by that name registered." For the first time in the last few days he seemed hesitant, really concerned. He put down his knife and fork. "With a new client I usually take very detailed notes. When you're handling other people's money you can't be too careful."

"Did he give you a check?"

"We hadn't gotten that far. We were still in the discussion stage. My take on the market. Different methods of asset allocation. The charity's goals."

"Charity?"

"Cahill's personal finances weren't the issue. He represents a California based charity."

"Don't they have investment advisors in California?"

"This may come as a surprise to you, Maureen, but I have something of a national reputation in my field. Or at least, did have, until your damn sketch showed up on front pages all across the country."

"I know all about national reputations. Unfortunately, I have one myself. But the fact is that the only place my sketch appeared was in the *Granite Run Chronicle*. It didn't even make it into the *Philadelphia Inquirer*."

"Are you serious?"

"You saw the television program last night. They showed my sketch of that Missouri kidnapper, but not the one I did that looked like you."

"That's right," he conceded.

"And when you went to your office this afternoon, did your secretary mention any appointment cancellations?"

"I thought it best to head trouble off at the pass. I had her clear my calendar for the week. But she did mention a request that I give a seminar at a financial planning conference in Detroit a couple of months from now."

"I rest my case," Maureen said.

Brody lounged back in his chair and almost smiled. "So this is still a local matter. Naturally, I'm pleased, but I'm sure it strikes you as unusual, seeing that this is a capital case and I'm a...a..."

"A Parrish? Unusual? Yes. Important? Probably not." Maureen gave him an arch look. "Your friend Chief Marsh most likely had something to do with it. But he won't be able to help you for long if you can't establish an alibi. This Cahill—did you get his card? The charity's name? Telephone number?"

"Yes to all three. You sound just like Marsh. Or Stanton." He pinned her with his eyes. "The police plan to get in touch with the charity tomorrow."

"Well then, you may have one more sleepless night ahead of you, but if that's the only problem..."

"It isn't." He took a deep breath. "This morning you mentioned hearing that I was acquainted with the victim, briefly, a few years ago."

Acquainted? That was a pretty cold way of putting it. "I was under the impression you saved her life."

"So you know about that too. Well, there's a little more to it. For a time we were...involved."

"Oh!" Maureen hadn't been prepared for that. But she should have been. Had she thought that two attractive teenagers had come out of the river clinging to one another, shaken hands and gone their separate ways?

"It's been over for years, but…" He groped for a word.

"But what?"

He pushed himself back from the table. "This is beginning to sound like an interrogation, Maureen. Which, if you remember, was not what I had in mind when I asked you to have dinner with me." He looked over at the paella she'd hardly touched. "Have you finished?"

When she nodded he said, "Good, let's get out of here." He took out his wallet, threw some bills down on the table and stalked off.

"I thought businessmen always paid with credit cards," she commented as she hurried to keep up with him.

"This isn't a business meeting." He gave her a scathing look. "Is it?"

Another crack about her having ulterior motives for going out with him. Well, she'd had just about enough of that.

He took off again and by the time she'd caught up to him he'd climbed the stairs to the sidewalk outside and had already approached the man in charge of valet parking.

She put her hand on his arm. "Brody, you're beginning to sound paranoid. If you're as confident of your alibi as you say you are why all the angst?"

"I'll take you home. We can talk there."

"I drove my own car."

"Damn. I just assumed you'd taken a taxi."

"For a single woman, the means to a quick getaway is often the better part of valor."

He rewarded her with a wry smile. "Prudent Maureen."

"Besides," she added, "You seem to have forgotten that I have a house guest."

For a moment he appeared confused, then the meaning of what she'd said dawned on him. "Ah, yes. The elusive Ms. Adams." He sighed, waved the parking attendant away and pulled Maureen's hand through the crook of his arm. "Come on. It's a beautiful night. Let's walk."

Apart from the patrons entering and leaving Tio Pepe's, and one or two people window shopping the antique shops across the street, Maureen and Brody had the neighborhood to themselves. The area still had an overall commercial character that was only beginning to give way to encroaching gentrification, and there was little pedestrian traffic at this time of night. For a few minutes, they strolled along in highly charged silence.

Maureen knew she should keep her mouth shut but she couldn't help herself. "Brody, you can't still believe I'm spying on you for Clay."

He didn't answer immediately but as they passed beneath a street lamp he maneuvered her into the shadows by one of the nearby buildings, braced his back against the wall and turned her to face him. He drew a long breath and then released it. "At the moment I don't give a damn why you're here. I'm just glad you are. We're not going to talk about Marsh or Stanton any more tonight, Maureen. We're going to talk about us."

"There is no us, Brody."

"I don't believe that, and neither do you." He touched her hair, combing through it, fanning it out around her face. She could feel the gentle tug against her scalp as he twisted his fingers in the strands. "Angel hair," he said softly. Then he cupped her chin in his palm and ran his thumb back and forth over her parted lips, probing gently between her teeth. "But this is not an angel's mouth."

Maureen couldn't breathe normally, couldn't pull away, couldn't stop him from easing her closer till she was standing full against him. Everything outside the soft defused light that encircled them faded away and the scene took on the eerie aspect of a movie reel being played out in slow motion. Maureen felt like a passenger trapped in an automobile that was careening inexorably toward a head-on collision.

A murder suspect was going to kiss her and she didn't think she was going to stop him. Didn't think she could stop him. Didn't think she wanted to stop him.

Then his mouth came down, down, down, and closed over hers and she stopped thinking altogether.

*   *   *

It was late when Maureen let herself into the condo and tiptoed past the door to the guestroom. Thankfully, Lisa had already gone to bed. The last thing Maureen wanted to face now was a post-date gabfest.

Despite the hour, what she wanted to do, needed to do, was paint. She hadn't had a brush in her hand since the night she'd first interviewed Lisa. Three days! Way too long a time for Maureen to be away from the kind of therapy painting provided. And much too short a time to let a man kiss her the way Brody had tonight. Not to mention the way she had kissed him back.

In the dark of her own room she stripped off the navy silk suit and embroidered vest she'd worn to Tio Pepe's, and her cheeks grew warm as she remembered the way Brody's eyes had glowed when she'd walked up to his table.

Later, under the street lamp, he'd slipped his hands under her jacket and caressed the skin of her shoulders and back, making the most incredibly seductive noises all the while. And she'd enjoyed every mind-numbing second of it.

In fact, he'd been the one to call a halt to it. Eyes half-closed, jaw clenched, he'd moaned into her hair, "I think it's time for us to call it a night. What a clever girl you were to drive."

Had she looked disappointed? Burrowed deeper into his embrace? He'd laughed and held her at arm's length. "Have you forgotten where we are? If we don't stop now we're going to be arrested for public indecency." Then he'd raised her hand to his lips and kissed her palm. "There'll be other nights, Maureen."

In the safety of her own home, in full possession of her senses again it was that promise that worried Maureen. What had Clay Stanton said? Rub a good looking man and a good looking woman together and you get sparks. Well, he hadn't known the half of it.

Fire was more like it. A roaring, out of control conflagration.

She and Brody were going too fast. There was no denying she was interested in him. More interested than she'd like to admit. But at this rate, they were going to end up in bed the very next time they set eyes on each other. And that wasn't her style. Never had been, never would be. She wouldn't allow it.

But the kiss and what had come after had been as much her fault as his. She'd been just another ready and willing female, and no doubt he'd know plenty of them before she'd arrived on the scene. And there'd be plenty more after she was gone.

Maureen pulled a stained artist's smock out of her closet, shrugged into it and made her way down the corridor that separated her bedroom from the studio. Once inside she switched on the bright overhead light and stood on the threshold gazing across the room at the large, almost completed canvas that was leaning against the opposite wall.

She'd come into this room just this morning when she'd been looking for Lisa and her glimpse of the painting had only served to magnify her fears for Lisa's safety. But as it turned out, it wasn't Lisa who'd been in danger. It was Maureen. In danger of losing her head over a man who was still a suspect in a brutal murder.

71

She must be out of her mind. She'd always had such disdain for those pitiful jail house groupies, who fell in love with criminals, wrote fan letters and sometimes even married convicts while they were serving time.

Had she started down the same foolish path?

Maureen walked around the room checking out her supplies, gathering up the fat tubes of paint, the brushes and crumpled rags, the turpentine and linseed oil, arranging them all on a battered little table that stood to the left of her canvas. Normally the familiar smells of the studio and getting ready to work would begin the calming process.

Not tonight.

She snatched up her palette and squeezed coils of rainbow colored oils around its' edge. She jabbed at one and then another with her brush, until she got the glowing scarlet she wanted for her little heroine's cloak, the lush green she wanted for the forest in which the wolf watched and waited.

She stared at the canvas. The wolf. He was the problem. Yesterday Lisa had called the painting scary. She'd been right. It was much too frightening for a children's book. Any child, even one as adventurous as Red Riding Hood, would run from an animal as terrifying as the one Maureen had originally conceived.

With determination she set to work correcting her mistake, investing her wolf with as much raw allure as her talent would allow, sleeking the brown pelt with gold and umber, softening the yellow eyes with flecks of green, hiding his talons and tail behind sprays of laurel and ivy.

That was the great thing about oils. In life you had to live with your mistakes. In art you could paint over them, make them disappear and put something better in their place.

She took a step backward and surveyed the changes she'd made. Yes, they would do nicely. Little Red might reasonably follow a wolf as intriguing and seductive as this one deeper into the woods. But Maureen knew better. She recognized what could be hidden behind a handsome facade.

Wasn't that one of the lessons fairy tales were meant to teach?

She put down her palette. Now she would be able to sleep. Just as it always had in the past, when her parents had been killed, when she'd become involved with a particularly gruesome case, painting helped her regain a measure of sanity and control.

She smiled and began to clean her brushes with the turpentine. She couldn't hope to make the mistakes she'd made tonight in Brody's arms vanish as if they never happened. But she could make sure they didn't happen again. He was still a murder suspect. She'd call him tomorrow and tell him that she wouldn't see him again. There would be no other nights.

At least, not until he had been completely cleared of any connection to Jeannie Starbuck's death.

*   *   *

Maureen. Maureen. Maureen. In the darknesss he stared at the ceiling of his room and repeated her name over and over again, like a mantra, like a lullaby. The sound of it both soothed and excited him.

He'd been so proud of her tonight. When she walked through the restaurant, so tall and graceful, every eye in the place was on her. And later, under the streetlamp, her lovely hair glowed like spun glass.

How he wanted her. Wanted to be inside her. Wanted to fall asleep in her arms. But the time wasn't right. She wasn't ready. He recognized that. But he could be patient. Although it seemed as if he'd been waiting a lifetime, he could hold out a while longer.

There would be other nights.

*   *   *

The next morning Maureen slept later than usual and decided to forget about her daily run.

Lately, she'd been letting too many letters go unanswered, too many phone calls go unreturned. That didn't reflect the professional attitude she ordinarily brought to her work. And what with the publicity she'd just received because of the Larkland case, she would soon be busier than ever, if that were possible.

And now that she'd decided to put Brody Parrish on a back burner for awhile, she'd have time to take care of all the little details she'd let fall through the cracks during the past few days. Besides, she felt guilty about leaving Lisa alone yesterday. Maureen didn't plan to make that mistake again.

Inviting Lisa to stay at the condo had been a mistake, a fissure in the wall of separation Maureen had been careful to maintain up until then. And once she'd let down her guard, the next thing she knew she was running off to see Brody. A bigger mistake, a wider fissure. First a witness, then a suspect. Pretty soon the so-called wall would be nothing but a pile of rubble.

But what was done was done. Mistake or no mistake, Lisa was Maureen's guest. She was here and she had a hunger for closeness that needed to be fed. Her crazy actions yesterday proved that. It was time Maureen paid some attention to her, made her feel welcome, secure. Gave her some assurances that she wasn't going to be asked to leave anytime soon.

For starters, something special for breakfast.

As Maureen had hoped, the odor of freshly brewed coffee eventually lured a sleep-tousled Lisa out of the bedroom and into the kitchen. Maureen had just finished whipping up a batch of paper-thin crepes and was putting a saucepan of sugared and spiced apples over a low flame to simmer.

"Good morning, Lisa. Breakfast will be ready in a minute," Maureen said cheerfully.

Lisa poured herself a cup of coffee and leaned back against the kitchen counter, watching Maureen set the table. "Jeez, you're bright and bushy-tailed for someone who got in so late last night."

"I hope I didn't wake you. I tried not to, but I'm afraid I'm not used to worrying about how much noise I make around here."

"Don't sweat it. I heard you come home but I didn't get up to check because I thought you might, you know, have someone with you."

"No," Maureen said. "I was alone."

Lisa shrugged sympathetically. "No chemistry, huh?"

Maureen spooned apples down the center of a crepe and thought about Brody and chemistry. About his hands in her hair. About the taste of his tongue.

"Hey, it happens," Lisa commented as she finished her coffee and went to refill her cup. "At least you got a dinner out of it."

Maureen watched Lisa move from the counter to the table. She couldn't take her eyes off the coffee cup in Lisa's hand. Yesterday, in the sink, when Maureen had returned from her run and found Lisa gone…

"The Granite Run cops want to go over the polygraph results with me this morning. Don't suppose you could give me a lift back there?"

"Sure," Maureen said thoughtfully.

"Hey, that's great. Maybe afterward, we could do somethin' together. Get our nails done or…" She stopped in midsentence and peered at Maureen. "Is there somethin' wrong? If you've got other plans I can always call a taxi."

"No. No. Everything's fine. Would you like some cream or sugar for that coffee?"

"Naw. Remember? I told you waitresses learn to take their Java straight. They need all the caffeine they can suck up." Lisa waved her mug in Maureen's direction. "How about you?"

"Black," Maureen said. "Especially with anything as sweet as fruit filled crepes."

While Lisa went to work on her crepes Maureen carried the empty saucepan over to the sink and ran hot water into it.

The sink in which yesterday morning there had been two cups. One half-filled with cold black coffee, the other with a sticky residue of sugar and milk in the bottom.

CHAPTER 7

This morning nothing could keep Brody from the river he loved.

The conditions for canoeing were perfect. The runoff from the melting snows in the Poconos filled the usually shallow Brandywine to its banks and produced a current swift enough for the kind of challenge he enjoyed. Most of the year it was little more than a creek, a gently curving ribbon of water that served as a decorative backdrop for summer picnics and winter sports. But in the spring, the river could be exciting and even dangerous.

Brody slipped the canoe free from the pier, pushed off into the dark water where the river was deepest and let himself be carried along past Granite Run toward the center of Chadds Ford, eight miles away. Coming back he would have to battle his way upriver but he looked forward to the only type of exercise he had any time or taste for.

For now he sat back and let the current take over while he gave some thought to last night and to what he was going to do about Maureen Lowe. Even as he frowned his groin quickened. Dammit, she was a piece of work. The rain-washed smell of her. That fine silky hair and creamy skin. Her immediate, passionate response to his kisses.

Her professional ties to the police. The affectionate way she spoke Clay Stanton's name. Her friendship with Lisa Adams.

Put them all together and they spelled trouble.

Women! They were like the river, one minute soft and inviting, the next minute unpredictable and treacherous.

The canoe drifted through a leafy canyon of dogwood and

sycamore, the sun streaming down through their whispering branches onto the green river below.

Green and unreadable, like Maureen's eyes in the lamplight last night.

Ah, last night. That was the problem. Something about it didn't fit. Tease her though he had, Brody hadn't believed for a minute a woman like Maureen could be had for the price of a dinner. He'd been prepared to invest as much time as it took. Getting there would be half the fun.

But because she'd been so utterly appealing, and because after the damn phone call he'd been desperate to forget even for a moment the accusation of murder hanging over his head, he'd made an exploratory move on her. For his efforts, he'd expected a few tension-relieving kisses.

What he got was an explosion. He'd been rocked back on his heels, wanted to consume her on the spot.

And an alarm had gone off in his head.

He'd pulled back. How many times did he have to get his fingers burned before he learned his lesson? Once, he'd had an excuse. He'd been a green, inexperienced kid. Since then he'd been careful where women were concerned.

They were all the same. They used their sexuality as bait and as attractive a lure as Maureen Lowe was, this time he couldn't afford to bite. Whatever she was after, and she certainly was after something, she wasn't going to get it from him. He'd made up his mind. He wouldn't see her again.

Through a swaying curtain of leaves the brown brick and gray wood shutters of the Brandywine Museum loomed off to his left. It would have been pleasant to spend an afternoon in its' austere galleries with Maureen, to hear her comment on the paintings in that lilting voice of hers, to pull her into a secluded corner and...

Muttering under his breath he executed a difficult sweep stroke and maneuvered the canoe into a hundred and eighty-degree turn. The hard work it took to get back to Granite Run and Riverbend fit his black mood. Again and again he rammed the paddle into the water till his shoulders and upper arms ached and perspiration oozed from every pore. Using the weight of his body to balance the canoe he thrust the paddle between his knees, tore off his sweatshirt and scrubbed at his neck, chest and underarms. Then he balled it up and tossed it into the bottom of the boat.

Only a few strokes from Riverbend he caught sight of his mother standing on the landing. She was getting around better every day, but what was she doing here? Though Victoria enjoyed the prestige attached to owning a house on the banks of the Brandywine, she'd never much cared for the river itself. The noisy little beasties that thrived in the lush growth along its banks were entirely too primitive for her tastes.

Brody glanced at his watch. He'd been gone a little more than an hour. It was only nine thirty, and though she was already perfectly dressed and groomed, the expression his mother's face was, to say the least, concerned.

What was so important that it couldn't have waited until he'd gotten back to the house? Had Paul called with news from California? But that was impossible. What with the time differences between coasts it was barely dawn in the West. He reached out and secured the canoe to the pier, then heaved himself up onto the landing. Victoria's gaze slid slowly to her left. Brody's eyes followed hers.

Maureen Lowe materialized from behind an ancient weeping willow. She wore jeans and a kelly green turtleneck, and her beautiful hair was tied back with a scarf. Tiny circles of gold shimmered at the tips of her earlobes.

Brody sighed. One look at her and his decision not to become involved evaporated like so much river mist. Cursing himself for a fool, he filled his eyes with her. Damn the consequences. She'd probably be the death of him, but what a way to go.

       *   *   *

Victoria Parrish waved Maureen toward one of the wrought iron chairs arranged around a glass-topped table on the terrace.

"While Brody is showering I hope you'll let me offer you some breakfast, Ms. Lowe. Fresh fruit, home baked breads? Since my stroke, I'm afraid our meals here at Riverbend are a trifle austere. Doctor's orders. But if you would like something you don't see, I'm sure Margaret would be more than happy to prepare it."

Maureen took one last look at the wide French doors through which Brody had just disappeared. He was gone but the memory of his bare, flushed torso still lingered. Had she imagined it, or had he preened just a little for her benefit?

She smiled to herself and took a seat across from Mrs. Parrish. "Nothing, thank you. I've already eaten."

"Oh, that's too bad. But you will join me for a cup of coffee or tea, won't you?"

"Yes, of course. Coffee would be fine."

While Victoria poured, the two women studied each other. Maureen felt a little like an insect under a magnifying glass but she put the time to good use doing some sizing up of her own. She could see the resemblance between mother and son. They shared the same tall, ramrod posture, the same shrewd, steely blue gaze.

Maureen was relieved when Mrs. Parrish finally ended the examination with a nod, as if she'd reached a conclusion of some kind. "If I remember correctly your parents died just a short time before my husband's heart attack. Of course their deaths were much more shocking than his." She sighed. "Terrible. Just terrible. I knew your father, you know." she said. "He was a fine police officer. A gentleman. "

"Yes, he was."

Victoria pursed her lips. "But as I recall, your mother kept to herself, didn't she? Seemed a bit uncomfortable in social situations. Avoided them, I thought."

Maureen was amazed. Though her parents and the Parrishs had barely known each other, Mrs. Parrish had formed a pretty clear picture of what Barney and Janice Lowe had been like. Surprisingly clear for a casual observer.

"My mother was a very private person," Maureen said.

"You're not much like her, are you?"

"Don't you think? I've been told I look just like her."

"Oh, I didn't mean physically. There's no denying you look like her. I meant, personality wise. From what Chief Marsh tells me you've chosen a very public way to make a living."

Maureen was a little uncomfortable with the direction the conversation had taken. "It wasn't public at all, until recently."

"But now it is, isn't it?"

Maureen placed her cup of coffee, untasted, on the table. "Mrs. Parrish, I didn't come here to talk about my problems. I came to talk about Brody's."

Victoria laughed. "Of course you did. But you'll forgive a mother's curiosity, Ms. Lowe, if I—"

"Please call me Maureen."

Victoria's mouth twitched slightly. "Maureen, then. Am I correct in assuming that you and Brody are seeing each other socially?"

"We had dinner last night."

"I hope he showed you a good time."

Maureen swallowed. "He did."

Victoria nibbled a slice of dry raisin toast. Then she shrugged. "Well, I can see for myself why Brody is interested in you. He's always had a fondness for blondes. But aside from those charms of which a mother might best remain ignorant, I'm confused as to your interest in him. Especially at this time, and because of your situation. You are the artist who drew the sketch that appeared in Monday's *Chronicle*, aren't you?"

"I am."

"And you've offered your hospitality to the young woman who's accused Brody of murder?"

"Mrs. Parrish, let me explain—"

"Please don't trouble yourself, Maureen. I'm sure you have good reasons for the things you've done. Any number of them. But my only interest is in how they will affect my son."

"I believe I'm in a position to help Brody clear his name."

The older woman sat back in her chair and fixed her guest with a chilly smile. "You're interested in the Parrish name, are you? How admirable. Perhaps you and I can be friends after all. If I read the situation correctly, we share a common goal. It is to your advantage as well as mine that Brody be exonerated as soon as possible. So I'm ready to hear how you can help us both get what we want."

"Just a minute, Mrs. Parrish. To my advantage? How?"

"Well, until he's out from under this ridiculous accusation his concentration on your relationship can hardly be as focused as you might like it to be."

Enough patrician beating about the bush Maureen decided. "Focused? Does it seem to you that Brody is focused on anything, Mrs. Parrish? It appears to me that he's ready to pursue any subject just as long as it has nothing to do with the murder charge. He avoids even the mention of Jeannie Starbuck's name." It suddenly struck Maureen how reluctant everyone seemed to talk about the victim. Even Lisa. It was almost as if her identity was incidental to what had taken place in her apartment last Saturday night.

But apparently Victoria Parrish suffered under no such restraint. "Jeannie Starbuck," she muttered. "That little bitch. Did you know her, Maureen?"

Maureen blinked. "No, I didn't."

"From the very first I tried to warn Brody about her, but he wouldn't listen. Up until he met her, he'd been so studious and dependable. Shy. Like your mother. But after the rescue people made so much of him, and the girl filled his head with such nonsense. Told him he was responsible for her, because he'd saved her life. Can you imagine it? Anyone with a brain could have seen that she had her hooks out for him. But he wouldn't hear a word against her."

Her expression softened and she suddenly looked tired. And older. Maureen recalled her recent illness and felt a momentary pang of sympathy.

"The young can be so headstrong," Mrs. Parrish said, almost to herself. "They don't understand how they can ruin their lives before they've even begun to live. They think their parents want to spoil their fun, are jealous of them, of all things. As if any adult would want to be seventeen again. To relive that youthful chaos, that pain..."

She glanced quickly at Maureen, and left the thought unfinished as the French doors flew open and Brody came striding across the flagstone terrace.

He stopped beside Maureen's chair. She raised her face to his. His hair was still damp from his shower and looked even darker than usual. There was a small cut, evidence of a hasty shave, in one corner of his mouth. He'd changed into a pair of chinos and a short sleeve knit shirt that echoed the blue of his eyes. But from now on, no matter what he wore Maureen knew she'd be remembering the bare-chested, graceful man who had leapt from his canoe onto the landing a few minutes earlier.

Everyone in Granite Run knew how proud the Parrishes were of their Delaware Indian blood. No matter how diluted, it added substance to their claim to being one of the area's "first families." But what with their fair skin and blue eyes, Maureen had always thought the claim absurd. Now, looking at Brody, she wasn't so sure. He didn't look as much like his mother as she'd originally thought. His paternal ancestry showed itself in his slashing cheekbones, the blacker than black hair, the unique tilt at the corner of his eyes.

He reached down, put his hand under her elbow and brought her to her feet. "You'll excuse us, Mother. I'd like to show Maureen the river walk."

Victoria shook her head. "Really, Brody, can't it wait? Maureen and I were having a most enlightening conversation. It might do you good to have some breakfast and listen to what she has to say."

But he was already on his way down the slope toward the river, Maureen in tow. "This won't take long," he called over his shoulder.

"We'll be back before you finish your coffee."

"That was extremely rude," Maureen protested as she stumbled down the incline after him. "You could have at least had a mouthful of something to please her."

They'd reached a stand of trees that screened the footpath from the estate. He swung her into his arms. "You're so right. But I have something other than zucchini bread in mind."

She reached up and pressed her fingertips against his lips, stopping them only inches from their target. "No, Brody," she whispered. "No."

He turned his head slightly, trailing the tip of his warm, clever tongue across her palm. "No? I didn't hear a 'no' last night, did I?"

Maureen squirmed inside the circle of his arms. He appeared to enjoy the process immensely, playing cat and mouse with her, first relaxing his hold, and then catching her to him again with an ease that made her gasp. "I'm serious, Brody. Last night was a mistake."

"I know a mistake when I see one. I've made enough of them. Take it from me, last night was no mistake."

"Then it was the wine, or the..." she couldn't help but laugh, "the mushrooms. Whatever it was, it has to stop."

"Lesson number one. Never laugh when you're trying to discourage someone from doing something." Brody lowered his head, began to nip at the curve of her jawline, his breath setting the tiny hoop earrings she wore aflutter.

She wanted to melt into him, wanted to rest her cheek on the top of that glossy, freshly washed hair. But she didn't do either of those things. Instead, she turned herself into a slim, still, sliver of ice.

Brody got the message. He straightened, released her and stepped back several paces, his features stiff with surprise. "Lesson number two," Maureen countered. "No means no."

"My apologies," he said coldly. "I was under the impression we were just taking up where we left off last night."

Maureen nodded. "All right, I deserved that. But one of the reasons I came here was to tell you there wouldn't be a repeat performance of last night's little after dinner entertainment."

He turned his back on her and walked a short distance down the path to where a fallen tree trunk had and been dragged to provide a natural bench. He sat down and glared across the water, a muscle doing double time in his jaw. "If that's all you had to say, a telephone call would have sufficed."

"Yes, I probably should have called first, but the fact is I have this ridiculous phobia about phones. They make me uncomfortable. I avoid using them whenever possible." She stopped short when she heard his snort of disbelief. "Never mind. It's not important. I had to drive Lisa Adams into Granite Run anyway. The police wanted to talk to her about..."

She caught herself just in time. She'd been on the verge of telling him about the questions Clay or the Chief were most likely putting to Lisa at this very moment. Questions about the polygraph results among them. But concerns about her own divided loyalties resurfaced and she changed her mind. "About yesterday," she finished lamely.

From ten feet away she watched him reach down between his feet and dig a palmful of pebbles out of the dirt. He tossed them back and forth in his hands for a time, then selected one and drilled it into the river. The pebble hit a broken branch being swept along by the current and then dropped into the swirling water.

"You don't take rejection very well, do you, Brody?"

"Does that make me unusual?" He turned to her with narrowed eyes. "Now, what exactly could the curious Ms. Lowe be thinking about now? Could it be motive, perhaps? Let's see, might the story go something like this? The murdered woman rejected my sexual advances last Saturday night, and I killed her because of it. Right? Well think again, Miss Marple. The word 'no' wasn't part of her vocabulary."

Maureen felt like she'd just taken a blow to the stomach. But it looked as if he was ready to open up at last. To deal with it. She had to keep him talking. "Then, I take it your relationship with Jeannie Starbuck was...an intimate one."

He'd flinched when Maureen said the name. "That would depend on your definition of the word intimate. When I met her I was, what, seventeen? Eighteen? She was a little older. Available."

"And grateful."

His eyes narrowed. "Grateful?"

"To you. For having saved her life."

He bared his teeth in a mockery of a smile, then turned away. "Oh, yeah. The famous rescue. Sure. Gratitude. It certainly looks that way, doesn't it?"

There was a sudden snapping of twigs, a rustling of the long grass a short distance into the woods. Maureen jumped as a covey of brown sparrows took noisy wing from a low hanging branch just above Brody's head.

"Jack rabbits," he said without looking up. "Mrs. Hartman puts food out for them." His eyes were on the river but his mind seemed a million miles away. Suddenly he turned toward Maureen again and in his eyes she thought she read regret, and then resignation.

"Jeannie and I met not far from here. She and a couple of friends rented a canoe up at Northgate, made it all the way down into town. Then they started horsing around and it capsized. Jeannie couldn't swim."

"I know how you met. I grew up in Granite Run. I read all about it in the newspaper."

"Well then, you know all there is to know, don't you?"

"That was a long time ago, Brody. Are you telling me that you and she dated for the next fifteen years?"

He looked down at his hands. "We went at it pretty hot and heavy for a couple of years. Then it seemed to wind down on its' own. I went away to school. She was a popular girl. One semester break I came home and she was married." He shrugged. "I pretended to be hurt and angry, but actually I was relieved to be off the hook."

He glanced at Maureen, gauging her reaction. "Are you sure you want to hear the rest?"

No, she didn't want to hear the rest. A few minutes ago, she'd been complaining to his mother about his reticence on the subject of Jeannie Starbuck, his relationship to her, his reaction to her death. But now Maureen never wanted to hear him say Jeannie's name again. Not in that rich, acid-etched baritone of his.

But she nodded anyway. "Go on."

He let fly with another pebble. "Last year she called me at my office in town. She'd gotten a divorce. I wasn't seeing anyone at the time. There didn't seem to be any reason for us not to get together for a drink for old time's sake. And one thing led to another, and... "

"Did you sleep with her?"

"What do you think, Maureen? You've had ample evidence over the past few hours that I'm no saint." He braced his elbows on his knees and steepled his hands in front of his face. "Yes. I slept with her."

"Who broke it off?"

"I did."

"Why?" There was that word again. Why couldn't she just stop asking questions if the answers made her feel so rotten?

"She wanted a commitment. I didn't see my way clear to making one. Not to her. Not ever. I couldn't get past the feeling that she was more interested in my pedigree than in me. When I told her it was over she accused me of using her, and she was right."

He shifted a little in Maureen's direction. "For whatever reason she was willing to continue the relationship under any terms I chose, but the day came when I couldn't live with myself anymore so I simply called a halt to it."

"It appears to have taken you a while to see the light."

Brody sighed. "Sex isn't an intellectual pursuit, Maureen. It makes people stupid."

Maureen studied the quivering ferns that grew in the rich silt along the river's edge. Was it possible that Jeannie Starbuck had carried the torch for Brody for fifteen years, settling for anything he was willing to give, in hopes of something more permanent at the end of the line?

She looked at the man and her pulse went into overdrive. Oh, it was possible all right. Wasn't she in a kind of thrall to him herself? Wasn't the whole town?

Everyone except Clay.

I always thought the guy was a three-dollar bill.

A shiver of dread rippled down her spine. Handsome Brody. Successful Brody. Rich Brody. Probably all that a woman could ask for, in and out of bed. What would it be like to have him, and then lose him? Not once, but twice.

It happened all the time. Violence following rejection. There was that famous murder case in Connecticut. A sophisticated, mature dean of a woman's college, who'd shot her on-again-off-again lover only after he'd decided to end their relationship once and for all.

Couldn't it just as easily have gone the other way? Suppose murder was the way the departing partner chose to end the affair?

Permanently.

"How did Jeannie react when you told her? Was she upset, angry? Did she threaten you?"

Brody shot up from the log and came toward Maureen, so obviously furious again that she had to steel herself not to back away. When he reached her side he stopped dead in his tracks and raked her face with his eyes, his expression bitter and full of...something. Disappointment?

What right had he to be disappointed in her?

"Why do I always feel as if I should have a lawyer present whenever we're together?" he said, and then stalked off.

*   *   *

From a window on Riverbend's second floor Brody watched Maureen get into her red Jeep Cherokee. A bright, spunky car for a bright, spunky woman. The image almost made him smile. Almost, but not quite.

She was most likely on her way to see Stanton, eager to fill the ears of her great, good friend with all the juicy details she'd gleaned down by the river.

Well, she was going to be disappointed. The police already knew everything he'd just told her. Immediately following the lineup Monday morning Brody had given them a statement. Not that he'd needed to. He and Jeannie Starbuck had probably been the stuff of Granite Run gossip for some time.

Why had he gone to such lengths to put himself in the worst possible light just now? Throwing his relationship with another woman in Maureen's face, beating her over the head with it, testing her.

Of course I slept with her. I'm no saint.

With every ounce of his being Brody wished he could go after Maureen and tell her it hadn't been exactly as he'd described it. When they were teenagers, Jeannie had called the shots, been the more experienced. It was only last year, when they'd gotten together again that she'd become the beggar, the whiner, the blackmailer.

Would saying he had sex with her out of pity, or to stop her mouth, have made him seem anymore heroic?

Heroic! Wasn't that a joke?

He braced his hands on either side of the window and followed the Jeep with his eyes until it disappeared from view. God, what kind of bastard had he become? He'd gone to bed with Jeannie more times than he could count and now she was dead, and all he wanted to do was forget about her and the last time they were together, and think about Maureen.

He heard movement behind him. He turned his head and found his mother standing on the threshold of her room, watching him.

"Is she gone?" Victoria asked.

He dropped his arms and straightened. "Yes."

"I'm sorry I couldn't wait on the terrace for you two to get back from your walk. Mrs. Hartman and I had some household matters to attend to. Of course, if Maureen had any breeding at all she would have waited to say good-bye to her hostess before dashing off like that."

Brody shrugged. "She was in a hurry when she left."

"She's very pretty, isn't she? That mop of blonde hair. Reminds me a bit of Jeannie." Victoria took a step toward her son. "But I'm prepared to make allowances for anyone who can help you, Brody."

"I told you before. I don't need any help. But if I did, I don't think we could count on getting any from Maureen."

"Oh, but we can, dear. She's obviously quite taken with you, and Lisa Adams is living with her. If I talked to Maureen, woman to woman, I'm sure I could get her to prevail upon Lisa to rethink her accusations."

Brody fought to keep the anger out of his voice. "You're not to talk to Maureen, Mother. Not to see her, not to tell her anything, not to ask her for any favors. I don't want her involved in any way. Do you understand?"

"Why, I believe I do. You don't trust her." With a self-satisfied smile, Victoria turned back into her room. "I knew I was right," she said smugly, barely loud enough for him to hear. "She is just like Jeannie, after all."

*   *   *

Yes, it would be a while. He had to keep that in mind for the time being. But one day soon he was going to have Maureen Lowe. Down by the river, her fair hair spread out on a bed of ferns and ivy creepers

She was worth waiting for. Worth the extra trouble. He'd seen the yearning in her eyes. She wanted him to use her. He would make her body answer his every need, and when he was done she'd clutch him to her breast and beg for more.

He'd put his mark on her and she'd be his forever, because after he'd possessed her no other man would be able to satisfy her

No other man would be able to take his place.

CHAPTER 8

As soon as Maureen stepped through the front door of the Granite Run Police Department she was greeted by a young officer who'd obviously been on the lookout for her.

"Lieutenant Stanton will see you in Interview Room A, Ms. Lowe."

"Not at his desk?"

"No, Ma'am. Interview Room A. If you like, I can show you where that is."

Ma'am? Maureen smiled. That was a first. Maybe Lisa was right about the glasses after all. "Thank you, I can find it on my own. Is Lisa Adams with him?"

The officer looked uneasy. "Lisa Adams. That would be the witness in the Starbuck case. I believe the lieutenant spoke with her earlier, but right now she's in with Chief Marsh."

"Is there a problem, Officer?"

"You should talk to the lieutenant, Ms. Lowe. He's waiting for you in—"

"Interview Room A. I'm on my way."

As she walked through the squad room, she saw two or three detectives look up, then suddenly become terribly interested in the folders on their desks. Something's happened, Maureen thought. Something about Bruce Cahill. Something about the lie detector test or the coffee cups. Something that will help Brody.

Though, after the scene at Riverbend she was at a loss to explain why she should care. Brody had all but ordered her off the property. He wasn't interested in her help. Didn't trust her.

But she did care. A lot. Even if there were never going to be an "us," she cared. She was her father's daughter. She knew Brody was innocent, knew it in her bones, and until he was out from under the dark cloud of suspicion hanging over his head, she'd continue to care. Hadn't she and Lisa together played a part in putting him there?

The setup in Interview Room A was more like it had been the night she interviewed Lisa than on the day of the lineup. Most of the folding chairs were stacked up against one wall and the long wooden table again dominated the center of the room. Clay was seated at one end of the table when Maureen entered and closed the door behind her.

He motioned for her to take a chair directly opposite his. "Sit down," he said curtly.

"Clay, I'm about to burst. What did Lisa have to say?"

Stanton rested his elbows on the table and tented his fingers in front of his face. "About to burst," he repeated. "Don't you think your interest in this case is a little extreme, Maureen? After all, your job was essentially over on Sunday night when you handed me your finished sketch."

His stiff posture and steely tone of voice struck Maureen as odd. She'd spoken to him briefly this morning when she'd dropped Lisa off. During a private moment she'd been able to fill him in about the coffee cups, explaining that she hesitated to question Lisa herself. The woman just became too emotional when Maureen did, so she'd decided to leave the questions to the police from now on.

So, what was Clay's problem? This morning he'd seemed his usual sweet, gruff self. He'd teased her about being a policeman's brat, always playing detective. Now, if anything, he seemed angry. But she didn't have anything to apologize for. She'd been dragged into this mess, kicking and screaming. Wasn't his last comment an echo of what Maureen herself had said just a couple of days ago?

"It was Lisa who invited me on board, Clay, when she asked me to take part in the lineup. Which at first, if you recall, I didn't want to do. You're the one who encouraged me to—"

He jabbed his finger in her direction. "No one told you to invite Adams to stay with you. That was your idea."

"I admit that was a mistake. But what's done is done. Right now, I'm more interested in hearing what Lisa told you about that straight line polygraph result. Not to mention those coffee cups in the sink the morning she disappeared."

He closed his eyes and began to massage his temples, as if trying to ease the pain of a headache. Maureen reached out to touch his arm but he pulled away from her and thrust himself to his feet.

"You might as well know that when I questioned Adams this morning she was able to explain away any concerns I had on either score. She said your obvious suspicions made her nervous so she took a Valium the morning of the test. She didn't realize it would affect the results. As for the cups, she thinks your imagination played tricks on you. She might have used two herself, but neither had anything in it but black coffee."

Maureen made a move to rise but Stanton loomed over her, the lips under his mustache set in a grim line.

"That's ridiculous, Clay. I'm an artist. Details like that don't escape me. Why would I have imagined a stained cup if one wasn't there?"

"Maybe out of some half-baked notion that it would help your boyfriend." he snarled.

"Boyfriend? Are you talking about Brody Parrish? He's not my boyfriend."

"What is he then? An acquaintance? Do you let all your acquaintances grope you in the middle of downtown Philadelphia?"

Maureen felt as if the man she had always regarded as a surrogate father had just struck her. "Downtown Philadelphia," she repeated. "How...? Who...?"

"When Adams wouldn't accept protection I put a man on Parrish. On Tuesday night he was followed to a restaurant called Tio Pepe's in Philadelphia. He was seen leaving with an attractive young woman who was familiar to the officer carrying on the surveillance. According to him, she and Parrish stopped in the doorway of a vacant shop and proceeded to put on quite a show."

Maureen dimly remembered the window shoppers across River Street on Tuesday night. The thought of someone spying on her and Brody during those reckless few minutes in his arms made her feel ill.

She fought back the bile that rose in her throat. "Clay, it's not really any of your business but I want you to understand. After Lisa's disappearance and the polygraph situation, I just felt there was something peculiar going on. I had to find out if I was being used to implicate an innocent man. I went to see Brody and was convinced that was the case. So when he asked me out there didn't seem to be any good reason to refuse."

Stanton grasped her arm and pulled her to her feet. "How about the fact that he's a murderer? That he stabbed a woman over and over again with a knife and watched her bleed to death? That wasn't a good enough reason to steer clear of him?"

"He didn't do it, Clay. He has an alibi."

Stanton released her and stepped back, his raised palms at chest level. Maureen felt sorry for the man. She could see him trying to bank the fire of his fury and only partially succeeding.

"His alibi is in the toilet. There's no California based charity. We checked. No charity, no prospective client named Cahill. Parrish made it all up. Not only that, but we've come across some forensic evidence in Jeannie Starbuck's apartment that could place him at the scene. If it pans out, and Marsh can be persuaded to do his damn duty, Parrish could be arrested this afternoon."

Forensic evidence? Hadn't Brody told her that he'd broken it off with Jeannie last year? Surely any findings that old would be worthless.

"He knew her. He might have spent some time in her apartment," she said, hating the tremor in her voice. "But that doesn't mean he killed her."

Clay shook his head, revulsion written all over his face. "Damn, if you don't sound just like Marsh. Listen to me, Maureen. Parrish is hustling you. You're not thinking clearly. I don't care how deeply involved with him you are, it's over as of now. Do you hear? Over." He turned away, his knotted fingers balled into fists at his side. "Every time I think about him putting his hands on you I want to strangle him. Thank God, your father isn't here to see this. To know who you let touch you."

Dangerously close to tears, Maureen's chin came up. She stepped around Stanton so that he would have to look directly at her. "How dare you say something like that and then turn your back on me. If my Dad were alive, he would never have spoken to me the way you just did. He would have understood that I'm a grown woman, capable of deciding who I see and don't see. He might not have been pleased with my choices, but he would have respected them because he respected me. Which you obviously don't."

She retrieved her purse from the table, slung it over her shoulder and headed for the door. "I'm going to get Lisa and take her home. When you think things over you'll want to apologize. You know where to reach me."

"Apologize! The hell I will," Stanton roared at her back. "And I refuse to have anything more to do with you until you come to me and say you've broken it off with Parrish. Do you hear me?"

"I hear you, Clay," Maureen sighed as she pulled open the door. "So must everyone else in Granite Run."

Her cheeks burning, Maureen marched down the gauntlet of detective's desks toward the chief's office, making a point to look everyone she passed right in the eye. Her pride wouldn't let her to do less, even though every occupant of the room must have gotten an earful of Clay's parting shot. And probably agreed that she was behaving like a fool.

Thankfully, the narrow blinds that covered the glass window in the Chief's door were shuttered. Maureen took a moment to square her shoulders and catch her breath before knocking.

She got a quicker than expected "Come in," in reply, and pushed the door open. Paul March was standing by a bank of metal file cabinets, a couple of manila folders clutched in his hand.

The tiny office was crowded but surprisingly neat. While space was at a premium, the furniture was a cut above the usual. Framed diplomas and awards decorated the walls, along with photographs of Marsh shaking hands with various community leaders. Including one with Brody.

"Nice place you've got here," she commented.

"'Tis a small thing, but mine own.'"

Maureen stared. She hadn't taken him for a man who could work literary allusion into his everyday conversation.

He grinned, stuffed the folders into a drawer and slammed it shut. "I get a kick out of surprising people with lines like that. They don't expect it from a small town cop." He settled himself behind his desk and gestured at a chair across from his. "Have a seat, Ms. Lowe."

Oh, no, Maureen thought. She was not going to sit still for another lecture. "If it's all the same to you, Chief, I'd rather not. I'm in a hurry. Where's Lisa Adams?"

Either Marsh didn't hear the question or he chose to ignore it. He rubbed his eyes with the thumb and forefinger of one hand. "Sounded as if Stanton worked you over pretty good in there. Tell Brody that the surveillance was Stanton's idea. I had nothing to do with it. He set it up on his own. When I found out about it this morning I called it off."

"Tell him yourself. If what Clay said is true you'll see Brody this afternoon." Maureen rested her palms on top of the desk. "Is the forensic evidence you've found compelling enough to get him arrested?"

"Naw. We don't have the equipment to run the tests needed so the state lab boys are handling them for us and we're not first in line for their attention. We don't even have preliminary results yet. But what we do have was enough to get a search warrant for Riverbend. Stanton and I will be heading out there in about half an hour. Christ! Isn't Victoria Parrish going to love that?" He sighed and began to massage the back of his neck. "Brody's got a lot of explaining to do about the alibi but a good criminal lawyer should be able to buy him another few days. The way I see it, his biggest problem right now is..." He stopped in mid-sentence and stared pointedly at Maureen. "I hope you plan to take Stanton's advice, Ms. Lowe."

Maureen's laugh was singularly humorless. "What? You and Clay, agreeing on something? Will wonders never cease."

"That wasn't meant to amuse. You would be doing Brody a favor if you removed yourself from the picture until he's out of the woods. Usually, he's as sharp and sure-footed as they come. But he's made some dumb moves lately. Really dumb. Going to your apartment Tuesday morning, and taking you out to dinner while he's under investigation for the murder of an old girlfriend. There are a lot of people here in Granite Run who owe Brody. People who'll go to the mat to keep this problem contained until he can be exonerated. But we sure could do with a little enlightened assistance here."

Maureen hung her head. There was no denying it. Her efforts to help Brody had only made things worse. He wasn't the only one who had made some dumb moves lately. "Let me put your mind at ease, Chief. When I last saw Brody I think he'd reached the same conclusion I had. That our...friendship wasn't going anywhere. Now, if you'll just tell me where I can find Lisa Adams I'll get out of your way too."

Marsh shrugged. "She left after I finished questioning her."

"Left? But I was supposed to pick her up and take her back to Philadelphia."

"She said you'd given her a key to your place. She called a cab." Marsh grimaced. "Umm, earlier, she may have overheard the surveillance officer reporting to Stanton. From what she said during our conversation I gathered she'd been able to piece together the gist of the situation and—"

Maureen's hand went to her throat. "You mean, Lisa knows about my seeing Brody?" She snatched her purse from where she'd left it and was already half way to the door when Marsh called after her.

"Yeah. And when she tore out of here awhile back, she was pretty pissed."

*   *   *

Actually, Lisa didn't appear that "pissed" when Maureen let herself into the condo later that afternoon.

She had spent the entire drive back from Granite Run trying to conceive of a way to calm her house guest's fears, and at the same time wring the complete truth out of her. She had finally hit upon an approach that might work.

Neither of us has been completely honest with the other, Lisa. I'm sorry about that, but I wanted to be Brody's friend as well as yours. I think we're both being used to frame an innocent man. Maybe if we discuss our concerns, frankly and openly, we can figure this thing out.

But one look told Maureen that Lisa didn't need any reassuring today. If anything, she appeared calmer and more in control than at any time since they'd met. More Valium?

"Well look who's finally arrived. My devoted protector," Lisa said airily, blowing twin streams of smoke out through her nostrils. From her perch on the living room couch she craned her neck to look past Maureen. "All alone? You didn't bring that bastard Parrish back with you so that he can carve me up like he did Jeannie?"

Maureen eyed Lisa thoughtfully. Where was the timid, wretched little waif that had so appealed to her protective instincts on the day of the lineup? "If you were truly afraid of Brody's showing up, Lisa, I doubt you'd be sitting here so coolly, awaiting your fate."

Maureen deposited her purse on the console in the hallway and cast a glance the small, black duffel bag on the floor nearby. "Planning to leave before we get a chance to sort things out? What are you running away from?"

Lisa waved a hand, scattering a trail of gray ash over one of the champagne colored cushions. "Well, for one thing I don't want to be around to see this pretty place get all messed up."

"That's a problem that's easily solved." Maureen took a saucer out of a kitchen cabinet, carried it into the living room and balanced it carefully on the arm of the sofa. "I didn't know you smoked," she said.

"Lots of stuff you don't know about me, Maureen. But when I talked about a mess, I didn't mean cigarette ash. I meant blood." She took one last drag, ground what was left of the cigarette into the saucer and leered at Maureen. "If I'm not around maybe he'll do you in my place. Just think about that for a minute. Do you remember my description of Jeannie's apartment after he got through with her? Blood

94

everywhere! Smeared on the walls, the carpet, the bed. Wouldn't all that red really clash with this ritzy color scheme of yours."

Suddenly, cracks began to appear in Lisa's newly acquired, cool facade. "You bitch!" she spat. "Why did you invite me here in the first place? To give me the third degree on the sly? All those smarmy questions. 'Tell me about growing up in California, Lisa. Had you seen Brody Parrish before the night of the murder, Lisa? How did you find a private investigator, Lisa? Do you take cream and sugar in your coffee, Lisa?' You've been pumping me for information and feeding it to Parrish all along. You've been in bed with him from the start. From the night I first described him to you. Who knows? Maybe before."

Maureen arched an eyebrow. "That's not true. I had my doubts about his guilt but I always believed you'd made an honest mistake when you identified him as the murderer. But, the way you're acting now suggests you may have had ulterior motives for everything you did."

"Bullshit. Why don't you face it, Maureen? Cut the goody goody act. We're two of a kind. We both get a charge out of screwin' guys who are dangerous. Hey, don't I know how that is? Puts a real, fine edge on it, don't it? Being just a little afraid? But lemme tell you, it gets old after awhile, watchin' out for your back all the time."

In the street below, someone tapped out a signal on a car horn. Lisa surged to her feet, made her way to the hallway. "That's my ride," she said. "I'm outta here."

"Leave the key I gave you," Maureen called after her.

Lisa dug in her jacket pocket and gave Maureen one last smirk. "Big deal. Who needs it?" she crowed. She tossed the key on the hall console and pulled open the door. "Take my advice. Start watching out for your back, girlfriend."

*   *   *

An hour later the atmosphere inside the condo still reeked of Lisa's venom.

Maureen retrieved the key from the console and discovered that Lisa had forgotten her luggage. The black duffel bag. She'd be back and, after the ugly things she'd said the thought of facing her one more time sickened Maureen. She stowed the bag in the bottom of the hall closet and then went from room to room erasing every other trace of the woman's presence.

She stripped the bed Lisa had slept in of its sheets and tossed them into the hamper. She replaced the towels in the guest bath and scoured all the fixtures till her hands felt glued to the scrub brush. She opened every window in the place, arriving on her last sweep around the condo at the sliding glass door that led out to the balcony.

Maureen spent what was left of the afternoon there, watching pewter colored clouds pile up behind Philadelphia's eastern skyline. How was the search of Riverbend and Brody's interview with the police progressing? she wondered. She had a feeling Paul Marsh would really light into Brody this afternoon, just to wake him up to the reality of his situation.

And Clay, with his attitude toward Brody—Maureen didn't even want to think about what a face-off between the two of them might produce.

The air was heavy and still, an atmosphere as dark as Maureen's mood. Finally, when lights began to wink on all over the city and thunder and lightning put in an appearance, she went back inside. Rain was already beginning to fall. A spring storm, Maureen thought ironically, as she went around reclosing the windows she'd opened earlier. What a nice, symbolic touch. The perfect way to end a day in which she'd had three angry confrontations with people who were important to her.

Or had been important to her.

Brody, Clay and Lisa. Was it possible she'd never see any of them again?

She went into her bedroom and stepped out of the jeans and T-shirt she'd worn all day, recalling the dark head and greedy mouth that had almost lain waste to all her good intentions this morning.

How far would Brody have gone there on the river walk if she hadn't stopped him cold with her ice princess routine? He had been laughing. She had been laughing. The kind of crazy laughter that bubbles up between two people when they are about to do something rash and wonderful. Something totally out of character.

Last night he was the one who put a stop to it. She was the one this morning. Weren't they a pair? Testing attraction's waters, while all the time holding a little back. Aware. Cool. Curious. Suspicious.

At least she had something to be reasonably suspicious about. Yesterday he'd been a murder suspect. Today he was a murder suspect with a discredited alibi. An alibi that didn't hold water was worse than none.

Why would an innocent person fabricate such an elaborate lie?

Why would a guilty person make such a sloppy job of it?

Maureen gathered up her clothes and carried them to the hamper in the bathroom. Then she got into the shower. After blow drying her just washed hair she went to her bureau and reached in for a pair of pj's, but her hand just happened to fall on a seldom used nightgown, a gauzy, white cotton thing whose spaghetti straps were forever slipping off her shoulders.

It had, though, one redeeming virtue. It made her feel sexy and desirable, even when there was no one around to desire her. Which would make this the perfect time to wear it, she decided as she lifted it out of the drawer.

She was ready to call it a night. She was as tired and as tense as she had ever been in her life. She'd just prepared a cup of herbal tea and carried it into the bedroom when the intercom buzzer sounded in the entry.

Maureen checked the clock on the nightstand. Ten pm? Was it Lisa, coming back for the forgotten bag?

The buzzer sounded again. Maureen put down her cup, walked into the hall and pushed the send button.

"Yes? Who is it?"

"Maureen, let me in."

There was no mistaking that voice. Or the fissions of pleasure and anticipation it ignited deep inside her. She pressed the button that released the downstairs lock, and went down the hall to listen for the elevator. When she heard it reach the fifth floor, she opened her door, stuck her head out and watched him come down the corridor.

The beautifully tailored suit he'd obviously worn to the police interview was rumpled, the top button of his shirt collar undone, and his tie was jammed into the breast pocket of his jacket.

He looked wasted, desolate and irresistible.

At the door he braced his forearms on either side of the jamb and leaned towards her, staring. Maureen didn't move. Let him stare. She felt as if she'd been waiting for his arrival all day, and had even dressed for the occasion.

He looked past her. "Is Lisa Adams here?" he asked, his voice thick and tight, as if it hurt him to speak. "Paul said there'd been some trouble between the two of you."

"She moved out this afternoon," Maureen answered, barely able to get the words past her own constricted vocal chords.

He cursed softly under his breath, and ran a hand back and forth over his mouth. "I need you, Maureen. If you don't want this to happen,

97

you had better slam this door in my face right now."

Maureen took a step backward, almost colliding with the hall console. He followed her inside, kicked the door closed behind him and reached for her. One hand slid into her hair and curved around the back of her head.

"Brody, I'm not sure…"

He pulled her closer. She could feel his lips trembling against hers.

"I promise, you won't be sorry. I'm sure enough for both of us."

Then he kissed her, and with a thrill, Maureen knew this wouldn't be like last night. He wouldn't stop. He was on fire. Ready to consume anything, or anyone, that got in his way.

CHAPTER 9

Morning after regrets?

Maureen lay with the fresh, clean light of dawn playing across her closed eyelids and waited for the pangs of conscience and regret that were surely going to surface.

She lay in her cool, neat bed, where he'd carried her after, not before or during. During had been up against the bookcase in the living room, and on the champagne colored sofa, and the pillow strewn hardwood floor.

What exactly, she asked herself, had gone on here last night? By not closing the door she supposed she'd given a sort of consent. But for the next couple of hours that had been all that was required of her. All, in fact, she'd been allowed.

She hadn't been forced. She'd been used.

She smiled to herself. A lot could be said for being made to feel...useful.

She opened her eyes. Useful. Of course. That was it.

I need you, Maureen.

That's why she'd let him in last night. That's why she'd taken Lisa under her wing. Maureen Lowe wasn't able to stand apart anymore. To simply sketch, and watch, and wait. The people she moved among were in trouble and she needed to help.

Needed to be needed.

The media had been the first over the "distance" wall. Then Lisa. Now, Brody. The wall was down. Maybe forever.

Could she handle it?

She could hear Brody moving around in the next room and was suddenly seized by the fear that he'd leave before they had a chance to talk. If there had been any talk last night, she couldn't remember it. Plenty of groans and sighs and even a strangled cry or two, but certainly not what anyone could call conversation.

Well, what did a sensible woman say to a man after an experience as intense as last night's? Thank you, could I have some more please? Maureen buried her face in the pillow to keep from laughing out loud.

But maybe laughter was the only way to deal with the whole, mindless, bizarre situation.

Keep it light. Keep it very, very light.

She sat up, wrapped herself in the sheet and hobbled over to the bedroom door. She poked her head out into the living room and was a little disappointed to see that he'd gotten all his clothes back on and was busily engaged in straightening things. Brody Parrish in the raw was a work of art. The men she'd been privileged to see naked before last night didn't belong to the same species.

Someday she was going to have to ask him to pose for her.

"Are you disposing of the evidence before making your getaway?" she inquired with what she hoped was just the right touch of whimsy.

He froze with an overturned lamp in one hand and her ruined nightgown in the other. "If you're thinking about having me arrested, you'll have to get in line," he replied, much too seriously.

So that was it. He hadn't been formally charged but he could see it coming and it scared him. Fear probably wasn't an emotion that a Parrish had much experience with, so he'd come to her to hide from it.

At least, for a little while. Remember that, Maureen. For a little while.

He righted the lamp on an end table and dropped onto the couch still clutching the handful of pulverized gauze. "I want you to know that I'm not particularly proud of my behavior last night."

Maureen made her way over to the couch, sat down next to him, and began to search under the cushions for her glasses. "You shouldn't be. You were an absolute beast."

She looked up and couldn't stop herself from running the fingertips of her free hand over his stubbled cheek. "You'll need to shave."

He grabbed her wrist. "You have every right to be angry with me."

"Is that why you were cleaning up? As a peace offering? Give me a break, Brody. Did I look like I wasn't having a good time?"

That earned her a smile. She could see him replaying last night's movie inside his head, and liking what he saw.

"You know what it was, don't you?" he asked.

"A marriage proposal?"

Two black brows shot up, like ravens taking flight.

She groaned. "That was a joke, Brody. A really bad joke."

"It was supposed to be an exorcism. I needed to stop thinking about you and concentrate on saving my ass. My alibi crashed and burned."

"I know."

He rested his head against the back of the couch. "Dammit! Once in a while I'd like to know something about this mess before you do."

It was the kind of remark he'd made before, but this time the accusatory tone was missing. Maybe last night had finally convinced him that she was on his side. Now he needed to be reminded that there was more than one way she could help.

"Where were you last Saturday night, Brody?"

He picked up a fold of the sheet and began to tug at it. "I have a feeling the exorcism didn't take. Let's try the bed this time."

Maureen clutched the sheet in both fists and retreated into a corner of the couch. "In case you haven't noticed, Brody, sex isn't the answer to everything."

Before she could catch her breath he was after her, trapping her between his arms. "Corners are always a mistake. I don't suppose I could talk you into an arrangement where we forget about everything else when we're together and just enjoy each other's company."

Maureen gazed into his elegant face, the skin drawn taut over the beautifully shaped head and cheekbones, the blue eyes that one minute exuded challenging humor, the next minute molten desire. It was the shifting contrasts in his personality that made him so magnetic. His mouth, hovering as always between a grin and a scowl, his voice making promises she knew now his body could keep.

In spite of all her good intentions, last night she had given herself to him completely, and if he touched her now she was afraid she would let him do anything he wanted. Again.

"What exactly do you have in mind? That I wait around here until you show up needing a little R&R?"

For a second he looked as if she had slapped him. Then he laughed and threw up his hands. "Lighten up, Maureen. The idea has a certain appeal but I'm not as much of a bastard as you want to believe. I just thought we could have some fun and get to know each other better before this whole thing blows up in our faces. Last night I thought I could get you out of my system in a couple of hours, but now we both know it's going to take more than that." He glanced at his watch. "What's your pleasure? Breakfast? Brunch? We could take in a movie or a gallery."

He held out his hand. This was not the same man who'd arrived at her door last night. This was the man from Tio Pepe's. Playful. Charming.

God, he made her dizzy.

He's a salesman, Kiddo. Charming people is what he does for a living.

"How about it, Maureen? Be my girl for today. Tomorrow they're going to lock me up and throw away the key."

"No questions about the case?"

"No questions allowed," Brody insisted. "That's part of the deal."

"Well, of course I'm tempted. But it does seem to me I've heard a line similar to yours in an old movie once. It went something like this— 'Mary Lou, honey, don't you want to make your soldier boy happy before he leaves for the war?" She threw a pillow at him. "You idiot! What are you trying to avoid? Who are you trying to protect? All you have to do to stay out of jail is to tell the police where you were Saturday night."

"I told them where I was, dammit. With Bruce Cahill, going over the parameters of a Charitable Remainder Trust. But now it turns out that there is no Cahill, and no California based charity."

Maureen inched back across the cushions until she was kneeling by his side. "Is that the truth, Brody? Because if it is, I was right in suspecting that this isn't just a case of mistaken identity. Somebody's trying to set you up. Is it the truth?"

"It is. But then a guilty man wouldn't hesitate to lie to you, would he?" He picked up her hand and brushed his lips across the inside of her wrist, his eyes never leaving hers. "What do you think? Are you sleeping with a murderer?"

Maureen studied his face, memory making her a weakling. Last night, that mouth, those lips, all over her, everywhere. Had she been afraid of him in the ugly way Lisa had suggested? Had fear put "a real fine edge" on their lovemaking?

She did a quick check of her reactions. No. She hadn't been afraid. In awe perhaps, but not afraid.

"You're not a murderer," she said softly.

"Good. I'm glad we got that out of the way." He hooked a finger over the edge of the sheet she'd tucked around her breasts. "Now we can get started on that fun we talked about."

She batted his hand away. "Brody, listen to me. You've got to get yourself a criminal attorney right away. A good one will find ways to delay your arrest. That's important. Once you're arrested, even your friend Paul Marsh won't be able to keep the story quiet. It'll be all over the newspapers and TV."

"I keep forgetting how well versed you are in police procedure," he muttered. "As a matter of fact, I have an appointment with a lawyer at Riverbend this afternoon. If I'd been able to talk you into spending the day with me I was going to cancel, but it's beginning to look as if I might as well go ahead with the damn thing."

He stood up, dragging her along with him. For some reason he seemed annoyed with her, which was ridiculous. Everything she'd told him was for his own good. Surely he could see that.

But annoyed or not, he couldn't keep his hands off her. He dug his fingers into her hair, held her head so that she had to look into his eyes and palmed the curve of her breast under the sheet.

He rested his forehead against hers. "Change your mind. Come with me."

"Where?" Her heart was racing. "Where?"

"To see the lawyer. To the police station. Wherever the hell I have to go today. Come with me."

The police station! Clay would go out of his mind if he saw them together. He was capable of making things more difficult for Brody, who was obviously still in denial about just how difficult things could get.

She braced her fists against his chest and shoved. "I can't spend the day with you. I have an important appointment myself."

He dropped his arms. "Break it."

"Break it?"

"Break it."

She stepped away from him, aware of how silly she must look with her chin in the air while at the same time struggling to keep the sheet from coming undone. "You'd like me to be your girl for the day? The whole day?"

"And night." He grinned. "Yeah."

His girl! Why, the arrogant, skirt-spoiled SOB. "Not a chance," she said, folding her arms across her chest. "Not a chance I'm going to pass up a spread in Philadelphia Magazine just to follow you around all day."

"Philadelphia Magazine is doing a story on you?"

"One and the same." She poked a finger into his white shirtfront. "If you call what we did last night sleeping, then you just slept with the top forensic artist in the country."

"I thought you didn't like publicity."

"The magazine will do the article with or without my cooperation. If I talk to them and let them take some pictures I may at least have some control over what gets into print."

"How long will the damn interview take?"

She looked up at him and laughed. "Don't pout, Brody. If that lawyer can keep you out of jail, and you'd like to come to dinner tonight…"

Something about his wolfish smile, and the way his fingers closed around her wrist, made her wonder who'd really come out on top in this last exchange. "Wait," she protested as he pulled her in the direction of the bedroom, "Neither of us has any time for this."

"Time for what? All I'm going to do is help you get dressed. I bet you've got one of those neat little power suits in your closet. Well, this afternoon, while the top forensic artist in the country is having her picture taken, I want her to remember whose hands snapped and patted and tucked everything into place."

*   *   *

Brody made it back to Riverbend late for his appointment, but in time to speak to Mrs. Hartman and his mother before they left on her first extended outing since her stroke.

"Mr. Wicklow arrived a few minutes ago, Mr. Parrish," the housekeeper said. "He's waiting for you in the library."

Brody couldn't hear Hayes Wicklow's name without frowning. He and Wicklow moved in the same business and social circles, but Brody disliked the other man intensely and sensed the feeling was mutual. In his opinion Wicklow was a foul-mouthed street fighter, a raunchy shark in a Brooks Bothers' suit. Brody had been surprised when Richard Bailey suggested Wicklow, and even more surprised when Wicklow had agreed to take the case.

Victoria Parrish caught her son's eye as she checked her reflection in the hall mirror. "You didn't come home last night, Brody," she said reproachfully. "You'll need to shave."

Brody ran a hand over his jaw, remembering Maureen's fingertips exploring his face. And other parts of his anatomy.

"Wicklow has seen worse," he said.

"Very well." Victoria sighed. "But promise me you'll be civil to the man. Richard Bailey and Paul Marsh say he's the best criminal lawyer in Philadelphia. And the soul of discretion."

Brody suspected that Wicklow's reputation for discretion was what had sold his mother on a man she wouldn't normally let through her front door.

"I'll listen to what he has to say with an open mind. That's all I can promise. Now, go on and enjoy your shopping. Just don't let her overtax herself, Mrs. Hartmaan."

He watched them leave, content that the housekeeper would look after his mother. The woman adored her employer, and this new demonstration of Victoria's continuing improvement elated Brody. It was another sign he might soon be able to move back to town. Much as he would miss Riverbend and the Brandywine, his mother's constant harping on his personal life made their relationship difficult. Sadly, they got along better the less time they spent with each other.

And he looked forward to showing Maureen his apartment. He wondered what she would think of it. It was very different than her place. All polished woods and dark leather. The thought of them lounging in his king-sized bed had him grinning as he headed down the hall to the library.

His girl. She hadn't liked that. Not one bit. God, he'd wanted her with him today, but he'd gotten a surprising kick out of the way she'd insisted on doing her own thing.

Sass to spare. But, hell, she'd seemed like a girl to him last night. Hair all loose and wild. No makeup. So soft and yielding under his hands.

He stopped grinning when he stepped through the library door. Hayes Wicklow had appropriated his desk, forcing Brody to settle for a visitor's chair in his own office.

The two men regarded each other warily. "I need a few minutes more to review Bailey's notes," Wicklow said.

Brody nodded, sat back and let his mind drift along more enjoyable lines.

Brody Parrish's girl.

He was beginning to feel possessive, territorial. His girl. His. Every mouth watering inch of her. He flexed his fingers, remembering how they felt splayed over the gentle swell of her belly, the graceful curve where her spine eased into her behind.

Had he been too demanding last night?

Did I look like I wasn't having a good time?

But at the very least, he had been thoughtless. More than a little out of his mind. Tonight he'd do better by her. Bring her a gift. Something pretty and frivolous. And when they made love, he'd go slowly, be gentle, ask her what she liked.

Tonight.

Across the desk, Hayes Wicklow glanced up from the yellow pad in front of him. "You know, Parrish, the look on your face isn't what I'd expect to find on the face of a man who's in as much trouble as you are."

"Sue me," Brody said. He wished Wicklow would go back to his notes and allow Brody further contemplation of the evening ahead.

But instead the other man kicked back in Brody's chair, rested one ankle on the opposite knee and smiled. "I'd say you looked more like a man who just had one hell of a lay."

Brody shrugged. Let the bastard think whatever he wanted. "Eat your heart out, counselor."

Wicklow arched an eyebrow. "Really? She's that good, is she?"

Brody's patience was wearing thin. "Exactly how much an hour am I paying you for this quiz show?"

"Not nearly enough, you horny jerk. Answer the question. Is Maureen Lowe worth risking your life for?"

Brody shot out of his chair, reached across the desk and grabbed the lawyer by the lapels of his very expensive suit. "I don't want to hear her name coming out of your filthy mouth again. Do you understand?"

"Shit. This is worse than I thought. You've fallen for the woman."

Brody released his hold on Wicklow and slumped back in his chair. He cursed under his breath. "How did you find out about her?"

"I had a little chat with your mother when I arrived. She mentioned that you hadn't been home all night. Her guess was that you were with..." Wicklow smirked and spread his hands. He leaned forward and began to sift through his papers. "I've run into the young woman in question a couple of times myself. In court. She and her work are impressive."

He picked up a photograph of Jeannie Starbuck and turned it in Brody's direction. "Your taste is improving, Parrish, if not your good sense."

Brody covered his eyes with his hand.

Wicklow shook his head. "I don't get it." His eyes did a slow circuit of the room. "Look at this place. Look at you. Marsh insists you're a numbers wizard, made him a bundle in the market. Cool. Sharp, he says. Well, when are you going to start acting like it? You think you can't lose this? Let me run a little scenario by you, so you'll get an idea of how royally you've messed up over the past few days. Picture yourself in a courtroom, on trial for murder, and a prosecuting attorney turns and points at you and says 'On Saturday night this man's lover was brutally murdered, and four days later he was breaking in her replacement.' How do you think that will play with a jury?"

"I want Maureen's name kept out of this."

"Does she want her name kept out of it?"

"What the hell does that mean?"

"She drew the sketch that brought you to the attention of the authorities, didn't she? She's got quite a rep already, but if you're arrested and convicted the media will give her part in the story a big play."

"She isn't interested in publicity," Brody said, but the memory of where Maureen was spending the afternoon rose up to gnaw at him.

"What is she interested in? Besides your skinny behind, of course." Wicklow picked up his yellow pad. "Paul Marsh tells me she's pretty chummy with one of his senior men. Clay Stanton. Is he your competition?"

Brody snorted. "He's old enough to be her father."

Wicklow chuckled nastily and cast a disbelieving look at the ceiling.

"Look," Brody said, "Forget about Maureen. You were hired to help me with a certain legal problem. Not with my love life. I'm a murder suspect. Remember? Aren't you interested in whether or not I killed Jeannie Starbuck?"

"Actually, that little detail is irrelevant. The question is whether or not the authorities can put together a conclusive case. They haven't been able to do that yet. That's why you're still walking around free. It's my job to keep it that way. Now, if they could add a reasonable motive to the other evidence they've accumulated..." Wicklow leaned across the desk. "By the way, you didn't have one, did you?"

Brody hesitated, looked down at his hands. He could feel the tension building up in his neck. Suddenly, he wanted to unload on someone, anyone, and here was Wicklow, who he didn't give a damn about, and who didn't give a damn bout him, coming through with the perfect opening.

"Oh, hell! Spill it," the lawyer demanded.

Brody took a deep breath. "You were wrong about Jeannie and I still being lovers at the time of her death. That ended more than a year ago. But a few months back, she did come to my office and ask for money."

"Money? We're not talking about a loan, are we?"

Brody shook his head.

"Blackmail? She had something on you?"

"Something. Yeah."

"Did you pay her off?"

"No. At first I thought I could work through the problem. Come clean. Set the record straight. It happened a long time ago and maybe people would understand—"

"Shut up!" Wicklow bellowed. "I'm not a priest. I don't want to hear your confession. All I want to know is, if the cops go to your bank, are they going to come up with any suspicious cash withdrawals or cancelled checks made out to the deceased?"

"Negative."

Wicklow checked his watch. "Damn! I'm due at a deposition in Chadds Ford in fifteen minutes. I can't deal with this right now."

He picked up his briefcase and shoved every paper on the desk into it. Then he stood and headed for the door, talking over his shoulder all the while. "The police obviously don't know about the blackmail attempt or you wouldn't be sitting here sweating. I'll call you tonight and we'll go over the Cahill business."

Brody got to his feet. "I won't be here."

The lawyer turned and stared at him. "Not Lowe again?" He sighed. "Parrish, you and I are never going to be best buddies. But I've been known to develop temporary affection for the people who pay me. I'd hate to see you end up in front of a judge. It's obvious you're not going to stay away from this woman, but do yourself a favor and watch the pillow talk. Okay?"

Brody wasn't prepared to make Wicklow any promises. Especially about Maureen. "I have a question," he said.

"Make it fast. I'm late."

"Jeannie had an ex-husband. Why aren't the police investigating him?"

"You underestimate them, Parrish. It's my understanding that they already have. But he has a couple of things going for him that you don't. He has an air-tight alibi, and no witness has identified him as the murderer."

*   *   *

The self-recrimination and doubts Maureen had expected to feel that morning unaccountably hit in the evening, just as she was adding artichoke hearts to a wild rice casserole.

She'd never invited a man to dinner at the condo before. Not even Pete.

Poor Pete. He'd tried so hard to get through to her. It might have worked out between them if she hadn't kept him at such a distance. A distance that he'd finally found unacceptable. But at the time, the "wall" had been intact and Maureen was just beginning to realize it had been a personal as well as professional wall.

But she was looking forward to tonight. On her way home from the interview with Philadelphia Magazine she'd stopped at a gourmet Italian deli and picked up a really good Chianti and some fresh bread sticks. She'd wrapped the bread in a checkered napkin, and placed it in the center of her tiny table, next to a riotous ivy plant in a wicker pot. A Caesar salad was chilling in the refrigerator and the combined aromas of butter browned chicken, garlic and sweet basil filled the small kitchen.

But for some reason, it was the artichoke hearts, the ingredient that was supposed to make this particular dish special, that did it. Suddenly it occurred to her that Brody wasn't coming tonight to sample her culinary skills, such as they were. He was coming for sex.

She put down her wooden spoon, covered the casserole dish and placed it in the oven. Wasn't that why he'd come last night? Wasn't that what she'd provided? A soft, warm, willing body for him to pour his fear, frustration and lust into? If she hadn't been available, wouldn't he have found someone else? After all, it wasn't as if he'd been half in love with her for fifteen years.

He hadn't even known she was alive until the morning of the lineup. True, there in the squad room, there had been sparks. But Maureen's college psychology classes had explained that sort of phenomenon. People often confused the adrenaline rush experienced in dangerous and exciting situations with sexual attraction. Strangers thrown together during natural disasters. Soldiers coming out of battle, falling in love with their nurses or the women they met in foreign cafes.

Try as Brody might to remain cool and confident, a murder charge was a new and dangerous situation for him. And there, at the beginning of it all, had been Maureen.

Her timing had been perfect. But, once Brody's innocence was established, and Jeannie's real murderer found, the attraction would evaporate along with the danger.

At least, for him.

And for her? What had he said in Tio Pepe's? They were adults, not children. Right? Maybe it would be best for her to think of their relationship the way he did. As a means to an end. A way to work past her ridiculous schoolgirl crush on him. A way to get over him and on with the rest of her life.

Just then the intercom sounded.

Maureen walked into the living room and pushed the receiving button.

As it had the night before, Brody's voice came over the line with all the warmth of a physical caress. "Maureen?"

"Come on up, Brody."

She waited for him at the open door, remembering what she had told herself this morning. Keep it light. That way you won't be devastated when it disappears.

Well, she'd try.

He sauntered down the corridor, looking tired but surprisingly jaunty, an airline flight bag slung over his shoulder and a gift-wrapped package in one hand.

"Did you see the lawyer?" she asked as he bent toward her.

He groaned into her hair. "First, say hello, Maureen. Then kiss me. Then, if we can't think of anything better to do, we can talk lawyers and magazine interviews."

It was amazing what the man could do during the space of a single kiss. Back her into the condo. Get the door closed behind them. Half carry, half drag her down the foyer into the living room.

Melt every bone in her body.

When they came up for air he was sitting on the arm of the couch and she was trembling in front of him, one hand braced against his chest, the other hanging on to the strap of the flight bag for dear life.

"Hello, Brody," she gasped.

"Now that's my good girl," he said drawing her closer.

"If you don't get off this 'girl' kick, Parrish, I swear, it's going to cost you." Maureen arched an eyebrow and fingered the strap of the flight bag. "What's this?"

He removed the bag and dropped it behind him onto the couch.

"Toothbrush and razor. A change of clothes."

"If I remember correctly, the invitation was for dinner."

He smiled. "You're calling the shots tonight, Maureen. If, after dinner, you decide that you don't want me to stay over, I'll go."

"Very noble. But I have a feeling you're not going to make that easy for me."

"Not on your life." His grin widened. He held the gift-wrapped package out to her. "Starting with this."

With a fingertip, she traced the familiar burgundy logo in one corner of the be-ribboned pink box. "If this is a black lace garter belt, I swear you're going to end up wearing it."

"You're not black lace."

"Oh, what am I?"

"Open the box, Maureen."

From under layers of flower sprigged tissue paper she lifted out a drift of silver gray silk. She shivered as the fabric cascaded over her palm, as weightless as smoke.

For a single moment, she was tempted to ask him if all his "girls" got lingerie, but she couldn't bring herself to do it. If it were true, she didn't want to know.

Had he read her mind? Was she so transparent? He cupped her face in both his hands. "I never realized that buying a gift for a woman could be so enjoyable. I made the saleswoman show me everything in the place. But when she brought this out I thought to myself, I want to make love to Maureen while she's wearing this."

He lowered his head and teased the corner of her mouth with the tip of his tongue until she opened to him. Where last night there had been fire, now there was only an aching sweetness that she hoped would go on forever. When he broke off the kiss she wanted to hit him.

He smiled down at her. "Wear it for me, Maureen. Ask me to stay."

She wished that he didn't look so sure of what her answer would be. "I don't know, Brody. I love my present, but you're awfully hard on nightgowns."

"Not tonight, Maureen. Tonight, I promise, if you let me make love to you, you won't know where the silk lets off and I begin."

*   *   *

He'd arrived about seven, but they didn't sit down to dinner until ten. By that time, the wild rice was a little dry but they washed it down with liberal doses of Chianti. Then Maureen gave him a quick tour of the condo and they went back to bed.

At two o'clock in the morning, looking down on a sleeping Maureen in the dark of her bedroom, Brody gave himself high marks for restraint. He'd been as good as his word. With a tenderness he hadn't known he possessed, he'd taken them both to a time and place beyond which neither cared a damn who was pleasuring who.

Not an altogether easy task for a man who had wanted this particular woman since the moment he'd laid eyes on her in the grubby squad room of the Granite Run Police Station. Wanted her during their argument in front of the condo. In the library at the estate. Under the street lamp in front of Tio Pepe's. On the banks of the Brandywine.

Wanted her now, this minute, as much as ever. Every man's fantasy. An endlessly desirable woman, totally vulnerable, totally available, to him, and only to him.

Almost too good to be true.

He could imagine what Wicklow would say.

In your dreams, Parrish.

No, there was definitely something going on between him and Maureen, over and above the physical. Something that had made her, he didn't like the sound of it but it certainly described the situation, a seemingly easy conquest for him, when he would lay money that under other circumstances, easy was the one thing she was not.

He laughed with her, and God knew he needed to laugh, even if it were only a kind of gallows humor. She turned him on, and after the last two nights, it pleased him to think that he knew her body better than she did herself. But what went on inside her head was still a mystery to him.

There were others, though, who thought they had a bead on her. Paul Marsh. Wicklow. His mother.

She's a friend of Lisa Adams and Clay Stanton. She's in the enemy camp.

I've seen the lady in court. Are you sure she wants her name kept out of it?

She's just like Jeannie.

Brody rolled over on his back and closed his eyes. Dammit. He'd like to keep his relationship with Maureen separate from the murder investigation, but it wasn't going to work. She wouldn't allow it. In the morning, that delicious mouth of hers would be brimming with questions as well as kisses. And when he'd let her get away with asking him about Jeannie, Maureen's inquiries had been as probing and insightful as any the police had made.

Brody reached down beside the bed, picked up his jeans and slipped out of the room quietly so as not to wake her. He couldn't think straight laying beside her, the tempting warmth of her body, the murmur of her breathing and the scent of their lovemaking all reaching out to him, filling him with renewed desire.

In the hallway he tugged on his pants, shoved his hands into his pockets and leaned against the wall peering through the arched doorway into the living room where they'd left on a light.

What could you learn about a person from where they lived?

Maureen's condo was attractively, if sparsely decorated. Spacious and uncluttered. Mono-toned, linen-covered furniture, almost seeming to float above bare hardwood floors. New, and relatively unlived in.

The lady traveled light. Not much to be learned there.

He glanced to his left, toward the guestroom, and felt himself tense. Maureen's initial connection to the case against him might have been pure chance. She was a forensic artist called in to interview a witness to a crime. But after that she'd accompanied the witness to the lineup, and then invited her into her home. Both actions involved choices. Choices Maureen had willingly made.

Why?

He turned to his right. Earlier in the evening, after dinner, she had shown him her studio. He dimly remembered being impressed and surprised, but he'd had a nice, mellow buzz on from the Chianti and Maureen's presence at his side, and hadn't really taken it all in.

It deserved a second look. He walked down the hall, pushed open the door, switched on the overhead light and sucked in a long, appreciative breath.

Here was where Maureen Lowe lived.

The studio was a cauldron of color and clutter centered around a large, fantastic rendering of the Red Riding Hood fairy tale. A number of other paintings lined the walls, bright corners peeking out from behind protective coverings. Underfoot a spattered canvas was anchored in place by a couple of rickety tables littered with stained rags, tubes of paint and tall jars holding every artist's tool and brush imaginable.

Brody leaned back against the doorjamb, gazed up at the unfinished painting and smiled. He was hardly an expert, but one didn't grow up a Parrish in Granite Run without acquiring some artistic discernment. He recognized talent when he saw it, and he was seeing it now.

It was obvious that Maureen had talent and ambitions that went beyond forensic art. Marsh, Wicklow and Victoria, he thought with growing satisfaction, didn't know Maureen as well as they thought they did.

He was on his way back to the bedroom when the telephone rang. The familiar stab of apprehension he assumed everybody felt at late night calls stopped him in his tracks. Maureen had mentioned having a particularly strong aversion to the telephone. Who would take a chance on disturbing her at this hour?

Another man?

She must have picked up the phone after the second ring. Brody could hear the muffled murmur of her voice coming from inside the bedroom. Somewhat amused at the jealousy he'd begun to feel and not wanting to intrude on her privacy, he waited impatiently in the hall.

After a few minutes the door opened and Maureen stood on the threshold, the dim light from the living room casting eerie shadows across her lovely features. She took a step toward him and staggered a little, catching hold of the doorframe for support.

Brody reached for her, pulling her into his arms. "Maureen? Baby, what is it?"

Against his shoulder her breath fluttered like the wings of a frightened bird. "It's…it's Clay. He wants to talk to you."

"Stanton? Talk to me? But…"

She tilted her head back and looked up at him, her green eyes huge, her skin as pale as the nightgown he'd given her. "It's Lisa, Brody. Lisa Adams."

"What about her?"

"Her body was found floating in the Brandywine an hour ago. Near Riverbend. The police are looking for you."

CHAPTER 10

At three o'clock in the morning, Maureen and Brody had the highway between Philadelphia and Granite Run almost to themselves. There appeared to be only one other car on the road, its headlights twin pinpricks in the darkness at least a half mile behind them.

But Brody drove the Jaguar with the same single-minded intensity he might apply to rush hour traffic. In the passenger seat, Maureen felt him growing more withdrawn and remote with each passing mile.

She touched his shoulder. "Brody, talk to me."

He darted a steely, sideways glance in her direction. "I never should have let you come. This isn't going to be pleasant."

"I don't expect it to be. But I have to find out for myself if my quarrel with Lisa had anything to do with what's happened. I should have kept my suspicions to myself a while longer. She was in an awful mood when she left the condo. Her life hasn't been easy. Maybe what she saw as my betrayal of her was the last straw. Maybe…"

"Suicide? You're thinking she committed suicide? Stop beating yourself up over this, Maureen. Lisa Adams was murdered, or the police wouldn't be looking for me in the middle of the night. And if you want my opinion, this only proves that she was never the innocent bystander you thought. At best, she was a hysterical attention seeker. At worst, a calculated liar. Either way, I was her victim. I'm sorry, but I'm having a hard time working up much sympathy for her."

Maureen sighed. "But I may be the last person to have seen her alive. The police will want to talk to me."

"I'm sure they will." Brody's tone was cold. "Tell me again what Stanton said when you picked up the phone tonight. His exact words."

"Why, I think it was 'Is Parrish with you?' Yes, that was it."

"Doesn't it strike you as odd that he'd expect to find me at your place?"

Maureen bit her lip, remembering the angry confrontation with Clay the previous day. "Lisa's body was discovered on Parrish property. The police were at the estate. You weren't there, so it seemed reasonable…"

"Reasonable that they call you? Did Stanton know I'd be with you, Maureen? Does he know about us?"

"Everybody knows about us, Brody." She watched his fingers tighten around the steering wheel. "The entire Granite Run police department, your—"

"How do they know? What do they know?"

"That we're seeing each other. Clay had a surveillance officer following you. The man observed us outside Tio Pepe's. He reported to Clay and—"

"My God! You knew someone was tailing me all this time, and you didn't tell me? Why the hell not?"

"It was only that one night. By the time I found out about it Paul Marsh had already called the surveillance off." Maureen turned and stared out the passenger side window, stung by his irritation at finding out that their affair was common knowledge. "I'm sorry," she said softly. "I didn't realize how important it was to you that our relationship remain such a deep, dark secret."

In the silence that followed she tried to occupy her mind with the sound of the Jaguar's tires eating up the asphalt miles, the scent of the car's fine leather interior, the dark tree shapes outside the window, silhouetted against the moonlit nighttime sky.

After several minutes, she felt his hand on hers.

"Maureen…," he began.

"It might interest you to know," she interrupted, "that your mother also has a pretty good idea about what's going on between us. At breakfast the other day she didn't hesitate to comment on the situation."

"Mother!" Brody swore under his breath. After a second, he brought Maureen's hand to his lips. "Baby, forgive me. She probably told the police they could find me at your place. Yesterday she went out of her way to mention your name to Wicklow."

Maureen whirled away from the window, her eyes wide. "Wicklow? Hayes Wicklow? Is he your attorney?"

Brody grimaced. "Yeah."

Wicklow. Maureen repeated the name to herself and felt a glimmer of hope. What a stroke of luck. The last time she'd seen the lawyer in action he'd been staggeringly impressive. Finally, something positive to latch onto. If anyone could help Brody through this, Hayes Wicklow could. "Brody, I've heard he can be brutal at times, but believe me, he has no equal in court. Prosecutors pale at the sight of him. You couldn't hope for a better advocate. You're fortunate to have been able to retain him."

"So everyone, including Wicklow, tells me," Brody growled.

Maureen leaned forward and studied his expression. So, the two men had butted heads already. It had probably been inevitable but that didn't change the fact that Wicklow was exactly who Brody needed at the moment. She reached for the car phone and held it out to him. "Call your lawyer. Have him meet us at Riverbend. You shouldn't talk to the police without his being there."

"Why? All I'm going to do is tell them the truth. That I never met Lisa Adams, much less had anything to do with her death. Why do I need Wicklow there, monitoring my every word?"

"You're paying him. Why not use him?"

With a grunt, Brody gestured toward the glove compartment. "His card's in there. Dig it out and dial the number for me, will you?"

After she handed him the phone Maureen settled back, closed her eyes and only half listened to the call. Brody's apology had eased some of the hurt she'd felt a few minutes ago, but it was obvious he still didn't trust her completely. Even after she had taken him into her bed, her body, he still suspected her of some sort of ulterior motives.

What did that tell her about the depth of their relationship? Mentally, she snickered at her own self-delusion. What depth? As far as he was concerned, his relationship with her was based on the same thing his relationship with Jeannie Starbuck had been. Sex.

Maureen had recognized that fact earlier in the evening, before he'd arrived at the condo. But later, wrapped in his arms and silver silk, she'd let herself forget.

When he snapped the receiver back into its cradle, she opened her eyes.

"That was Wicklow's answering service," he said. "Someone from Riverbend called him a few minutes ago. He's on his way there now." He glanced up into the rearview mirror. "For all we know, those may be his headlights behind us."

At the next off ramp Brody took the Granite Run exit and a few streets later turned down the winding rural road that led to Riverbend. Just before they reached the driveway of the estate he pulled the car onto the shoulder of the road and switched off the ignition.

From there, they could see into Riverbend's courtyard, where a number of police cruisers and an ambulance were parked, doors open and colored lights flashing.

Brody removed the car keys from the ignition, slipped them into Maureen's hand and curled her fingers around them. "I'm getting out here. I'll walk the rest of the way. You take the Jag and go back to Philadelphia. If there's anything I think you need to know, I'll call."

"What's this all about, Brody?"

He twisted around in his seat and looked at her. "You misunderstood what I said earlier, Maureen. I never meant to keep us a secret. I asked you spend yesterday with me. Remember? But I'd hoped to keep what's happening between us separate from the past, and...," he turned his gaze on the house, "...from the kind of thing that's going on in there. I know I rushed you into things, but from the moment I saw you I knew you were going to be different than the other women I've known. You were going to be...important."

He leaned forward and tucked a stray strand of hair behind her ear. "I was right. So, go home, Maureen. There's no way that the media isn't going to get hold of this now, with a second body, and this one found right here at Riverbend. You know what the tabloids will make of your involvement with me. It won't be pretty."

The press! Maureen had forgotten all about them. Every self-protective instinct she possessed urged her to take the keys and run. She could imagine the snickering headlines and soundbites. Murder suspect discovered in love nest with police artist. That would be the least offensive. Any self-respecting gossipmonger could do better than that.

But she couldn't run, couldn't leave Brody to the wolves. She tucked the keys back in his hand.

"I appreciate your wanting to protect me, but I have to talk to the police. If Lisa were murdered, I'm not just someone you spent the night with, Brody. I'm your alibi. And I have no intention of disappearing on you the way Bruce Cahill did."

*   *   *

Their fears about the media were borne out the minute they stepped through the front door of the estate.

Paul Marsh had just hung up the phone in the entry hall. After coming forward and shaking their hands, he nodded in its direction. "That was Rick Steele over at the *Chronicle*. He's getting calls from all the news services. Someone tipped them that a big story was about to break in Granite Run. They've been monitoring our police radio." He combed his fingers through his thinning hair. "Reporters and TV people are going to be crawling all over this place in a couple of minutes."

"It was bound to happen, Paul," Brody said. "I appreciate how you've handled things so far. I won't forget it. I know it's been difficult."

"Hey, you weren't the only reason we kept things quiet. Granite Run's voters have an aversion to this kind of publicity. It's bad for property values. Not to mention the tourist trade."

"Can you keep the bastards away from the house? I can take whatever they dish out but there's no reason my mother or...," He slipped his arm around Maureen's shoulder, "...or anyone else should have to put up with them."

"All I can do is put a police barricade across the driveway. Riverbend isn't fenced. I don't have the manpower to keep reporters or curiosity seekers from circling around through the woods."

"That's trespassing."

"Yeah, well, respect for private property isn't always the first concern of the fourth estate." The chief shrugged. "I'll do what I can."

Clay Stanton came out of the parlor just in time to hear Marsh's promise. Brody felt Maureen stiffen at his side, but after she and Stanton shared one long glance, full of fury on his part and distress on hers, they broke the eye contact.

"I think we have more important things to do than keep Riverbend sacrosanct," Stanton snarled.

"Having the media overrun what may be a crime scene isn't going to help the situation, Stanton. Tell someone out front to head them off. Now!" Marsh turned his back on his lieutenant and fished a small notebook and tape recorder out of his pocket. "Why don't we find a quiet place to talk, Brody. It'll be in your best interest to give me a statement now. That way it won't look as if you tailored the facts to fit the circumstances."

"I'd like to check on my mother first."

Already at the door Stanton paused and glared back at them. "That won't be necessary. Both the Chief and I talked to her. She's fine."

Brody glared at Stanton. "Am I under arrest, Paul?"

The chief waved his hands. "No. No. Until the coroner completes his examination we can't be sure about the time or cause of death. Things look suspicious, but there's always the chance that there could have been an accident."

Stanton's nasty chuckle escaped no one.

"Clay, I gave you an order," Marsh exploded. "Get the hell outta here!" Then he nodded in the direction of the library. "Make it fast, Brody. Your mother is in there with Mrs. Hartman. They're been very helpful."

"That's right. Told us exactly where you could be reached," Stanton chimed in smugly. "Not that it was any big secret," he added before he stepped outside and slammed the door behind him.

Fists clenched, Brody made a move to go after him but Maureen put a restraining hand on his arm. "Don't, please. That last remark was for my benefit, not yours."

That was just the point, Brody thought, looking down at her hand. Stanton's comment was the first of many she'd hear or read during the next few days. Wicklow had been right. Once she presented herself as his alibi the press would play her up as Jeannie Starbuck's "replacement."

Perhaps even suggest she was the motive for murder.

Inwardly, Brody cringed. The thought of Maureen's name being mentioned in the same context as Jeannie's made him want to hit something or someone. But he was the one at fault. Nobody else. He'd put her in this position. He'd gone to her, made love to her. It had been stupid and cruel of him to involve her in his life when he was under suspicion of murder.

If only there were a way to keep her out of it. If only he didn't need an alibi.

Dammit! What was happening to him? What had become of the calculated detachment he'd brought to all his relations with women since that first youthful fiasco with Jeannie? Since when had Maureen Lowe's reputation and welfare become more important to him than his own?

He took her arm and led her over to the Chippendale settee against the wall. When she was seated, he hunkered down in front of her. "Listen to me, I've got to see to my mother. Wait here. Don't talk about tonight to anyone until I finish with her. Not even Paul."

A few feet away Marsh coughed discretely. "If you were with Ms. Lowe all evening, Brody, her statement will be as important as yours."

Brody reached up and touched Maureen's face. "From now on I

mean to take better care of you," he whispered. He turned and looked over his shoulder. "I'm sorry, Paul. Neither Maureen nor I will be making any statements until Hayes Wicklow puts in an appearance."

*   *   *

Victoria and Mrs. Hartman were so engrossed in the view from the windows overlooking the terrace that neither one of them was aware Brody had entered the room.

The housekeeper was still in her bathrobe and slippers but Brody wasn't surprised to find his mother fully dressed. He walked up behind them, looked past their shoulders and drew in a ragged breath.

Outside, through the gently swaying trees a short distance to the left of the family pier, he could see a fan of bright light and five or six dark figures, bending and rising, slowly, deliberately, as if taking part in a well choreographed dance. The light rained glittering spangles on the black, moving water below. If Brody hadn't known that in the midst of it all lay a body, he might have thought the whole scene beautiful in a surreal sort of way.

"So close to the house," he said softly.

Victoria gave a startled gasp and turned, burying her face in her son's shoulder.

"Oh, Mr. Parrish," the housekeeper cried, "Your father must be turning over in his grave. A murder! At Riverbend!"

"Be still, Margaret," Victoria snapped. "No one has said anything about a murder. At least," she peered into Brody's face, "not to me."

"Are you all right?" he asked.

She raised her head and stepped back. "Now that you're here, I'm fine." Thank God, it was true. Brody could see that she was pale but her back was straight and her voice steady. The past few months had taught him that she possessed an amazing reserve of energy for a woman of her age, and an absolute certainty that, given enough time and money, she could bend any situation to her will.

That conviction had served her well during her recovery. But very soon she was going to have to face the reality that some situations and people were easier to control than others. Even time and money had their limitations. Sometimes there just wasn't enough of either.

What was going on down by the pier was a perfect example of what might lie ahead for them all.

"If you feel up to it, Mother, I'd like to hear what happened here tonight."

Victoria nodded toward the housekeeper. "From what Margaret tells

121

me, the telephone rang about two o'clock."

"It was Chief Marsh, Mr. Parrish. He was very apologetic about waking us, but he said his lieutenant had received an anonymous call from someone who claimed to have taken his girlfriend for a midnight canoe ride on the Brandywine."

Brody frowned. Two anonymous calls? One to the press and another to the police. Coincidence?

"The caller said that while they were drifting past Riverbend..."

Victoria raised a slender fist. "The gall of some people. Using our river in the middle of the night. Can you imagine, Brody?"

Not only could he imagine it, he had done it himself. Granite Run's teenagers had always considered a sail the perfect way to end a hot summer date. But summer was still a couple of months away. Anyone who'd grown up in the valley should have known it would be dangerous to challenge the nighttime currents around Riverbend so early in the season.

"We don't own the river, Mother," he said. "Go on, Mrs. Hartman."

The woman fumbled nervously with the belt of her robe. "The caller told the lieutenant that while they were passing the house they saw what looked like a body caught in the reeds along the shore. They steered close enough to see that it was a woman and, by the looks of things, she was...dead."

"They found the body around midnight? Why did the police wait until two o'clock to call?"

"The caller claimed that his girlfriend didn't want her parents to know what she'd been up to, so they didn't report their discovery right away. He said there was obviously nothing that could be done for the woman. But later, after he'd taken his girlfriend home, he got in touch with the police. When the Chief called here he and the lieutenant were already on their way." Mrs. Hartman's lips began to tremble. "That's when I decided I'd better wake your mother. I hope I did the right thing."

"I don't think you had any alternative," Brody assured her.

Victoria sighed. "Paul seems quite positive the body he found in the river is that of the woman who claimed to have witnessed Jeannie Starbuck's unfortunate end."

"His identification is probably as good as anyone's. From what Maureen told me, Lisa Adams was a newcomer to Granite Run and something of a loner."

"Maureen again," his mother said. "I must admit, at first, I really didn't approve of your attachment to her, Brody. But now it seems she may prove useful if the police foolishly try to blame you for Ms. Adams' sudden demise."

Brody shook his head, marveling at his mother's amazing talent for euphemism. Unfortunate end. Sudden demise.

But hadn't he, in a way, been doing the same thing? Avoiding the truth. Hoping he wouldn't need to do anything more than deny his guilt. Using Maureen to forget.

And if Stanton had been telling the truth his mother was the one Brody had to thank for dragging Maureen's name into it tonight.

"Are you the one who told the police that they could find me at Maureen's place?" he asked.

"Why yes, Brody, I am. I knew it would make you angry but I felt it was in your best interest. Which is always my first concern, Dear."

He gritted his teeth and swallowed down the anger that rose like burning bile in his throat. His best interest? Or hers? Before her stroke he would have raised the roof at yet another instance of her interference. Not that it would have done any good. He had just about reached the conclusion that she was past learning. Still, if his and Maureen's relationship were to continue he would have to lay down the law to his mother. Soon.

But not tonight. He was exhausted...and there was a body down by the river.

"I suppose you called Wicklow too," he said wearily.

"Of course," Victoria replied smugly.

*   *   *

Maureen was examining the painting that hung above the Chippendale settee when Hayes Wicklow finally put in an appearance.

She checked her watch. If it had been his car behind them on the highway tonight he should have arrived long before this.

After a short, whispered conversation with Chief Marsh Wicklow came to stand by her side. "Good evening, Ms. Lowe. Let me introduce myself. I'm..."

"I recognize you, Mr. Wicklow. I was in court when you defended Vic Ross."

"I remember. You were responsible for the sketch that got Ross arrested, and I might add, ultimately convicted."

"He was guilty."

"So the jury concluded." Wicklow took a step closer and peered at the painting Maureen had been studying when he'd arrived. "I must admit I've never understood the value some people place on paintings and sculpture. Are you impressed with this particular work?"

"Not in the least."

Wicklow raised an eyebrow.

Maureen turned away from the painting and sat down. "A minute ago I was pacing up and down the hall, trying to keep myself occupied while Brody talks with his mother." She shrugged. "I just happened to notice this wasn't the same painting that had been hanging here a couple of days ago."

"Any significance to that?"

"Probably not. Victoria Parrish is a collector. Perhaps she likes to move things around every once in while." Maureen took another quick glance over her shoulder. "Though why a serious collector would replace an important work with anything this mediocre is a mystery to me. Especially when the subject of the first painting was Riverbend itself."

"Speaking of seriousness and mysteries," Wicklow said, "Has this latest development finally made Brody aware of how desperate his situation is?"

Before she could reply, Brody himself exited the parlor with his arms around the shoulders of his mother and her housekeeper. Just one look at his poor haggard face was all the answer Wicklow needed. Brody could never look other than elegant, but his eyes were almost black with fatigue, and worry dragged at the usually taut skin around his mouth.

Maureen thought back to earlier in the evening, and to the man who'd made such wonderful, languid love to her, and she wanted to drop her head into her hands and cry. Instead she stood and started toward him.

Victoria frowned when she saw Maureen approach, and Brody shook his head and waved her and Wicklow away. "I'll be with you in a minute," he said before shepherding the two women in his care down the corridor and toward the stairs.

At the foot of the staircase Paul Marsh was conferring with a group of men who'd just come through the front door. Some of them, Maureen noticed, were in uniform, some in civilian clothes. Two or three of them had trouser cuffs that were stained and damp. One was carrying a camera.

"Pretty damn impressive, isn't he?" Wicklow said, close to her ear.

Maureen felt her color rise. "Who?" she asked defensively. "The photographer?"

Wicklow chuckled. "Parrish. I couldn't help noticing your reaction when he came into the room a few seconds ago. I think I may have misjudged you, Ms. Lowe. You're in love with him, aren't you?"

Maureen turned and stared at the man standing next to her. This was the first time she'd ever seen Hayes Wicklow outside a courtroom. There, he could be a smooth-talking snake charmer one moment and a ruthless bully the next. And according to courthouse gossip, he was also a man who could turn the air blue with his longshoreman vocabulary.

Only the snake charmer was in evidence tonight. And, so far at least, he hadn't uttered one word that couldn't have been spoken at a convention of nuns.

Watch your step, Maureen cautioned herself. "Brody and I only met a few days ago," she said.

"I didn't ask how long you've known him. I asked if you're in love with him."

"I don't think that has any bearing on the case, counselor."

"Well, you haven't wasted your time in the courtroom, I see. I'll withdraw the question for now. I only hoped that, if you did happen to care for him, you might assist me in curbing some of his more self-destructive tendencies."

"Self-destructive tendencies? You're going to have to explain yourself, Mr. Wicklow."

"He sometimes talks too much, Maureen." Wicklow took a step closer still. "May I call you that?"

Maureen nodded. She tried to avert her eyes and found she couldn't. There was something about that working class face combined with that Ivy League educated voice that was utterly hypnotic, and he knew it. Was he as successful with women, she wondered, as he was in the courtroom?

He shrugged. "How shall I put this? Brody is only guilty of what I call the arrogance of innocence. Like so many falsely accused people, he is so self-righteous, so sure of himself and his reputation that he's ready to fire off statements and answer questions that haven't even been asked. Ready to confess to real or imagined past sins that have nothing to do with the problem at hand."

"I assume you're talking about the statement he gave to the police on the morning of the lineup." This time Maureen was able to move a short distance away. "But now that you're on board, I'm sure you'll see to it that he's more circumspect."

Obviously aware of her retreat he smiled, inclined his head and scrutinized her from under raised eyebrows. "Of course. When I'm around. But there are parties to which a lawyer may not be invited. Let's say, for the sake of argument, that during some tender moment Brody felt the need to confide in you something that you might later be required to repeat on the witness stand. Would it be presumptuous of me to ask you to discourage him from making such revelations?"

"That doesn't sound like advice you'd give someone you believed cared for Brody, Mr. Wicklow."

"Please, call me Hayes. I want to believe you care, Maureen. I want to believe the evidence of my own eyes. But I've learned to be skeptical even of that. Men have been known to trust faces as pretty as yours to their eventual sorrow."

Pretty! Maureen dragged her fingers through her hair. He had to be kidding. She must look like a bag lady. She felt as exhausted as Brody looked. All she wanted to do was curl up in some dark corner, go to sleep, and not wake up until this whole ugly nightmare was over. One thing was certain, she was in no shape to debate anything with the likes of Hayes Wicklow.

"You said self-destructive tendencies. Plural."

"Yes, well, this second problem could be even more damaging than the first. Have you or he given any consideration to this? If Brody is innocent, then someone is going to a great deal of trouble to frame him."

"I mentioned that possibility to him yesterday." Maureen said.

"What was his reaction?"

"He changed the subject." With a kiss, she recalled.

Wicklow nodded. "Pure and simple denial. Which isn't difficult to understand when you consider the kind of hatred it would take to fuel such an undertaking. Brody must have a clue as to the identity of his enemy. But he's either deliberately ignoring the obvious, or protecting someone." Wicklow glanced down the hall. "We'll talk more about this later. Here comes our friend now."

During their conversation Brody had come back downstairs and joined the group of men at the other end of the corridor. Just as they had seemed about to disperse, the front door had opened and Clay Stanton reentered the room. There had followed a few minutes of heated conversation and now Brody was coming down the hall toward Maureen and Wicklow.

The look on his face made Maureen's blood run cold.

"The news isn't good," he said when he came to a halt in front of them. "The police can't be positive until after an autopsy, but it looks as if Lisa didn't drown. There are bruises on her neck."

Lisa, strangled. Maureen was rocked back on her heels by shock. And shame. No matter what Brody thought, this might not have happened if she'd dealt more gently with Lisa this afternoon.

"Time and place of death?" Wicklow asked.

"The criminalist is pretty sure she was killed somewhere else and dumped in the river," Brody replied. "As for the time, her being in the water will make it harder to determine, but they think the medical examiner will be able to pinpoint it later today."

"Did Marsh ask you to make a statement?" Wicklow demanded.

"Yes, but I refused."

Wicklow raised his eyes to the heavens. "Hallelujah."

"I thought you'd approve." Brody reached out and touched Maureen's cheek. "I told Paul that neither of us would be making any statements until they'd fixed on an approximate time of death."

"Brilliant," the lawyer crowed. "You're finally displaying some of that intelligence you're reputed to have."

"I don't understand," Maureen began. "Wouldn't it be best to get the statements over and done with now, while everything is fresh in our minds?"

Brody shook his head. "This is my call, Maureen. If Lisa Adams were murdered while we were together last night, we're simply buying time. But if she died before seven P.M., you won't have to make a statement. We'll be able to keep your name out of it."

"I'm going to have another talk with Marsh," Wicklow said and started to leave.

"Wait," Brody said. "There's more."

Wicklow sighed. "There always is. Spit it out."

"Lisa didn't have any identification on her, but Stanton came across her purse and luggage a quarter of a mile down the river walk."

"And...?" the lawyer prompted.

"There was fifty thousand dollars in cash in her suitcase."

CHAPTER 11

For the next few seconds Hayes Wicklow proceeded to live up to his reputation for colorful invective. Brody leaned back against the wall and allowed the lawyer some time to blow off steam. Finally, after a glance at Maureen's astonished face, he put an end to it. "That's enough, Wicklow."

"Fifty thousand dollars," Maureen repeated. "Where would Lisa have gotten that kind of money?"

"Where indeed. And in cash." Wicklow snapped. "You know what this looks like, don't you, Parrish?"

"Like someone paid her to disappear."

"Someone? That's rich. Which particular someone do you think the authorities will finger?"

Brody shrugged. "Me."

"You fool. If you tried anything like that I'll…"

"Thanks for the vote of confidence. I didn't do it."

Maureen stepped between them. "Wait a minute. Trading accusations and denials won't get us anywhere. Let's try to make some sense of this. First of all, the money could have been Lisa's to start with. She claimed to have been down on her luck, but she was able to foot the bill for a private polygraph test on her own."

The angry flush that had accompanied Wicklow's outburst faded as quickly as it had appeared. "A good point. But, fifty thousand dollars? In cash?"

"Even if the money wasn't Lisa's, even if it came from someone else, wouldn't it be ridiculous for the police to assume that Brody both bribed and murdered her?"

Wicklow nodded. "It would seem a bit like overkill, wouldn't it?"

"Just in case anybody is listening," Brody growled, "I didn't do either. I never met the woman."

"Of course," Wicklow continued, "they might theorize that Lisa accepted the bribe and then refused to leave. Or asked for more money and had to be silenced permanently."

Brody watched Maureen push her glasses up into her hair and frown in concentration. He was becoming familiar with her gestures and expressions. He could tell that she wasn't about to concede anything. It felt damn good knowing she was on his side, having her argue on his behalf. With no makeup and her hair all disheveled she looked like an earnest teenager struggling with a tough math problem. She must have been a corker when she was a kid. How was it possible that they'd lived in the same town for years and he hadn't noticed her? Age difference or not, he must have been blind.

"You're saying that someone is supposed to have handed Lisa fifty thousand dollars, and when she wouldn't go through with the terms of the bribe, killed her and left the money to be discovered by the police? That would have to be a pretty dumb someone if you ask me." She crossed her arms. "Brody's no fool."

Wicklow smiled. "So, what are you suggesting? That we're dealing with two different people here? A briber and a murderer. Each acting without knowledge of the other? Each having a separate motive?"

"Neither of which is me," Brody said.

"Yes, yes. We hear you." The lawyer narrowed his eyes and glanced over his shoulder. "Perhaps we should run that premise up the flagpole and see if the cops salute."

Brody pushed himself away from the wall. "Do either of you amateur gumshoes realize that it's almost six A.M.? I don't know about you, Wicklow, but Maureen and I need some rest if we're going to be in any shape to face what's coming our way later this morning."

"You're right. You can expect the police to do a number on you, Parrish. It's their job. You're their prime suspect. Correction. Their only suspect. Marsh won't be able to cut you any more slack. With this second murder he's going to have to come down hard on you to avoid a charge of favoritism by the press." The lawyer shook his head. "The introduction of the media into this equation multiplies our problems. We're all going to have to dance around this one very carefully."

Brody turned and glared at the group still standing at the other end of the corridor. "I know the cops need access to the crime scene, but before I go to bed I want them out of here."

"I'll talk to them. But you do understand that when they leave their next stop will be to wake up a judge?"

"I know," Brody said.

Maureen yawned behind her hand. "I'll call a taxi to take me home."

"That won't be necessary. I'll be glad to drive you back to Philadelphia," Wicklow offered.

But Brody had other plans. "No. Stanton said there's already a cadre of reporters and cameramen out front. I want to keep them in the dark about Maureen for as long as possible. I've asked Mrs. Hartman to make up one of the guest rooms for her."

"Brody, I'm sure Hayes isn't going to stop and talk to any reporters. He'll drive right through the front gate and…"

"Hmmm. Much as I would enjoy your company on the trip home, Maureen, I think Parrish is right. Anyone who leaves here now is going to be photographed and followed. Once the press finds out about you they won't give you a moment's peace."

"Whether or not that's true I can't stay here indefinitely. All I have with me are the clothes on my back."

Brody scrubbed his hand across his jaw. "Humor me this once, Maureen. It'll only be for a few hours. Just until the coroner fixes on a time of death."

Maureen dropped onto the settee. "Oh, all right. I'm too tired to argue. But understand, one way or another, I'm out of here sometime today."

"Agreed," Wicklow said. "Parrish, after you show Maureen to her room you and I will send the police packing."

"No," Maureen cried, then lowered her voice. "Get rid of the police first." She clutched Brody's sleeve and looked up at him, her eyes wide and pleading. "At this stage in the game I know I'm being ridiculous, but I don't want Clay to see us go upstairs together."

Brody looked down at her hand. Despite the tension between her and Stanton a few minutes ago, she still cared what he thought. Brody groaned inwardly. He'd put her in this awkward position. He, with his absolute certainty that no one would take a murder charge against him seriously. He'd led this spunky, intelligent woman into an embarrassing situation.

He should let her go, should tell Wicklow to get her out of here. But couldn't they both see how impossible that was? For Maureen there was more at stake now than exposure to the media or Clay Stanton's attitude.

Brody covered her hand with his. "Wait here for me. This should only take a minute." He turned to his lawyer. "Come on, Wicklow, it's time you did something to earn your fee."

"Later, Maureen."

"Goodbye, Hayes."

The two men started down the corridor together. "That's one bright girl you've got there," Wicklow said under his breath.

Brody's lips twitched. "She doesn't like being called a girl."

"I'll file that away for future reference. By the way, does this desire to keep her close at hand suggest a concern for more than her reputation?"

"It does."

"Her physical well being? Her safety?"

"Possibly. This is the second woman with a close connection to me who has been murdered."

"And once Maureen steps out that door she'll be publicly connected to you. If it would set your mind at ease I could arrange for a body guard."

"That won't be necessary," Brody said.

Wicklow grinned. "Yes, I imagine that's a territory you've already mapped out for yourself."

When they reached the bottom of the stairs Wicklow smiled engagingly at the police and spread his hands wide. "Gentlemen. Isn't it time we left and let Mr. Parrish get some rest? I think we can all agree that he has a difficult day ahead of him."

*   *   *

Brody led Maureen to one end of the upstairs hall and opened the door into a small guestroom.

She stepped inside and looked around. "Brody, this is exquisite."

Everything about Riverbend was dazzling, but like many of the homes built in the eighteen century, the grand spaces on the lower level were designed to entertain and impress. The family rooms and sleeping quarters upstairs tended toward charming if somewhat more cramped and haphazardly proportioned.

But with eclectic taste and mismatched pieces, someone had turned this low-ceilinged, fan-shaped space into a tiny jewel of a room. A simple box spring and mattress had been pushed diagonally into one corner, but from the ceiling above a crown canopy rained thick, ecru-colored lace down onto a green moire spread. Two large *bombé* chests flanked the bed, their heavy presence undaunted by all the lace, or by the shallow crystal dish of rose petal potpourri that rested on the surface of one of them. An ankle-length green velour robe had been draped across a bentwood bench at the foot of the bed.

Maureen walked over, picked up the robe and buried her face in its lush folds. She felt dizzy with fatigue, overwhelmed by the beauty and elegance of her surroundings. Momentarily speechless, she looked up to find Brody still standing in the doorway, watching her reactions. Why didn't he come to her? Didn't he realize how out of place she felt? How only his embrace could make her feel really welcome?

"There's a larger guest room at the other end of the house, but I thought an artist would get a kick out of this place. At one time it supposedly belonged to the daughter of the house, but there hasn't been a female born into the Parrish family in three generations." He nodded toward the chests. "I think there are towels in one of those drawers. I'm afraid this room doesn't have a connecting bath, but there's one right down the hall."

Maureen sank down on the bed. "I'm sure I'll survive. Aren't you coming inside? I don't bite."

Brody lifted an eyebrow and Maureen felt her color rise. "Well, sometimes perhaps, in the heat of passion." She held out her hand. "But I promise, this won't be one of those times. I just need to be held for a minute."

He shook his head. "Not a good idea, Maureen. It wouldn't stop there."

She dropped her hand. "I'm sorry. I didn't mean to turn into a hysterical female on you. At a time like this you have more important things on your mind than me and my stupid nerves."

"That's not it. You're not hysterical or stupid, and there's nothing I want more this minute than to crawl into bed with you. But not here." Brody leaned against the doorjamb, one foot in the room, the other in the hallway. He stared down at the floor between his feet. "I brought someone to Riverbend, once."

A thin blade of jealousy sliced between Maureen's ribs. Up until a few days ago jealousy had been almost unknown to her. Now it was becoming all too familiar. "Jeannie?" she asked stiffly.

"Yeah. It was a stupid, teenaged thing to do, but she had a thing

132

about this house. She knew my mother didn't care for her. I think Jeannie saw it as a way to get back at Victoria. Sneaking in here after my parents had gone to bed, and then sneaking out again before they woke up. Unfortunately we got caught, and there was hell to pay."

"I'm surprised you went along with her."

"I was seventeen. Drunk on hormones."

Maureen looked down at the moire spread. Would there be hell to pay this morning, when Victoria Parrish woke to find another of her son's lovers at the breakfast table? "Maybe I shouldn't have stayed, Brody. I can still call a taxi."

"No. I want you here." He paused. "Does it frighten you when I talk about Jeannie?"

"Of course not."

"It should."

"Why?"

"For God's sake, Maureen, stop being so naive. I'm suspected of her murder." He shook his head. "You ought to pick your friends more carefully."

Jealousy gave way to embarrassment. "What you mean is that I ought to pick my lovers more carefully."

"You were taking an awful chance."

"You didn't murder anyone, Brody. I knew that from the beginning."

"Nonsense."

Maureen studied his face for a moment, made an important decision and patted the bedspread. "Come sit down, Brody. It's time I let you in on a little secret." When he still hesitated, she sighed. "I guarantee, this will make you smile."

Once he'd made up his mind it didn't take long for him to reach her. Only a stride or two, his dark head barely missing the light fixture in the ceiling as he passed under it. When he sat down he put his arm around her and dragged her down onto the bed along with him. They lay there silently for a few seconds, face to face.

"Make me smile, Maureen," he said.

It's now or never she thought, and took a deep breath. "The other day in the library, you asked if our paths had ever crossed when I lived in Granite Run."

"I remember," he murmured, the fingers of one hand exploring her lips. "You said they hadn't."

"Yes, well, I lied. In a way, they had. I was in Brandywine Park the day you saved Jeannie Starbuck's life. I saw the whole thing. The boat overturning, and you diving into the river and…"

Suddenly, she was as shy as the twelve year old she'd been then. Before he could say a word she hid her face in the warm curve of his neck. "Right then, I developed the most horrendous crush on you, Brody. For months after the rescue I would walk along the tow path out there and hide at the edge of the woods hoping to catch a glimpse of you. And at night, I dreamed that it was me you saved, not Jeannie."

She chanced a glance at his face. He wasn't smiling. Why on earth not? He should be laughing at her. Teasing her. Not looking as if it were the end of the world. "Hey," she said. "Relax. I got over it. You went off to college and I grew up. I forgot about you. Sort of. Until the day of the lineup."

"When you recognized me and decided that a hot-dogging swim team jock couldn't possibly off someone. Was that your reasoning? Your logic?"

"Brody, you risked your life when everybody else just stood there. The town council gave you a medal."

"I didn't risk anything," he interrupted. "I was a good swimmer. It never even crossed my mind that I was taking a chance."

"Stop it. Just because you were on the swim team doesn't mean that there wasn't any danger." She hesitated. She was beginning to feel like she was in a time warp. She'd had this discussion before. Only then it was with…? Was it Clay? God, she was groggy. She had to get some sleep. They both had to get some sleep.

She reached up and covered Brody's mouth with her hand. "Can we please not argue about this? It's very noble of you to downplay your role, but whether you were a hero or a showoff has nothing to do with the point I was trying to make. I just wanted you to understand, before you went off to your own room to brood about it, that for me you were never some good-looking stranger. I knew you. Knew all about you. I don't make a habit of falling into bed with every man who comes knocking at my door."

His arms tightened around her. "I never thought that."

"Oh, I think you did." She sighed and snuggled closer. "But it doesn't matter anymore. I'm glad I told you, and now that I've had my hug and said my piece, I can go to sleep with a clear conscience." She felt his lips move against her forehead.

"You don't know me as well as you think you do, Maureen," he whispered as her eyes drifted closed. "Not yet, anyway."

134

*   *   *

He hadn't planned to kill Lisa. Not at first. But in the end her death had become inevitable. She was an obstacle, one he couldn't get past. She stood between him and what had become almost as important to him as his original goal.

Maureen.

His feelings for her were growing more complicated with each passing day. In the beginning, they'd been what any man might feel for a desirable woman. Physical lust. The need to possess. To dominate.

But now, he wanted more. He wanted her to know him. To accept him. Not as the insipid phantom she saw in his place, but the real man. Powerful. Cunning. Worthy.

Maureen was worthy. She'd proven that. She wasn't like other women. Women who cut and ran once things got a little difficult.

The desire to reveal himself to her now, to make her a partner in everything he'd planned, was overwhelming. Unfortunately, there were other tests she still had to pass.

The time wasn't right. But it would be. Soon.

*   *   *

The sound of rain trickling off the eaves of the roof woke Maureen. She opened her eyes and turned her head on the pillow. To the left of the bed, through a lace-curtained window, a pale watery light filtered into the room.

For a brief, panicky second she didn't remember where she was. Then, in a rush, it all came flooding back. Lisa's murder. The drive to Riverbend. The police. Her silly little confession. Brody's arms around her as she fell asleep.

She sat up and looked around, the edge of the spread sliding off her shoulders. She hugged herself against the morning chill and tried to get her bearings. Obviously, sometime after she'd fallen asleep Brody had gotten up, covered her with the spread and the robe and left.

Left her in a strange room, in a strange house, in a strange situation. With a sick feeling in the pit of her stomach. She remembered his strange reaction to her confession. It had been a mistake to tell him. He'd probably taken her story as an attempt to turn their little fling into something more serious, and as soon as he could, before she could make any emotional demands on him, he'd escaped.

I don't fall into bed with just any man who comes knocking at my door. Maureen cringed. What a fool she'd been. He'd never asked her for any assurances in that regard.

135

She pushed the robe off her feet. Suddenly, she was angry with herself. And with him. What was she supposed to do now? Wait here until he could find a way to sneak her out of the house before his mother found out she'd spent the night? Parade downstairs on her own and face her hostess looking like the wrath of God?

There wasn't a mirror in sight, but one look at her wrinkled slacks told Maureen all she needed to know about her appearance.

She crossed the room to the window and pushed aside a handful of lace. While she'd been asleep it had rained, and stopped, but the air still held a suggestion of drizzle, and every so often a fat droplet fell from the roof above and splattered on the outside sill. Below and to the left of the window she could just make out a square of puddled flagstone terrace.

And Brody standing at its edge looking toward the river.

As always, the mere sight of him set her pulse fluttering. He was dressed in a pair of khaki slacks and what appeared to be a brown and black flannel shirt. She couldn't see his face, only the top of his dark head, but she sensed rather than saw the tension in his shoulders, the belligerent way his fists were jammed into his pockets.

If he looked up and saw her what would his reaction be? Would he smile or frown? Suddenly, it was very important for Maureen to know. She struggled to open the window, but the rain-swollen wooden frame refused to budge. She rapped on the glass but he was too engrossed in the view to hear her.

What had so captured his attention?

From her vantage point she could see more than he could of the Brandywine as it emerged from the forest on one side of the estate and flowed past the family pier. But when the river entered the woods on the opposite side of Riverbend, its waters disappeared again behind a curtain of glistening, wind-whipped treetops. All she could make out, through the swaying branches and leaves, was a glimpse of florescent yellow ribbon.

Maureen shivered. Police crime scene tape. Was that what had Brody so intrigued? So irritated?

When she glanced down at the terrace again he'd disappeared.

Maureen turned back into the room, no closer to a decision as to what she should do than before. Only then did she see the folded piece of paper propped up against the bowl of potpourri.

She walked over and picked up the sheet of heavy, cream colored paper. Next to the bowl was a small green marble clock. She squinted at it. Without her glasses she could barely make out the tiny roman numerals on its face. Nine o'clock. She'd been asleep for almost three hours, and during that time Brody had left, and then he, or someone, had come in and placed this note by the bed. The idea that someone had been prowling around the room while she slept made her uneasy.

She unfolded the note.

Maureen, Victoria Parrish had written in a small, neat hand, *if you wake up in time please join us in the parlor for a light breakfast. You will find everything you need to freshen up in the bathroom down the hall, and if you leave your clothes on the bed Mrs. Hartman will press and have them back to you by the time you return.*

Maureen's heart thudded against her ribs. Below Victoria's delicate signature was a dark scrawl she had never seen before. But like his smile, his voice, his handwriting was unmistakable. She would know it anywhere.

Darling, it read, *you are expected, and welcome.*

Under that was a bold, slashing initial. *B.*

Maureen refolded the elegantly scented notepaper and touched it to her lips.

Darling, he had written. Coming from him the word was almost a kiss.

*   *   *

Anything anybody, male or female, could have possibly needed to freshen up had been laid out on the vanity of the little bathroom down the hall. Paper wrapped bars of French milled soap. Unopened bottles of skin lotion and shampoo. A hair dryer. A razor. Toothpaste. Even a flagon of unisex cologne. It was a more elaborate display than any Maureen had come across in all her travels, even in four star hotels.

Wrapped in the green velour robe, she stared at her reflection in the steam-misted mirror above the sink. Despite having had less than three hours sleep, Brody's note and the needle spray shower she'd just taken had left her feeling invigorated and ready to face anything the day might hold in store.

In fact, she could hardly wait to get back to the guestroom to see if Mrs. Hartman had accomplished the promised miracle with her clothes.

She had. When Maureen came downstairs her black silk blouse and wool slacks were as presentable as they had been when she'd pulled them out of her closet immediately following Clay Stanton's three A.M. phone call.

Had that only been this morning? It seemed like a lifetime ago.

Lisa's lifetime.

Brody was just coming through the arched doorway leading into the parlor. His face lit up when he saw her. None of the tension she'd noticed in his stance on the terrace was now evident. He grinned as he bent over her. "You smell delicious," he whispered. "I wish we could have taken a shower together." He tucked her hand into the crook of his arm and led her to where Victoria was sitting. "Mother," he said. "Maureen is here."

"Yes, Brody, I see her. My eyesight is as good as it ever was. Sit down, my dear. If I remember correctly you take your coffee black. Brody, bring our guest a dish of fruit and whatever else you think she might enjoy."

Victoria passed Maureen a cup and the two women waited in silence while Brody went to the credenza across the room and returned with a plate heaped high with fresh strawberries, wedges of cheese and miniature muffins.

He took a seat at Maureen's side and balanced the plate on his knee. "We'll share," he said with an almost imperceptible wink.

His posture was solicitous, his words and glances openly attentive, even flirtatious, but Maureen couldn't help noticing the guarded expression in his eyes. She nibbled on a wedge of cheese and stole a glance at her hostess's face. Victoria was doing her best to appear comfortable with the situation, but Maureen was convinced that Brody had given his mother strict instructions as to how his guest should be treated.

Expected and welcome, his note had read. But the unwritten message had been—don't worry. This won't be a repeat of Jeannie Starbuck's reception.

Maureen wondered just how long they were all going to pretend this was just an ordinary breakfast on an ordinary day. She put down her cup. "I saw you from the guest room window earlier this morning, Brody. I tried to get your attention but you were too interested in something down at the water's edge to hear me."

The plate on his knee trembled slightly. She put her hand out to steady it and looked up to see what was wrong, but he had busied himself with his coffee.

"Was someone there?" she asked.

He shrugged. "I saw some movement under the trees. Thought it might be a cop or a reporter but I was mistaken. It was only a doe foraging for food."

Victoria smiled. "Our Mrs. Hartman has a tender spot in her heart for animals. She often leaves scraps down by the river for them to find when they come for a drink."

Maureen remembered the sparrows that had made such a commotion in the tall grass down by the riverwalk on the morning after Tio Pepe's. "Perhaps you should tell her to stop for the present," she suggested. "The police won't appreciate having their crime scene disturbed."

"That's their problem," Brody said grimly, just as Mrs. Hartman appeared in the doorway.

"What is it, Margaret?" Mrs. Parrish asked.

"That Lieutenant Stanton is here again. He wants to talk to Mr. Parrish."

Victoria threw up her hands. "Doesn't it occur to these people to call first," she said irritably. "Well, I suppose there's nothing one can do but cooperate. Show him in, Margaret."

An involuntary gasp escaped Maureen's throat. Not Clay. She wasn't sure she was ready to face him again. Not after the look she'd seen in his eyes a few hours ago. For one chilling moment she'd actually been afraid of him. Afraid of Clay. The idea was ludicrous, but lately he'd seemed like a stranger to her.

Brody must have noticed her alarm. He was already on his feet, calling after the housekeeper's departing back. "Mrs. Hartman, wait. Tell Stanton I'll see him in the library."

He handed Maureen the plate. "It's me he wants. There's no need for everybody's breakfast to be ruined. Wait here. This shouldn't take long."

With narrowed eyes Victoria watched her son leave the room. "Brody's concern for our appetites is quite touching, isn't it? I hope you were comfortable in the guestroom he chose for you. It's difficult to heat that end of the house but the room's location does allow for a great deal of privacy. Perhaps that was the motivation."

Maureen decided to ignore the suggestive edge to Mrs. Parrish's comments. In fact, she could almost sympathize with the older woman's attitude. After all, Brody had formed bad attachments in the past, one of them leading to the predicament he now found himself in. Why wouldn't his mother question the advisability of any new involvement? If nothing else, the timing was lousy.

Besides there were more important issues Maureen wanted to broach with her hostess.

"It's a beautiful room, Mrs. Parrish. Brody told me a bit of its history. That it once belonged to a Parrish daughter."

"There hasn't been a Parrish daughter in a very long time."

"So he said. Not many sons, either."

Victoria touched her napkin to her lips. "My husband was in his fifties when Brody was born. He didn't want any more children. I was disappointed, of course, but..." Across the room the French windows rattled in their frames. "Listen to that wind. It's going to wreak havoc with my daffodils."

"No uncles or cousins?" Maureen pressed.

Somehow Victoria managed to look both annoyed and smug. "Until I came along the Parrish women weren't a particularly productive lot. Brody and I are all that is left of the family."

Well, that had been a blind alley. Hayes would be disappointed. There didn't appear to be any family member who might profit financially or otherwise from Brody's being found guilty of murder. No one who could have been mistaken for him because of a family resemblance. No one whose identity he might feel honor bound to protect.

Victoria frowned. "What brought on this sudden curiosity, I wonder? An interest in who will inherit Riverbend when I die? Has your relationship with my son progressed that far?"

Maureen sighed and shook her head. Time to change the subject. She wasn't ready to confront her own questions about her relationship with Brody, much less his mother's. "My only interest in Riverbend is as an artist, Mrs. Parrish. I couldn't help noticing that your private collection rivals that of some of the best small museums in the country."

"If you said that to flatter and impress me, you've succeeded. My husband and I shared a passion for collecting. He had an amazing eye and loved to encourage talent before it was universally applauded." The chill disappeared from Victoria's voice, and she gestured toward a familiar rural scene hanging above the credenza. "Do you see that early Wyeth over there? It was my husband's pride and joy. I myself favor the Hudson River School. So much warmer." She raised an eyebrow. "Your interest in fine art surprises me. Is there a style you prefer?"

"My tastes tend toward the contemporary," Maureen said. "But I can understand your appreciation of the naturalists. Especially when you own one of the best. I was surprised to see that you'd taken *Autumn at Riverbend* down from its prominent place in the entry. If I owned it,

I would never..."

"It's being cleaned," Victoria said, just a little too quickly.

Maureen recalled the clear, pure colors, the absolute clarity of the painting in question when she'd last seen it four days ago. "Cleaned," she repeated.

"Yes." Victoria stood. "We appear to have finished all the coffee. I'll ask Margaret to bring us another pot."

"Mrs. Parrish, why...?" Maureen began. But before she could frame the rest of her question Brody had walked through the door, an official looking piece of paper in his hand.

Mrs. Parrish went to him, touched his arm. "Is Lieutenant Stanton still here?"

"No, Mother. He's on his way to Granite Run Security. I'm to follow him in the Jaguar."

"The bank? I don't understand."

Brody crumpled the paper in his fist and looked past his mother's shoulder. "Maureen, I know you would rather avoid Stanton, but I want you to come with me."

"That's a court order, isn't it, Brody?" Maureen said, getting to her feet.

He nodded, his face grim.

"A court order?" Mrs. Parrish echoed. "For what?"

"The police have gotten permission to examine our bank accounts, Victoria. Mine and yours."

The color drained from his mother's face. "What do they expect to find?"

"Stanton didn't see fit to share that piece of information with me. But I imagine they expect to find a withdrawal. Of fifty thousand dollars."

CHAPTER 12

The first thing Maureen noticed when she and Brody stepped out of Riverbend's front door was the avid faces of the reporters who had set up shop behind the wrought iron fence, their cameras, pencils and microphones at the ready. They looked for all the world like zoo animals waiting for their keeper to deliver the next meal.

She and Brody being the next meal.

Some of the reporters called out to Brody as he helped her into the Jaguar's passenger seat. But he pointedly ignored them, circled the hood, pulled open the car door and settled himself behind the steering wheel.

He fastened his seat belt, leaned across the console and checked hers. "I'm sorry about this, Maureen. I'd hoped the weather would have dampened the media's enthusiasm, but it looks like Stanton's sudden arrival and departure has them chomping at the bit. They know something's up."

She shook her head. "It's not your fault. It was bound to happen. My spending the night only postponed the inevitable."

He fired up the ignition and eased the stick shift into gear. "Yes. But I'm glad you stayed just the same."

She looked at him out of the corner of her eye and recalled his note. "So am I."

For several seconds he stared out through the windshield, then he turned to her and grinned. "What do you say we give the bastards a run for their money?"

Something about that sudden smile of his made her grip the edge of her leather seat. "Brody, please, don't do anything crazy."

"Naw," he said, stepping lightly on the gas pedal and slowly maneuvering the car down the driveway, past the police barricades and out onto the public road.

It was only when the mob surged toward them that he allowed the Jag's powerful engine to roar into life. The startled reporters stopped in their tracks, then parted in front of the car like a wave coming up against the bow of a ship. Their angry, astonished faces reappeared at the side windows, mouths moving and hands beating against the glass.

Cameras flashed furiously next to Maureen's face as the Jaguar shot past.

"Let them eat dust," Brody crowed.

Maureen twisted around in her seat and looked behind her. "They're running for their cars."

"By the time they get started and turned around, we'll be halfway to town," he said gleefully.

For the next few miles he looked so pleased with himself that Maureen had to smile. She watched him drive and wondered, not for the first time, if she could get him to pose for her. He would be a difficult subject to capture on paper or canvas. One moment—cool and demanding, almost to the point of arrogance. The next—needy, passionate. Even reckless.

Two men for the price of one. What more could an artist, or a woman, ask?

Well, maybe a tad more continuity, she decided, as they pulled into Granite Run Security's parking lot and the exhilaration he'd displayed on the drive over abruptly deserted him.

With good reason. Clay Stanton had already arrived and parked his marked police cruiser in front of the bank where it could easily be seen from the street. The press wouldn't have to look too hard to find them once they got to town. One pass up and down Granite Run's main drag would do it. They wouldn't even need that if someone on the police force had tipped them off about the court order.

And it was a pretty good bet someone had. Clay Stanton, for instance. Brody drove to the back of the parking lot, to a series of spaces normally reserved for employees. Not that choosing a spot here would do much good if anyone decided to check out the lot. The Jag would have a hard time hiding among to its more dowdy neighbors.

Brody released the door lock and started to get out. "Come on," he said. "Let's get this over with."

"I'm going to wait in the car, Brody."

"The hell you are. I'm not leaving you out here alone."

"Be reasonable. Clay will just give you more grief if I walk in there with you."

"I can take whatever Stanton dishes out, and you can't avoid him forever, Maureen."

"I know. I know." She sighed. "Brody, I've never known Clay to act like this. Whatever happened to make you two dislike each other so much?"

Brody shook his head. "I don't dislike the man. Up until a few days ago I had a great deal of respect for him."

"But you supported Paul Marsh in the election, even though Clay was the more experienced candidate."

"That was strictly a business decision, Maureen."

"Business? I don't understand."

"Look, people here like having a local police force. It's a status thing. We're one of the few small towns in the valley that does. Chadds Ford and all the rest are serviced by the state police." He nodded in the direction of the bank. "I'll grant you, Stanton is a good cop. But Granite Run doesn't...didn't have much crime."

He swallowed hard and Maureen could see the effort it cost him to continue. "Up until last weekend we had what? One or two bodies a year? Suicides, or tanked up drunks plowing into trees. Here, the chief of police has to be more of a politician than a cop. Someone who can mediate between the homeowners, the small business people, the no-growth activists and all the rest of the special interest groups." He glanced her way and raised an eyebrow. "Does that sound like something your hard-headed friend in there could handle?"

Maureen sighed. She had to admit that Paul Marsh fit Brody's idea of a police chief to a T. Still, she wasn't entirely satisfied with his answer. She cocked her head to one side. "Then, what has Clay got against you?"

"Besides the election results? Isn't it obvious? You. Us."

"No. It preceded us. It was there on the day of the lineup."

"Well, in a town like this the citizens are often more affluent than their public servants. Maybe it's just a case of reverse snobbery on Stanton's part. It may not be me. It may be the name or the money."

Maureen nodded. In the back of her mind she could hear her father and Clay arguing politics while she did her sixth grade homework.

"Yes. That could be it. But I have a feeling there's even more to it than that."

She studied Brody's face. His gaze slid away from hers, toward the bank. "You're questioning the wrong man. The one with the answers is inside that building."

He was right. She was behaving like a coward. And right now, he had more important matters to deal with than her squeamishness about facing down Clay. She reached for the door handle. "Let's go," she said.

As they approached the bank's entrance he took her hand. His grip was like iron and his palm was damp. Maureen looked up and was surprised by the tiny beads of perspiration that had begun to collect just below his hairline.

"Brody, what is it? Clay isn't going to find anything incriminating in your bank records, is he?"

"It's not my records I'm worried about, Maureen."

*   *   *

Once inside the bank Maureen didn't have time to question Brody about his last remark, but it certainly left her with something to think about while she paced outside the bank manager's office.

Inside the glass-enclosed cubicle she could see Brody, Clay and the manager, Mr. Pauling, standing around a conference table. A computer prompt blinked on a nearby monitor, eager for its next command, while Clay frowned over reams of paper a printer had just spit out into his hands.

Maureen tapped her foot impatiently. They'd been in there for forty minutes. Hadn't they gotten around to Victoria Parrish's records yet?

"You're Maureen Lowe, aren't you?"

Maureen spun around, expecting to confront another camera. Instead, she found herself facing a thin, fiftyish woman, with a paper cup in her hand. Earlier, when Maureen and Brody had walked past the teller cages, Maureen had noticed the woman and thought there was something vaguely familiar about her.

The woman extended the paper cup. "Would you like some coffee?"

Maureen shook her head. "No, thank you. I've already had my quota of caffeine this morning. Any more and I'll go off like a Roman candle."

"You don't recognize me, do you?"

"I'm sorry. I know we've met, but I can't seem to recall who you are."

"I've worked for Granite Run Security for a long time. Your daddy used to bring you in with him when he made deposits. You were just a kid."

Maureen smiled. "Of course. I remember now. I used to think you had the nicest name. It was, don't tell me, it was...Juanita, wasn't it? Juanita...?"

"Swann. Juanita Swann."

"Of course. Hi, Juanita. It's nice seeing you again."

Juanita colored slightly and studied the contents of the paper cup. "I feel bad about not having dropped you a line when your parents died. It was just such a shock, them murdered like that. And in Miami, of all places. Well, you know how it is. I kept putting off writing and then you moved away, and..."

"Don't trouble yourself, Juanita. I understand."

They stood nodding at each other, and it began to look as if they had run out of things to say, when Maureen suddenly recalled something her father had told her about the Swanns. "Wait a minute. You and your husband had a child, didn't you? A little girl about my age. She had cerebral palsy. How is she?"

Juanita beamed. "My Amy. She's doing fine. Works downstairs in data entry." She took a deep breath and looked past Maureen's shoulder, into the bank manager's office. "I saw you come in with Mr. Parrish. Is he a friend of yours?"

"Yes, he is."

"He's a good man. He'd be awfully angry if he knew I was telling you this, but he helped me and Amy when my husband ran out on us. Mr. Parrish found her a special school, and then pestered Mr. Pauling into giving her a job here at the bank. He's a real good man. I don't believe a word of what they said about him on the news this morning. He never hurt those women." She shook her head. "Not Mr. Parrish."

So, Juanita Swann was one of the people Paul Marsh had told Maureen about. One of the people in Granite Run who "owed" Brody. One of the people who would go to the mat for him.

How many more of them were there?

She glanced around the bank lobby. The place was strangely quiet for a Friday morning. Just one or two customers in front of the teller cages. "You know, Juanita, there's a lot of reporters looking for Mr. Parrish. I half expected them to have turned up here by now."

Juanita grinned and waved the paper cup in the direction of the

146

front door. "Don't worry. Bernie Nicks is taking care of them."

"Bernie Nicks?"

Juanita repeated her gesture with the cup. "Over there. The security guard."

Maureen followed the older woman's directions, and saw through the bank's glass entry doors the imposingly large figure of a man in a dark blue uniform, legs braced wide, hands clasped behind his broad back. There seemed to be some kind of melee going on in front of him.

"Bernie likes Mr. Parrish, too." Juanita said. "Well, I think I'd better get back to work. Looks like Mr. Fazio needs to make a deposit. Why don't you go relax in one of those big easy chairs over in the escrow department until Mr. Parrish is finished." She started off toward the tellers' cages. "Keep in touch," she called over her shoulder. "Send me a Christmas card."

Oh, I will, Juanita, Maureen thought gratefully. *I certainly will.*

*   *   *

The first man to exit the bank manager's office was not Brody, or Mr. Pauling. It was Clay. And the first thing he did was amble over to the escrow department and take the chair opposite Maureen's.

With deliberate care she chose a fashion magazine from a stack of periodicals on the table between them and began to leaf through it.

Clay braced his elbows on his knees, and after a series of stretching exercises during which he audibly cracked the bones in his neck, he brought his chin to rest on top of his clasped hands.

They sat there for the next few minutes, waiting each other out.

"First round to Parrish," Clay said finally.

So this was how they were going to handle it. No apologies, no explanations. As if the telephone call and the scenes at the police station and Riverbend had never happened. Maureen placed the magazine back on the table and folded her hands in her lap. Okay. He was a proud man, and it was hard for him to admit he was wrong. Making the first move was probably as far as he was willing to go. If she held out for anything more they might never speak again.

That disturbing thought made up her mind for her. "You didn't find anything," she said. "No fifty thousand dollar withdrawal?"

"Nope. Nothing in Parrish's personal or business accounts, and no loans against his credit cards."

"And Mrs. Parrish's records?"

"Clean."

Maureen exhaled the breath she felt she'd been holding for the last

147

hour.

Clay shrugged. "Listen, I never said the guy wasn't smart. Just that he's guilty." He twisted his neck from one side to the other again, and in the process caught sight of the security officer's broad back in the doorway. "Bernie Nicks keeping the press at bay, huh?"

"Brody has a lot of friends, Clay."

"Every last one of them bought and paid for. Hey, I saw you talking with Juanita Swann. I know that story too. Big deal. Parrish has suits in his closet probably cost more than her kid's education. And Bernie's operation? Wanna bet a tuneup on Parrish's fancy car would more than cover it?"

"When you don't like someone it's easy to take everything he does and twist it around until it fits your preconception, isn't it, Clay? When did you become such as cynic? What did Brody ever do—?"

"He murdered two women, that's what he did."

"No. That's not it. There's something else. I know it. You recognized Brody from Lisa's description and my sketch, and yet you had the *Chronicle* put it on the front page, then sat back and waited for the calls to come in. You took a chance on the man you believed to be guilty getting away, just to see him publicly humiliated. Why?"

Clay grinned. This time it was not a pretty sight. "Guess you could call it poetic justice."

"Run that by me again."

He stared at her for a long time before answering. What was the problem? Why didn't he just come out and say it, whatever it was?

"Clay, for God's sake, what?"

He threw up his hands. "Agh! It would be a waste of time and breath. I can see it in your eyes. You think you're in love. You'll just go running off to him with the story, and he'll pat you on the head and tell you it's a lie, and you'll believe him."

"Try me."

He leveraged himself up out of the chair and stood looking down on her. The grin was gone, replaced by an expression that could only be described as sad. Sad and worried. "No. You're not ready. But you will be. Soon. You'll start noticing things. Catch him in one lie and then another. Then you'll come to me, ready to hear the truth. But don't wait too long, Maureen. I don't want to see you get hurt."

He turned and started for the door. "Your daddy would have wanted me to look out for you."

*   *   *

Shit! Brody thought, his eyes riveted on the little scene being played out in the escrow department. *I just get past one damn hurdle unscathed, and here's another one in my face,*

He'd expected that sooner or later Clay Stanton would want to set things right between himself and Maureen. If his feelings for her were only half what they seemed, their estrangement must be tearing him apart.

It hadn't surprised Brody when the older man had left the bank manager's office and made a beeline for where Maureen was sitting, but understanding what was probably taking place out there didn't make it any easier to watch.

Dan Pauling came and stood by Brody's side. "What if Stanton comes back with more demands?"

"Give him whatever he asks for," Brody replied.

"Is that a good idea, Brody? Perhaps you should talk with your lawyer before giving the police carte blanche?"

Brody flicked a reluctant glance in the bank manager's direction. "They have a court order, Dan. There's nothing we can do about it. Besides, I didn't see anything on the books that they can hang me with. Did you?"

"No, but it's rotten that they can put people like you and your mother through something like this. Reputation used to count for something."

"It's their job," Brody said, with a weary sigh.

He knew Pauling was trying to be supportive, but he wished the man would just go back to doing whatever bank managers did and leave him alone. All he wanted to think about was getting out of here, taking Maureen some place and losing himself in her softness, then sleeping for a week.

That is, if she would have anything more to do with him after Stanton got finished talking to her. And answering her questions.

God, just look at the expression on the man's face! Was it possible that Wicklow was right? That the aging cop had a thing for Maureen? Well, wouldn't any man with an ounce of testosterone left in his system respond to her?

If Stanton did have a yen for Maureen, Brody would lay money she was totally unaware of it. Just as he suspected she was unaware of the other male interest she'd stirred up.

As in Hayes Wicklow's case, for instance.

I'd be glad to give you a ride back to Philadelphia, Maureen.

As if there'd been a snowball's chance in hell that Brody would have let that grinning leprechaun drive off with her.

But then, she didn't sleep with just any man, Brody remembered, smiling. He would never tell her of course, but her assurances in that regard had been unnecessary. On the evidence of their lovemaking alone he'd come to the conclusion that she hadn't been with more than a couple of other men in all her twenty whatever years.

That realization had excited him more than he would have imagined. That, and the fact that what she lacked in experience she more than made up for with enthusiasm and a sort of innocent wantonness that both surprised and delighted him.

He exhaled a long breath. Thank God! Stanton was finally leaving. Apprehension eating away at his gut Brody waited for Maureen to turn around and look in his direction. When she did his knees went weak with relief.

She was smiling. It was a puzzled little smile. But it was a smile all the same.

Brody put his hand on the bank manager's shoulder. "Dan, is there an employee's entrance or back door to this place?"

*   *   *

"Where are we going?" Maureen asked.

While they'd been inside the bank the sky had cleared and the day had turned balmy. Once they'd gotten out of the parking lot and left the surprised reporters once again behind, Brody lowered the window on the driver's side and hung his arm out over the door. The sun felt good on his skin.

But he knew something that would feel even better.

"Our friends in the media are going to think we're headed back to Riverbend. But I have other plans." He smiled and lifted her hand to his lips. "You've never seen my apartment here in town."

"I'd forgotten you had one," she said.

"Yeah, well, I haven't set foot in it for months. When my mother was taken ill I decided to move back home until she was on her feet again. But the landlord has been keeping an eye on the place for me."

He pressed Maureen's hand against his thigh. "I think you'll like the apartment. But first we'll stop and pick up some supplies. A jug of wine, a loaf of bread and thou. Not necessarily in that order."

"Sounds like a party. What are we celebrating? Clay's failure to find any unusual withdrawals from your mother's accounts?"

He turned her hand over and began stroking her wrist with his thumb. "Look, Maureen, I admit I had some concerns along those lines. But happily, nothing came of them. If that doesn't satisfy you, and I can tell by the look on your face that it doesn't, we can discuss Victoria's past transgressions and what you and Stanton were so busy talking about, later. Much later. Right now, all I have on my mind is," he wiggled his eyebrows suggestively, "lunch."

Maureen stared at his long, elegant fingers. All she had to do was nod, and in a few minutes they would be working their magic on other parts of her anatomy.

This is crazy, she thought. *He doesn't have time for this. I don't have time for this. I have to get back to Philadelphia. I have to get back to work.*

But her spine was turning to mush. "Oh, all right," she said helplessly. "I seem to be developing an appetite myself."

*   *   *

They decided to forget about the wine and bread.

Maureen had a quick, kaleidoscopic impression of his apartment. Fruitwood and mahogany, with a tapestry twist. Not the usual bachelor pad. Not for a man who'd grown up with Riverbend's deep, jewel-rich colors and mellow woods.

It was almost a repeat performance of the night he'd shown up at the condo uninvited. Only this time they both participated in the frenzy. On the way to his bedroom they raced to get themselves and each other undressed, leaving a trail of discarded khaki and silk in their wake. And, between the cool paisley sheets, Maureen's hands and mouth proved as cunning and explorative as his. They were torn between wanting the wanting to go on forever and an urgent, desperate drive toward climax.

Finally, gratefully, climax won out.

A minute or so later Maureen rolled over on her back and gazed silently up at the ceiling. It was hardwood, just like the floor, here and there dotted with knotholes that resembled eyes. Curious, thoughtful eyes that had observed what had gone on here for the last half-hour.

She started to get up. From behind, Brody snaked an arm around her waist and pulled her back, burying his face in her hair.

"Don't go, Maureen. There's nothing out there better than this," he murmured sleepily.

God, he was good. Was there a woman alive who could resist a man who said the things Brody did? Maureen burrowed into the curve of his body and they lay nestled together like two spoons in a cutlery drawer until his relaxed breathing made her think he had fallen into a much needed asleep.

Maureen brought her hands up to her face and inhaled greedily. If she never spent another moment in his arms she wanted to remember the taste of him, the smell of him, forever.

"Fahrenheit," he said.

She turned in his arms. He was grinning at her across the pillow.

"What did you say?" she asked.

"Fahrenheit is the name of that cologne you're snorting."

"How...apt," she said. To her surprise and chagrin, her lips began to tremble. "Brody, we can't go on like this."

"Why not? Seems to me we're getting pretty good at it."

"We're going to kill each other," she said and then the idiotic tears started to flow in earnest.

He gathered her into his arms again and held her while she shook like a frightened two-year-old beset by invisible monsters. "Shss, Baby. Shss. Maureen. It'll be all right."

"I don't know what's the matter with me," she gasped between sobs.

"I have a good idea what's the matter," he said, more serious now. "You're feeling guilty because Jeannie and Lisa are dead, and a little while ago, it felt so damn good to be alive."

Maureen wiped her eyes and went back to staring at the ceiling.

She couldn't help thinking that this was the first time she'd heard Brody Parrish say anything that even remotely suggested pity or sympathy for either of the dead women.

*   *   *

While Brody slept, Maureen took a leisurely tour of the apartment that had been only a lovely blur an hour before.

Surprisingly, it was smaller than her condo, but everything in it, the furniture, the fixtures, the luxurious towels in the tiny bath, whispered money and taste. The colors were jewel tones, emerald and ruby, but in each room there was a single spot of surprising brightness, like the lemon yellow love seat in the library at Riverbend.

In Brody's living room it turned out to be a huge, pickled pine hutch pushed up against a tapestry hung wall. It drew Maureen like a magnet. She couldn't resist running her hands over the raw wood surface, examining the beautifully bound books on its shelves, and the contents of its tipsy antique drawers.

Inside one of the drawers, protected by soft blue fabric, she found a set of silver pieces. Sterling not plated, the pattern baroque, masculine, cut deeply into the gleaming metal. She picked up a knife, weighing it in her hand, mentally comparing it to the serviceable stainless steel in her kitchen in Philadelphia.

"I'm going to want to see your search warrant, inspector," Brody said from the bedroom doorway.

Hurriedly, Maureen replaced the knife. "Oh, Brody, I'm sorry. I didn't mean to snoop. It's just that it's all so beautiful. I couldn't resist."

"That was a joke, Maureen," he said, walking over to a wide leather easy chair and settling into it. "Everything here is meant to be touched and used, not just admired."

Maureen dropped onto his lap. "Even the tenant?"

"Especially the tenant." He nuzzled her neck and then leaned back to examine her face. He pulled her close and covered her mouth with his.

The kiss was staggering. Overwhelmingly intimate. Possessive in a way that stunned her.

It took a few seconds for Maureen to think clearly. Defensively. Making love with Brody Parrish was one thing. Surrendering herself to him, belonging to him, like the tapestry and silver, even for the short time this was going to last, was something else entirely.

She braced her hands against his chest. "And you?" she said. "Did you get enough rest?"

"Enough to what?"

"To talk."

He groaned, stood her on her feet and then followed suit. "Why do I think I'm going to need a drink to handle what's coming?" He walked over to the hutch and took a bottle of Scotch from behind one of its doors and poured a generous shot into a heavy crystal tumbler. "Want to join me?"

She shook her head.

"I didn't think so." He raised a salute in her direction.

The glasses in Maureen's kitchen cupboards were just glass. But Scotch, in diamond-cut crystal? That was Brody. Beautiful, costly, and dangerous. To her, and to himself. He was using her and the whiskey, just as Hayes had suggested. To avoid dealing with some harsh truths.

For his sake, and hers, she couldn't let that continue.

She walked over to him and put her hand on his arm. "You shouldn't drink on an empty stomach."

He knocked back the Scotch in a single swallow, then gave her a long, hard look. "Don't worry, Maureen. I'm many things, but not an alcoholic." He put the bottle back behind its little door. "But you're right. When a man is about to undergo the third degree he needs to keep a clear head." He folded his arms. "Okay, copper. You won't need the rubber hose. What do you want to know?"

"Well, for starters, why don't you tell me about your mother's 'past transgressions.'"

CHAPTER 13

Brody didn't reply immediately, but stood with his arms folded across his chest, his expression bleak and withdrawn.

Maureen wondered if pushing him to answer questions now was at all fair. Despite the fact that he'd fallen asleep after they'd made love, it had only been for an hour or so. That meant that during the past two days, while under intense stress, he'd had very little rest.

Exhausted as he was, might he end up telling her something he shouldn't? Something that, as Hayes had suggested, she might later be asked to repeat in court. Under oath.

Talk about being caught between a rock and a hard place. Professionally, Maureen wanted to help Brody. Personally, she wanted to know everything about him. But there was always the chance that the answers he gave would lead them down paths better left unexplored at this time.

Finally, after several seconds of silence, Maureen shook her head. "All right. Forget I asked. Maybe there's an another way to handle this. I've seen Victoria in action a couple of times now. I think I can make an educated guess as to her 'past transgressions.'"

Brody raised an eyebrow. "Guess away."

"Well, for starters, how about this?" Maureen took a deep breath and then plunged ahead. "I did a lot of thinking while I was waiting for you and Clay to finish up that business at the bank. I got to wondering about something you told me about your first breakup with Jeannie. When you came home from college and discovered she'd gotten married, had your mother anything to do with that?"

He studied her thoughtfully for a moment or two, then sighed. "You never cease to amaze me. You're good. Really good. Your father and Stanton would be proud."

"Come off it, Brody. When I first offered to help I told you I had the instincts of a cop. Remember?"

"Yes, you did. And if it walks like a duck, and quacks like a duck, it's a duck."

Maureen turned away. Not the same old suspicions again. Not now. Not after everything they'd shared.

Before she could finish the thought Brody groaned and pulled her into his arms. "I'm sorry, Maureen. You didn't deserve that. I guess you're going to have to learn to live with the fact that I'm convinced people, women in particular, can be as devious as hell. And I've come by that conviction honestly, having had more than enough experience to back it up."

"Was that a lesson learned at your mother's knee, Brody?"

He laughed grimly. "Yeah. Your guess wasn't exactly a shot in the dark, was it? You're too smart not to have picked up on Victoria's exaggerated view of the importance of the Parrish name in the grand scheme of things. She believes it's her sacred duty to protect it from anything or anyone who might damage it. In her opinion my youthful relationship with Jeannie threatened to do just that. No matter what I said to the contrary, and no matter how often I said it, she was certain I'd end up marrying Jeannie. So Victoria went about insuring that would never happen. She financed a wedding, a honeymoon, and a down payment on a house for the happy couple."

"The happy couple?"

Maureen felt Brody stiffen. He dropped his arms and began to pace the room, looking for all the world like a caged animal, evidencing the same kind of tension he always displayed whenever he was forced to discuss his relationships with Jeannie or his mother.

He stopped at the window and stared down into the street. "Jeannie and some other guy she was seeing while I was away at school."

Maureen watched him from where she was standing. "Jeannie was willing to marry just anyone?" she asked. "But I thought you said that she was after you to make a commitment to her?"

Brody shrugged. "A bird in the hand."

"God, this sounds like something out of a soap opera. How did you find out about your mother's part in it?"

"The lesson wouldn't have had the proper impact if I weren't aware of how it was accomplished. Victoria was proud of what she'd done. She told me. It proved what she'd been saying all along—that Jeannie was a cold-hearted little manipulator. What Victoria didn't realize was that she'd just revealed herself as one as well."

"You must have been furious."

He sighed. "I wish I could say that I was, but I'd allowed the situation with Jeannie to drag on too long. I was relieved to have it over and done with, and more disappointed in Victoria than angry."

"But, if you felt that way about Jeannie, why had you continued to see her?"

"It's difficult to explain, even to myself. I suppose I felt as if I owed her something. Attention. A good time. Something."

"You owed her? That doesn't make sense. You're the one who saved her life. She owed you."

He turned around and leaned against the wall, his hands in his pockets. His eyes rested on her face for a long moment, as if he were seeing her for the first time. Then he smiled. Not his usual dazzler, but slow, thoughtful, and equally as riveting. "You know, I often ask myself how I could have missed noticing you when we were growing up. I bet you were a pretty kid. Had lots of friends. Right?"

Maureen nodded. Her childhood had been wonderful. No grist for the therapy mill there. "What has that got to do with you and Jeannie?"

"Do you remember anything about me? I mean, before the famous rescue scene in Brandywine Park?"

"I was only twelve, Brody. As self-absorbed as any child, I suppose. I don't think I was aware of much outside my own secure little world."

"Well, I was a geek, Maureen. A shy, skinny teenager, all ratty hair and pimples, with a beak like a knife and not a friend in the world besides my over-protective parents and teachers. The only place I didn't look and feel awkward was in or on the water. When people my age thought about me at all, I was that rich punk kid from Riverbend who attended a snotty prep school in Hershey."

Maureen stared at him. He was so incredibly attractive that what he was saying seemed ridiculous. He had to be exaggerating. But then she recalled how she'd described the rescue to Clay.

This gawky, Ichabod Crane type came loping out of nowhere.

"But after the rescue I was the town hero," Brody continued. "It was a pretty heady experience. When people looked at me then, I saw admiration in their eyes. And Jeannie made it clear that she was interested in me. She was a looker. Popular. She saw to it that I was invited to parties. Suddenly I had friends. By the time I left for college a year later, everything had changed. I'd changed."

"And you felt Jeannie was responsible."

"Yeah."

"But grateful or not, you still didn't want to spend the rest of your life with her."

"Gratitude only goes so far. We had nothing in common except the sex, and as young and horny as I was, I knew even then it wasn't enough."

"Then, in a way, your mother did you a favor. She got you, how did you put it, off the hook?"

He winced. "Young men don't appreciate their mothers doing them that kind of favor. What Victoria did made me realize that to have any kind of private life I was going to have to leave Riverbend." He made a sweeping gesture with his arm. "So after graduation I moved in here. End of story."

No, that wasn't the end of the story. Not by a long shot. If it had been, they wouldn't be standing here now. Brody wouldn't be suspected of murder. He and Maureen might never have met.

What was that line from the song? Circles within circles. Wheels within wheels.

Maureen walked over to where Brody was standing and looked past his shoulder down into the street. Below was Chafey Road, a quiet, tree-lined boulevard on the outskirts of Granite Run's compact little business and social district. The town's only hotel, the Waltham Inn, was across the street, along with a couple of charming little restaurants. And Brody's office.

Not a bad place to live. Convenient. And he'd done wonders with the apartment itself. But it wasn't Riverbend.

Brody must feel a little like Adam, forced out of paradise.

She turned to him. "How was your relationship with your mother after you left?"

"Strained." His voice was flat and unemotional. "We had breakfast together at Riverbend every Sunday and I took a turn on the river. She came into town once a week and we had lunch. That was the extent of it. Until her stroke."

"When you moved back home."

He raked a hand through his hair. "She needed me, and I'd experienced such a sea change after the rescue, that I thought

158

something as dramatic as a stroke might work the same magic on her. Soften her attitudes, give her some perspective on things. And it actually seemed to have happened until Jeannie's murder, when I began noticing some backsliding on Mother's part. Then, this morning, when Stanton found the fifty thousand in Lisa's purse, I thought to myself, dammit, here we go again."

"It must have been a relief to find that there hadn't been any large, unexplained withdrawals from her accounts."

"It was." He reached out and swept Maureen into his arms again. He looked down at her, his eyes searching her face. "Turn about is fair play. Now, I'll ask the questions."

"Having seen you rescue Jeannie was my only secret, Brody. You can ask me anything now. I'm an open book."

"Then you won't mind telling me how this morning's little chat with Clay Stanton went."

She shrugged. "There's not much to tell. Clay and I are speaking, but that's about all. On certain subjects we've agreed to disagree."

"He didn't offer any explanation for the grudge you think he has against me?"

"He's decided that I'm not ready to hear about it. Yet."

"I don't know if I care for that 'yet.'"

"His word, Brody. Not mine."

They stood for a while, feeling safe in each others arms, willing the moment to last, fearful of what lay ahead. After a time he bent and whispered close to her ear, "It looks like it's you and me against the world, babe. Do you know what I think we ought to do now?"

She shook her head and pushed him away. "God, you're insatiable!"

He threw back his head and laughed. "Weren't you the one who told me sex didn't solve everything? I'm starving, Maureen. I was going to suggest we send out for pizza and a six pack."

Once again, he'd surprised her, thrown her off balance. She was going to miss this funny, alarming, mercurial man when this was all over. If she didn't watch out he would ruin her for any other man, if he hadn't already. She ought to cut and run now, before it was too late.

But of course, it was too late, wasn't it? Had been since Wednesday night.

If you don't want this to happen, Maureen, you better close this door in my face right now.

She hadn't closed the door, and now she had to face the

consequences. "I make a mean pizza myself, Brody," she said.

"I forgot. You're a woman who cooks. How did I get so lucky? But there's not much in the kitchen. We'll have to hit the supermarket. Give me a minute to get dressed and we can..."

"We don't need to go shopping. I have everything I need in Philadelphia."

"In Philadelphia?"

"Brody, I have to go home."

"You are home. I knew you were uncomfortable at Riverbend. That's why I brought you here."

"Here?" She glanced around wildly. "You expect me to stay here?"

He rested his cheek on her hair. "We'll stay here. Together. Look, I could hardly wait to show you the place. I've been picturing you here for days. You said you thought it was beautiful."

She backed off, tried to put a little distance, physical and emotional, between them. "It is beautiful, and I love that you were anxious for me to see it. But what you're suggesting is impossible. I have a job. A life. I've got to go home. Change my clothes. Read my mail."

"Dammit. I'll buy you whatever you need. Clothes, shampoo. Art supplies. Whatever. Make me a list and I'll go get them right now."

"You'll do no such thing. Brody, are you listening to yourself? Do you have any idea how that sounds?"

He reached for her again. "Stay with me, Maureen. You heard what Wicklow said. The police are going to come up with some reason to pull me in. Even if it's just to keep the press off their backs. We've got two, three days at the most. Stay with me. Sleep with me, eat with me, use this bright, cop-like mind of yours to help me figure out who's trying to set me up. Oh, I know. You and Wicklow have decided I'm not ready to deal with that ugly little detail. But I'm ready. Or will be, if you'll stay with me."

The world was full of manipulators, Maureen thought. Not all of them cold-hearted, and not all of them women. "Brody, I want to. I do. But, living here, letting you buy me things, is impossible."

"Ah, now I understand. It's your feminist sensibilities that are getting in the way. You're not a girl, and you don't like the idea of being kept, huh?" He grinned. "Okay. I get the message. I'm a millennium kinda guy. So, how do you feel about keeping me?"

"What?"

"If I get dressed, right now, and drive you back to Philadelphia, will you let me stay at your place? Will you buy me clothes and shampoo?"

She had to laugh. "You would do that?"

"I'm a desperate man. I'll do whatever it takes to be with you, Maureen."

For now, Maureen reminded herself. For two or three days at the most. Either way, if he were arrested or cleared, that was all they were going to have. She supposed she could afford two or three more days out of a career, out of a lifetime, for the man she'd been carrying around inside her head and heart for over a decade.

"God, you're a tough sell," he prodded.

"Hmm. Not as tough as I ought to be." Maureen sighed. "Is there a lease? Where do I sign?"

"Here," he said, and kissed her.

*   *   *

Brody refused to believe that any of his clients, past or present, could be responsible for his problems. But because Maureen insisted, they stopped at his office before leaving Granite Run and picked up a computer printout of his client list, intending to go over it when they reached Philadelphia.

But once they arrived at the condo he was too hungry and tired to face the long list immediately, and too impatient to wait for Maureen to prepare the promised pizza. Instead, he stood in front of the open refrigerator, scooping up cold chicken and artichoke casserole with a spoon and chug-a-lugging milk from the container.

Maureen leaned against the kitchen counter, shaking her head. "If the head waiter at Tio Pepe's could only see his favorite patron now."

He finished off an apple, walked over to where she was standing, and rested his forehead against hers. "I'm sorry, babe. I'm so groggy I can't even think straight. We can have the pizza tonight."

"Brody, you look as if you're about to pass out. Go to bed."

"What about the list?"

"We'll look at it after you've rested."

He reached for her hand. "Come with me. To sleep. I swear, just to sleep."

"No, I'm not as tired as you are, and there are some things I need to get done around here." She gave him a little push in the direction of the bedroom. "Go," she said and watched him stagger off.

First, Maureen cleaned her glasses. Then she turned her attention to the mail she and Brody had just brought up from the mailbox in the lobby. There was very little of interest in it. An unsolicited credit card. Supermarket flyers. A couple of catalogs. All fodder for the round file.

161

The only thing of any importance was an emotional thank you note from the kidnap victim in Larkspur. Reading it, Maureen felt renewed pride in the work she did, and anger at the nameless someone who was trying to use her to frame Brody.

She picked up the pencil and pad she kept by the telephone, switched on the answer machine and flopped down onto the couch. It had been a slow morning. Only two messages. The first, from a small police jurisdiction in California.

Maureen breathed a sigh of relief as she listened to the gruff male voice of the chief identifying himself and describing a long-standing case he could use her help on. Not a rush job, he said. Call anytime during the coming week. His department was willing to fly her out to the West Coast at her earliest convenience.

When the second message came on she stopped scribbling and sat up a little straighter.

"Hi, Maureen. It's Pete. It's Friday morning, and I have a new show opening tonight. Are you free for a late supper with the gang after the gallery closes? If you can make it, just show up around nine. We've missed you." There was a long pause. "I've missed you."

Pete Hauser. A couple of months ago she had almost married him. They had come that close, but then she'd backed off. Why? And why had he let her squirm out of it so easily?

Even his proposal had been so Pete. "Shall we get married next month or do you have too much work lined up?"

That was Pete. Make no demands Hauser, he laughingly called himself.

Make no demands, don't push, don't break down any walls.

After her retreat, they'd drifted apart. But there was still a residue of feeling there. Maureen had heard it in his voice. Had felt it too.

She found herself staring at the wall across from the couch. A lovely taupe color with white woodwork. Elegant and simple, she'd always thought. But, after seeing Brody's apartment she began to wonder if it wasn't just a bit stark. How different she and Brody were. Sterling and plate. Crystal and glass. There wasn't anything in his apartment that would fit in here.

Well, maybe, the tapestry. The wall would be a great backdrop for it. And, of course, that wonderful hutch...

Maureen sighed and got to her feet. She checked her watch. What was the matter with her? She was wasting precious time daydreaming when there were places she had to go, things she had to find out. Fast.

162

She went into the bedroom and started to change out of the clothes she'd put on immediately after Clay's three AM telephone call.

Brody was asleep on the bed, breathing deeply. Before having flung himself down on the mattress he had kicked off his shoes, unbuttoned the top button of his khaki slacks and tugged his flannel shirt free of the waistband. The lines of fatigue that had been etched into his face the past couple of days were softer in repose, though his dark brows were still drawn together in a frown.

Maureen studied him. He looked the way he never did when he was awake. Vulnerable.

She continued to stare while she pulled on a white T-shirt and jeans. She lifted a navy linen blazer out of the closet, put it on and then went and knelt by the side of the bed. She touched his hair and smiled. Now she understood why he kept it so short. In even the few days that had passed since the lineup it had begun to curl a bit around his temples and ears. Not a look a careful, self-styled "numbers" man would favor.

A geek? That was hard to believe. Maybe once, but not anymore.

"Brody," she whispered. "I'm going out for a while."

He groaned and shifted his weight toward her without really waking up.

Maureen watched him thoughtfully for another second or two, then turned and opened the nightstand drawer. Just in case he woke up before she got back her "kept" man ought to have his own key. The key that had once been Lisa's. Maureen placed it and a note with the condo's elevator code next to the wallet Brody had thrown onto the bureau.

Then she went to see Pete Hauser.

*   *   *

The Hauser Gallery wasn't as trendy or avant-garde as most of its competitors on South Street. But over the past five years it had carved a nice little niche for itself in the Philadelphia art world, especially among those who, like its owner, still harbored a taste for realism.

When Maureen walked through its front door at four o'clock in the afternoon, Pete Hauser was supervising the setting up of a new exhibition.

She called his name and he turned, his face brightening when he caught sight of her. He came forward with outstretched arms.

"Wonderful. You got my message." He bent his sandy-haired head and kissed her cheek, then pulled back and gave her a long once over. "God, you look good. But, you're early. The others won't be here for a while, and you know how these openings go. I'm not going to be able to break free until we shut the place down around nine."

The eagerness in his voice and face shamed her. Even if he hadn't called, she would have come. Not for his sake, but for Brody's. "Pete, I know you're busy but I need your help."

Immediately, his expression turned serious. "Then, forget busy. All you have to do is ask, Maureen. Anything."

She nodded toward an arched doorway in the rear of the gallery. "Do you mind if we go into the back room? There's something I'd like to check out in your permanent collection."

"Not a problem. But it's the permanent collection I'm highlighting tonight. Come and have a look." He took her arm and drew her over to a wall where two of his assistants were busily arranging and re-arranging a series of paintings. "Tonight's a kind of a celebration. I've just acquired a work I've been after for years."

Maureen stared at the wall, at the three prominently displayed paintings, two of which Pete had owned for as long as she'd known him. The third she'd last seen hanging in the entry hall at Riverbend.

She couldn't believe her eyes. This was more than she'd dared hope for.

Maureen turned to Hauser. "Victoria Parrish sold you *Summer*," she breathed.

He grinned happily and lowered his voice. "Well, you know how things are among collectors. I'm not supposed to reveal the name of the seller, but the identity of the former owner wasn't exactly a state secret, was it?"

"Pete, what did you pay for it?" Maureen bit her lip. There'd been an urgency in her voice that she hadn't been able to disguise.

He raised an eyebrow. "Has this anything to do with the help you need?"

"I know it's not the kind of question one asks, but I have to know. It's important."

"I said I would do anything for you, Maureen, and I meant it. But we have a problem here. To get the painting I had to agree not to discuss the particulars of the sale." He shrugged. "Of course, if you wanted to try and guess the price, and got close, I might not be able to hide my surprise. Unfortunately, the chances of that happening are close to nil. I got lucky this time and—"

"How does fifty thousand dollars sound? In cash."

"How in hell could you...?" He cocked his head to one side. "That sounds like an unbelievably good guess. Especially since you know the painting is worth a good deal more than that."

"Not if the seller were in a hurry, Pete. Not if he or she insisted on cash. The complete set would be worth a fortune. Far more than the total price of each individual painting added together. So the owner of two paintings would be in a great position to bargain."

Hauser nodded. "As I said, an amazingly good guess."

"Thanks, Pete, and congratulations. And good luck in getting the Brandywine to part with 'Autumn.'"

Hauser shook his head. "Now, why do I think that's an exit line? Why do I think you're not going to be here when the gallery closes?"

Maureen put her hand on his arm. "I'm sorry, Pete."

"No apology necessary. Except for this painting, it's been the story of my life. A day late and a dollar short." For a moment he studied her face, then he sighed and reached up to straighten her glasses. "Or in our case maybe it was a day early, huh?" He hesitated again and his eyes got suspiciously bright. "I told you a few minutes ago that you looked good, Four-eyes. That was an understatement. You look great. Fabulous. Like you've finally met someone you're ready to make some room for in your life. Anyone I know?"

*   *   *

"You should have called," Hayes Wicklow said as he showed Maureen into his office.

"So your secretary informed me. But I've yet to feel completely comfortable with disembodied voices coming at me over coaxial cable. And I was so excited about what I've found out that I wanted to see your face when I told you."

Wicklow looked uneasy. "I just meant, I might have saved you the trip. I was about to leave for Granite Run when my secretary buzzed and told me you were here."

"What trip? I only live a quarter of a mile away, Hayes."

"Oh. I didn't realize you'd returned to Philadelphia." He frowned. "Did Parrish bring you? Where the hell is he? I've been trying to reach him for over an hour."

Maureen walked over to the dark leather chair in front of Wicklow's massive mahogany desk and sat down. "Brody is at my place."

"What's he doing there?"

"Sleeping."

"Sleeping," Wicklow roared. "Dammit. I thought I could count on you to get the man focused, Maureen. His situation is precarious. Can't you two keep your hands off each other long enough to—"

"Calm down, Hayes. Believe me, you're going to want to hear what I have to tell you. I know where Lisa's fifty thousand dollars came from."

Now she had his attention. He dropped into the chair behind the desk and drilled her with his eyes. "Maureen, listen to me. What you just said has very serious implications. Anything you've learned from Brody is not covered by lawyer-client privilege. I warned you about that."

"Brody doesn't know anything about the money. That's why I came to you. I'm not sure how he'll react when he finds out. It's not something he's going to want to hear. And there's a question in my mind as to whether the information will help or hurt him." She leaned forward across the desk. "That's why I wanted to talk to you first."

Absentmindedly, Wicklow began to massage the arms of his chair. "Give me a moment to think," he sighed. Finally, he exhaled and threw up his hands. "God, I hope I don't regret this. Go ahead. Tell me. Everything."

Maureen told the lawyer about her conversation with Victoria Parrish that morning, about her suspicions regarding the Gresham painting, and about her visit to the Hauser Gallery. But she didn't tell him everything. She kept to herself what Brody had revealed about his mother's earlier payments to Jeannie Starbuck. That had been a private conversation between Maureen and Brody. If Brody wanted Wicklow to know, he could tell him himself.

Wicklow listened with his arms folded on his desk and his eyes closed. When Maureen finished he looked up and shook his head. "I have to hand it to the woman. Here she is, recovering from a stroke, hasn't been let out of the house more than a couple of times since, and she's running around selling paintings, bribing witnesses and God only knows what else."

Maureen nodded. "I have a feeling Mrs. Parrish had some help from her housekeeper," she said.

"Undoubtedly. But you were right to be concerned about what you've found out. This might look as if Brody's mother bribed Lisa Adams to recant, or leave town, because she knew her son was guilty."

"You don't think Victoria or Mrs. Hartman could have had anything to do with Lisa's death?"

"What? Strangled Lisa? No. It's not beyond the realm of possibility but I doubt the two of them together would have had the strength. Even if they had, Parrish would still have Jeannie Starbuck's murder on his plate. Poor guy. He doesn't need this. Not now," Wicklow finished with an uncharacteristic burst of sympathy. He stood. "Come on, let's go and wake Brody up."

"Oh, Hayes, he's exhausted. Why don't we let him sleep?" Maureen hesitated. She didn't like what she saw in Wicklow's face. "What did you mean when you said, 'not now.'"

He stared at her for several seconds, then looked quickly away. "An hour before you showed up I had a call from Paul Marsh. The preliminary results of the forensic tests are back. Things don't look good. The police want me to bring Brody in."

CHAPTER 14

Maureen snatched the receiver from its cradle after the very first ring. "Brody?"

"It's Hayes, Maureen."

"Oh. Hayes." She tried to disguise her disappointment. Not to mention her fear. "Is Brody with you?"

"No." There was a chilling hesitation at the other end of the line. "He's being fingerprinted and photographed. They've arrested him."

Arrested. Brody behind bars. The image refused to compute. Maureen looked down at the bed on which she was sitting. He had been here a little more than an hour ago, angled across the mattress, the sheet twisted around his torso, his shirt open to expose the dark hair on his chest.

He'd been visibly shaken and strangely silent when Maureen and Hayes had awakened him. Obviously, for all his brave talk about expecting to be arrested, he never actually believed it would happen. What had Hayes called his attitude? The arrogance of innocence? Yes, that had been a pretty accurate description of Brody's take on things the past few days.

That is, until late this afternoon.

Then like a man in a trance, he had straightened his clothes, swept his things off the bureau into his pocket and with what amounted to only a few slurred monosyllables, said goodbye and left with Hayes.

Maureen gripped the receiver tighter and covered her mouth with her hand to keep a sob from escaping. Oh God, why had she listened to them? Why hadn't she insisted on going with them to Granite Run?

"I'll be there in thirty minutes," she said once she'd composed herself.

"No, Maureen. You will not come here tonight." Hayes spoke slowly, as if trying to get through to a child or someone in shock. "Even if Brody wanted to see you, and he doesn't, the police won't allow you anywhere near him right now. Do you understand?"

At any other time Maureen would have resented being talked to like this, but at the moment she had to admit Hayes was right. There was no logical reason for her presence at the Granite Run police station tonight. She'd just be a distraction, an annoyance. Hayes needed to focus on his client's best interests, not on comforting and explaining things to her.

"Hayes, I know you're busy. Just tell me what they've got on him and I'll let you go."

Maureen heard the lawyer sigh. "The test results are pretty damaging. From what I understand, fiber samples recovered from Jeannie Starbuck's apartment match up with those from a couch and carpet at Riverbend. A bartender from the Crocodile Grill now 'seems to recall' seeing Brody there last Saturday night. The police think that information, along with your sketch and Lisa's identification, add up to probable cause. And they're right. They have more than enough to hold him."

"You're going to get him out, aren't you, Hayes? He's not going to spend the night in a cell?"

"You know as well as I do that there's no bail schedule for capital cases. I need a goddamn judge to set an amount, and it's Friday night. Judge Richmond is on call but I haven't been able to reach him yet." Hayes lowered his voice. "Look, Maureen, I don't want to make too big a stink about this. Paul Marsh is risking his badge by not transferring Brody to the county facility immediately. The holding cells here in Granite Run are not exactly rooms at the Ritz, but they're a hell of a lot better than anything Brody would have to endure in a county jail."

The county jail! Before being hired by the Granite Run Police Department Maureen's father had put in a year as a prison guard. The experience, he'd once told her, had made even him, a stickler for procedure, hesitate before arresting and sending anyone there.

Maureen swallowed. "How is Brody taking it, Hayes?"

Wicklow actually chuckled. "The arrogant SOB has raised steely-eyed anger to an art form. The inmates in the county lockup are lucky he's not joining their ranks tonight. If one of them made a move on Brody he'd do some serious damage himself."

There'd been something akin to admiration in the lawyer's voice.

"You've gotten to like Brody, haven't you, Hayes?"

There was a pause. "I'm not paid to like him. I'm paid to defend him."

"I think you like him. Attitude and all."

"You think too much, Maureen. Get some rest and come down here tomorrow morning. If I can arrange bail you'll be here when he gets out. If I can't, then I'll lean on Paul one last time and get you in to see your man. That's all I can promise. Do we have a deal? You'll stay put for now?"

"Yes. Goodnight. Oh,…Hayes?"

The lawyer groaned. "God, you're hard to get rid of. What now?"

"What about Mrs. Parrish?"

"Mommie dearest doesn't know anything about this yet. When I get through here I'm going over to Riverbend to pick up Brody's passport. He's going to have to turn it in to get bail. I'll break the news to Victoria then, and if I think she's up to it, I'll confront her with the information you dug up about the sale of the painting. Is that all right with you?"

"I trust your judgement, Hayes."

"Do you? Thanks for the vote of confidence. When all this is over and done with I hope I'll have deserved it. See you tomorrow."

For a couple of seconds after Hayes rang off Maureen stared at the cold, hard receiver in her hand. Then she gingerly returned it to its cradle. When was the last time a phone had brought her anything but bad news?

God, she felt so restless, so on edge. She trusted Hayes, was glad that Brody had someone of that man's skill and tenacity on his side. But it had been Brody's voice she'd longed to hear. Brody's smile she longed to see. His hands she longed to touch.

She sank back onto the mattress, curled her fingers into the sheet and drew it around her.

Fahrenheit. It smelled ever so faintly of Fahrenheit.

All of a sudden Maureen lost her battle with tears. Two days. They were supposed to have had two days.

*   *   *

The press had already stationed themselves outside the Granite Run Police Department when Maureen pulled up in front of it on Saturday morning.

Hayes had given her some suggestions on how to deal with the reporters and cameramen. Head up, eyes front and absolute silence. "Don't even give them a 'no comment' to quote," he'd ordered.

Well, here goes, she thought, and barreled right through them like they were a swarm of pesky insects. Flashbulbs popped and a few shouted remarks filtered through the cocoon in which she'd wrapped herself.

"Who's the blonde?"

"Wasn't she in the Jag with Parrish yesterday?"

"Isn't that Maureen Lowe?"

"Ms. Lowe, wasn't it your sketch that first brought Parrish to the attention of the public?"

By the time the questions had become personal she'd reached the front door. Someone inside pulled it open, and once she was through, slammed it shut behind her.

"Thanks," she said and turned, only to find herself staring directly into Clay Stanton's stony face.

"Did any of them recognize you?" he demanded.

"Yes."

He grimaced.

"It was inevitable, Clay. And no wonder, what with all the stupid publicity I've received the past few months. Besides, any one of them could have run into me during a previous case." She waved a dismissive hand. "Some of them saw me with Brody at Riverbend yesterday. Our friendship is going to come to light. I'll live with it."

"You say that now, but once he's convicted you'll sing a different tune."

"Talk about a rush to judgement." Maureen shook her head and turned away. "I didn't come here to argue with you, Clay. I have better things to do with my time."

"Look, if your name comes up we'll just do what the politicians do. Stonewall it. You never had a "relationship" with Parrish. You were keeping an eye on him because you'd gotten close to Lisa Adams and were naturally interested in seeing that justice was done." He put a hand on her shoulder. "We'll use the arrest to explain your presence here today. You were asked to come in because the witness is deceased, and it was your sketch that originally brought him to our attention."

She swung back on him. "Is that the spin? Is that how you've decided to think about this?"

"It's how you should think about it. You made a mistake, but if you use your head you can still make it work to your advantage." He actually smiled. "Take my word for it, the media will eat it up."

Maureen studied him with narrowed eyes. Clay's interest in the media's take on things was something new. Or was it? She'd always wondered how the publicity about her had gotten started in the first place. She hadn't sought the attention. In fact, up until then she'd avoided the spotlight as much as possible. Could Clay have been responsible? Could he have been the one who alerted the press to the part she'd played in some of those earlier high profile cases?

Was it possible that in some twisted way Clay had thought he was helping her? Furthering her career? That he'd brought her into this case because he knew it was going to turn into something big, knew Brody was going to be implicated?

But that was preposterous. How could he have known?

Maureen raised a hand to her throbbing head. She glanced around the lobby. Behind the gray Formica reception counter a cluster of uniformed officers and plainclothes detectives had gathered, watching and listening to the little scene by the door.

All the questions she wanted to ask Clay would just have to wait until some other time.

She marched over to the desk. "Is Hayes Wicklow here?"

A baby-faced sergeant, caught in the act of eavesdropping, flushed. "He's in with his client, Ms. Lowe."

"Then I'd like to speak to Chief Marsh."

"I'm afraid he's unavailable too. Right now he's busy with a citizen."

"Isn't there someone around here who can take a statement?" she demanded.

The young man's Adam's apple did a jig. He looked past her shoulder. "The lieutenant is next in charge, ma'am."

Clay stepped closer, slipped his hand under her arm. "Come with me, Maureen." He nodded to the sergeant. "We'll be in one of the interview rooms, Ripley."

"Room B is occupied. Wicklow and Parrish are in there."

"Then we'll use A."

When they reached their destination he pulled out a chair for her. "Now, what's this all about?" he asked.

Maureen sat down, folded her hands in her lap and waited until he'd settled himself at the head of the table. Just like a father or teacher dealing with a recalcitrant schoolgirl, she thought, and wondered if he remembered this was where they'd traded angry words just a few days ago.

"I want to make a statement," she began, and then stopped. "Shouldn't you be tape recording this, or at least taking notes?"

He shrugged. "It's a good idea to discuss what you want to say, first. Before you go on record. Just to get things clear in your mind. Then, if you still want to, you can write out your statement yourself. Or we can tape it. Whichever you prefer." He spread his hands. "Whenever you're ready, Maureen."

Again, she hesitated. She wasn't sure exactly how official an off-the-cuff statement was supposed to sound. Well, all she could do was say what she'd come to say, in the most simple and straightforward way possible.

"I want to advise everyone involved in Brody Parrish's arrest that he couldn't have murdered Lisa Adams. I saw her, alive, late Wednesday afternoon. Mr. Parrish visited me at my condo in Philadelphia that night, sometime around seven PM."

Maureen looked down at her hands. Heat flared in her cheeks. As Clay had said, this was for the record. She wasn't telling him anything he didn't already know. But a part of her still felt as if she were throwing it in his face that only a few hours after he'd ordered her not to see Brody again she'd been in his arms.

She took a deep breath and forced herself to go on. "He stayed until almost noon the next day. If you'll talk to Hayes Wicklow I believe you'll find that he and Mr. Parrish had a one o'clock appointment at Riverbend that lasted until three that afternoon. After that he—"

Clay cleared his throat. "Parrish has been arrested for Jeannie Starbuck's murder, not Lisa Adams.'"

Maureen sighed. "Are you trying to tell me that this department isn't working on both cases with an eye to their being committed by one and the same person? That Jeannie Starbuck's murderer wasn't the only one with a reason to kill Lisa?"

"That remains to be seen. But using your own logic, it would follow that if Parrish killed Jeannie, he killed Lisa. Can you at least admit that, Maureen?" Clay spoke with such sweet reasonableness that Maureen was nonplussed. No longer angry, he cocked his head to one side, the picture of gentle concern. "The evidence in the Adams case is still being developed, but consider this. The coroner's investigation so far suggests that Lisa died sometime between eleven PM Thursday and one o'clock Friday morning."

"Well, there you are. Brody couldn't have done it. He was at my place from around seven until you called."

"Was he? Now, Maureen, stop and think before you answer."

"Of course he was. You called there. You spoke to him yourself."

"So I did. At three AM. When exactly did you two turn in?" he asked, his lips just a bit tighter than before.

"Exactly? I'm not sure. Around ten."

"Am I wrong? Didn't my phone call wake you up?"

"Yes, it did. I was asleep."

"Was Parrish in the room with you? If I remember correctly you had to leave to look for him."

"He was just outside the bedroom door. In the corridor."

"Was he dressed?"

Maureen had a quick vision of Brody in jeans. She didn't think he'd been wearing anything else, but she'd been so upset at the time that she hadn't noticed. "Clay, what are you getting at?"

With a fatherly smile he kicked back in his chair. "That it only takes an hour or so to get back and forth between Granite Run and Philadelphia, and it appears that you can't answer for your friend's whereabouts between, say ten-thirty and when I woke you at three AM."

Maureen pushed herself to her feet. "I should have known better than to talk to you. Where Brody is concerned you see everything from a distorted point of view."

"There's evidence to support my point of view."

"Oh, don't talk to me about fiber samples. Bruce Cahill was in the library at Riverbend. He could have picked up threads from the couch and carpet on his clothes and shoes. He could be the killer. Why aren't the police looking for him?"

"Because he's a phantom, Maureen. A figment of Parrish's very active imagination. There's not a single person in Granite Run, or connected to that California based charity Cahill supposedly represents, that's ever seen or heard of him."

"That's not true. Mrs. Parrish saw him."

"His mother?" Clay sneered. "Now, there's an unbiased witness. The court will certainly give a lot of weight to her testimony."

It was no use. She was wasting her time trying to convince him. "You're not being honest with me, or yourself, Clay. You made up your mind about who killed Jeannie before you had a scrap of evidence to back up your suspicions."

"And I suppose you didn't have a preconceived idea about his guilt or innocence from the beginning?"

Maureen rubbed her forehead. "You're right, I did. But at least my feelings were based on fact, not personal prejudice. The best way to predict future behavior is by examining past behavior. With my own eyes I saw Brody save Jeannie's life. It's inconceivable that he would then turn around and..."

A weary smiled began to spread across his face. "The big rescue, huh? That's what makes him incapable of murder? Well, it's time you and everybody else in this town faced up to the truth. It was a fraud, Maureen. A setup. Parrish never rescued anyone."

Maureen stared at Stanton, open-mouthed, eyes wide. Fraud? Setup? The ugly words rang in her ears. And it suddenly hit her that Clay had been hinting at something like this all along. She'd simply refused to process the information before.

What I always wanted to know was how the canoe happened to tip over in the first place.

But it wasn't true. Couldn't be. Clay was lying. He was furious because she'd slept with Brody. He'd say anything to ruin Brody in her eyes.

Stanton stood. "Christ. What does it take? You still don't believe me, do you?"

Fighting angry tears, Maureen shook her head.

"All right," he said. "Don't take my word for it. Ask the bastard yourself."

*   *   *

Hayes hesitated with his hand on the doorknob of Interview Room B. He studied Maureen's face. "Are you okay?"

She took a deep breath and straightened her shoulders. Hayes wouldn't want her to upset Brody any more than he probably was already. She had to calm down or Hayes might call a halt to the meeting. She couldn't let that happen. "I just had another go-round with Clay," she said. "But I'm fine. I want to thank you for getting me this chance to see Brody."

The lawyer squeezed her arm. "It's Marsh you should thank, not me. But remember, there are guidelines I promised him you and Brody would adhere to. This door has to remain ajar and you and Brody can't touch. Other than that," he pushed the door open and winked, "you have ten minutes. Make the most of it."

He left, leaving Maureen to step across the threshold alone.

Brody was leaning against the far wall, his hands shoved into his pockets. He looked up when she entered but didn't make a move toward her. They stared at each other for a second or two without saying a word.

"Wicklow told me you wanted to see me," Brody said at last. "I had a bet with myself you wouldn't show. Obviously, you have more nerve than I gave you credit for."

Nerve? What did he mean? Had he thought that she'd run and hide once he was arrested? Maureen took a step in his direction. She gestured vaguely with her hand. "The rules make this so awkward."

He cocked his head and smiled grimly. "Seems as if we've come full circle, doesn't it?"

"Full circle?" Maureen repeated. He was talking in riddles.

"This is where we began." His glance swept the room and then returned to settle on her face. "And it appears that this is where we end."

If Maureen's eyes had been closed she wouldn't have believed this cold expressionless voice belonged to him. "I don't understand. Are you angry with me, Brody? Why?"

"I'm not angry with you. You were just doing what was expected of you. What even I had expected of you when I was thinking rationally. So neither of us should have any complaints. After all, we both got what we were after, didn't we? You got another notch on your charcoal pencil and I had a good time."

He looked down at the floor, and his voice softened. "A very good time. So much so that, if by some miracle I get out of this alive, I could be tempted to give it another whirl. What do you say, Maureen? Is it a plan? Of course, just to keep you honest I'd have to be careful not to fall asleep when you're around."

Her arms stiffened at her sides, her fingers curling into fists. Maybe Brody wasn't angry, but she was fast approaching flash point. "Would you care to explain that last remark?"

"Well, if I remember correctly there were a couple of times yesterday when I did just that. Fell asleep and woke up to find you playing Nancy Drew again. First, when I caught you in my apartment searching through my things, and later, after you pumped me about my mother and then decided to check up on how the Parrishes managed to lay their hands on enough cash for a fifty thousand dollar bribe without it showing up in their bank records."

Why, he was deliberately misconstruing her actions, Maureen thought desperately. Had Victoria gotten to him with some trumped-up story? "How did you find out about my going to the gallery?"

"Wicklow gave you away, without realizing it. He thought I should know what my mother had been up to. Told me how you went to Hauser and wormed the particulars of the sale out of him. Guess I'm not the only sucker for your charms."

Maureen didn't want to believe this was Brody speaking. He was parroting what someone else had told him, waiting to see her reaction. They'd settled the spying issue back in his apartment.

Hadn't they?

"Have you spoken with your mother?" she asked.

He grimaced. "I called the poor, silly woman this morning, and told her to go to Paul and tell him everything about her involvement before someone else did. She's in his office with him now."

Ah, someone else. That's you, Maureen told herself. So, the Parrishes were closing ranks, and Maureen was on the outside, looking in. Well, she'd known this would happen eventually. It was just a bit sooner than she'd expected. But she wasn't going to cry. Wasn't about to give anyone, not even him, that satisfaction.

He looked up at the ceiling. "Oh, please, Maureen. Don't give me another one of those patented 'Brody, how can you think such things about me' looks. They worked in the past, but I'm immune now. Save them for Wicklow. He's still making excuses for you. But I imagine I've had more experience with dishonest women than he has."

"Don't worry, Brody. I'm through trying to convince you that I'm not some kind of police spy. I have an aversion to being where I'm not wanted, so I'll leave. But before I do, I think you owe me the answer to one last question."

"I never said I didn't want you, Maureen. And if memory serves, the only way I was ever able to stop you from asking questions was to kiss you."

They stood, looking into each other's eyes for a long moment, memories of kisses, mind-reeling, bone-melting, never-again kisses, hanging in the air between them.

Finally Maureen forced herself to speak. "Clay just told me that the time I saw you pull Jeannie out of the Brandywine fifteen years ago wasn't a rescue. It was a setup designed to make you look like a hero. Is that true?"

Brody pushed himself away from the wall and took a couple of steps toward the dark, tinted window that separated Interview room A from Interview Room B. "Is Stanton in there, Maureen, waiting to hear what I have to say? Waiting for me to give him a motive for murder?"

He gazed at her, waiting, and smiled his beautiful, reckless smile. "What the hell. I always figured he suspected. Even back then. Yes, Maureen, the famous, award winning rescue of Jeannie Starbuck by Brody Parrish, scion of the much esteemed Riverbend and Granite Run Parrishes, was indeed a hoax. A fraud. A lie. And, what's more—"

But Maureen had heard enough. Almost more than she could bear. She turned and rushed from the room.

*   *   *

For some minutes after Maureen had left, Brody remained standing in front of the glass, studying his reflection on its cloudy surface. When he heard a footstep in the doorway he turned quickly and glanced over his shoulder, half-hoping, half-fearing she'd returned.

"Your mouthpiece and the chief are waiting," Stanton said from the doorway. "The three of us are handling your transfer to County."

Brody inclined his head toward the glass. "Did you get an earful?"

"Didn't hear anything I didn't already know."

"Yeah," Brody said. "I always wondered what kept you from blowing the whistle all these years."

Stanton couldn't resist a smug smile. "Well, you know, at first I thought, hey, it's a rich kid's prank, and nobody got hurt. Right? So what's the big deal? And after awhile it just gave me a charge, seeing how easily you'd fooled everybody when they damn well should have known better. I mean, come on. In the spring the Brandywine can be a pisser, but come summer, except for maybe around Riverbend, it's hardly more than a creek. Am I right?"

Brody nodded, and Stanton laughed derisively. "Of course, I made sure you knew I knew. It sorta made us co-conspirators, didn't it? Our dirty little secret. Ours and Jeannie Starbuck's."

The older man took a couple of steps into the room. "It felt great, let me tell you. Think of it. Me, your average run-of-the mill cop, having something on you, the biggest damn fish in the Granite Run pond." He shook his head. "Now, a couple of times there, you looked so miserable I was afraid you might own up and spoil the fun. And you did surprise me when you supported Marsh in the election. I'd expected you to give me the nod just to keep me quiet. Truth was, I was beginning to wonder if I'd misjudged you until you hauled off and killed Starbuck. What happened? Did she threaten to expose the less than heroic hero?"

Brody wiped a hand across his mouth. "I don't suppose it ever occurred to you that I might have been among those fooled? That, for reasons of her own, Jeannie set up the 'rescue,' and let me think of myself as hero for only as long as it suited her?"

A flicker of confusion flashed across Stanton's face. His eyes narrowed, and he spent some seconds staring at Brody. Then he shook his head. "No way." He jabbed his finger into Brody's chest. "You're lying, you murdering scum. You're just trying to cop some sorta plea."

Brody batted the older man's hand away. "Get out of my face, Stanton," he growled. He knew he was about to say something he would later regret, but he couldn't help himself. Hell, he'd already said more than he ever meant to. Fat lot of good it did him. "I wonder which upsets you more?" he sneered. "Jeannie's murder or Maureen's interest in me."

The two men stood toe to toe, glaring at each other, neither giving an inch. Finally, Brody exhaled wearily. "Look, forget that last crack. I was out of line. I know how much you care for her. That's why I feel I can ask you a favor."

"You're going to ask me for something? Are you out of your mind? You're talking to the wrong man. You've had all the favors you're going to get from the Granite Run police."

"It's not for myself. It's for Maureen."

Stanton's face went white with anger. "You forget about Maureen, you hear? She knows the truth. She doesn't want to have anything more to do with you. I told you this morning, and I'm telling you again, she'll help us fry you. Whadda ya think of that, hero?"

Brody inhaled sharply. The reminder of Maureen's betrayal hit him again like a blow to the gut. But he still had to get through to the old man. Had to make him understand. Had to get him to act.

"Listen, you asshole, I'm worried about her. First Jeannie, then Lisa. The past few days I've had a premonition Maureen's in some kind of danger. That's why I wouldn't let her out of my sight. Goddammit! You're a cop, man. You were her father's best friend. Keep an eye on her, that's all I ask."

Stanton snickered. "Who are you trying to snow this time, Parrish? Me? You forget, I had your number a long time ago. As long as you were running around scot-free and she thought the sun rose and set in that pretty face of yours, Maureen was in danger. But now? I don't think so. Come on," he gloated. "We're wasting time. You have a date with a jail cell, courtesy of the county. And this time it's not going to be one of Granite Run's tidy little holding rooms. No sir. It's going to be the real thing. The whole enchilada. A stinkin' mattress, a scummy toilet, and with any luck at all, a very friendly roommate."

CHAPTER 15

Fraud. Hoax. Lie.

The words, delivered in Brody's silken rasp, echoed inside Maureen's head as she moved around the bedroom, pulling clothing from the closet and bureau drawers and tossing it into her carry-on bag.

She had to get away. She couldn't stay here. Not tonight. When Lisa had stormed out of the condo it had taken very little time for Maureen to scour it of every last vestige of the other woman's presence. But it was proving more difficult to banish Brody's ghost.

Everywhere she looked she saw him. In the kitchen, his arm draped over the refrigerator door. In the living room, his long legs stretched out across the couch. In the bedroom... Even the solace of painting was denied her. He was in the studio too, laughing at her from behind the wolf's seductive gaze.

Getting out was the best idea. And thanks to the Chief of Police of San Brava, California, she had some place to go, and something useful to do when she got there. She certainly hadn't been any use to anyone around here.

Not to Lisa, to whom Maureen had promised friendship and protection. With suspicion and doubt she'd driven Lisa away, straight into the arms of her murderer.

Not to Clay Stanton, who'd invested in Maureen's talent and discretion, much to his sorrow. Her actions during the past week had cost her his affection and admiration, both of which had been dear to her.

Not even to Brody, whom she'd wanted to help most of all. Her amateurish efforts on his behalf had provided his accusers with even more evidence than they already had to convict him. She'd shown them how Victoria Parrish had acquired the money to bribe Lisa. Even if it had been without Brody's knowledge, what did that say about his own mother's belief in his innocence?

Maureen closed her eyes, reliving those last terrible minutes at the Granite Run Police Station this morning. Before she'd even asked Brody about the rescue, he had been on the attack. And after she'd asked, he didn't hesitate to ridicule her gullibility, even to the point of providing the authorities with a motive for Jeannie Starbuck's murder. Hadn't he all but admitted that she'd threatened to expose him as a bogus hero? A phony?

For a moment Maureen stopped packing and stared into space. Guilt and shame were consuming her, eating her up alive. Why couldn't she cry? It would be so much better to get it all out in one cleansing bout of tears than to carry around this cold, dead weight where her heart should be.

Even now, with her emotions frozen, she couldn't stop what Brody had called her "cop-like brain" from spinning. Why, when he'd never trusted her completely, had he let her into his life? Made love to her? Done whatever it took to keep her by his side?

Well, she didn't have to think too long and hard to come up with an answer to that one. He was a man, and the sex had been good. And free. She'd gone to Riverbend and practically thrown herself at him. Why would he have turned down what was there for the taking, no strings attached?

How it must have amused him to hear her confess to having had a "crush" on him, to feeling as if she had known him for years. How on earth had he kept from laughing out loud?

You don't know me at all, Maureen.

Strange. That night at Riverbend, it was almost as if he had tried to warn her himself. As if he as well as Clay, had been trying to get through to her, to get her to see past her blind, schoolgirl infatuation all along.

Why? Was it possible that Brody cared for her? That he wanted her to know the truth? To know him? To love him?

Love. What did love have to do with them? Neither of them had ever mentioned the word in the other's presence.

Maureen flung an extra pair of glasses into the suitcase. She had to stop trying to find excuses for him. He was a liar and a cheat, and possibly, probably, a murderer.

No. She didn't believe that. Just because the man wasn't the hero she'd wanted him to be, did it follow that he was a monster? Prince Charming or the big bad wolf? Talk about irrational, black and white thinking! When was she going to grow up?

But now that her eyes had been opened she couldn't just ignore all the evidence, could she? Lisa's description, the bribery attempt, the fiber samples, the motive, the disproven alibi.

God, she simply had to get out of here. She was going around in circles, driving herself crazy. Thank goodness she'd been able to get a ticket for the eight PM flight. With the West Coast time difference in her favor she'd arrive in California around ten tonight. Plenty of time to get to her hotel, take the sleeping pill she was certainly going to need, and crash for the night. Then in the morning she could rent a car and head south to San Brava.

Maureen stood in front of the bed and stared down at the contents of her suitcase. She'd packed all the clothes she would need for a two day trip and still had room to spare. Now, what else...?

Ah, yes. What good would a forensic artist be to San Brava's police department without her pads and pencils? Maureen kept the tools of her trade in a briefcase she stored in a closet just inside the front door. She left the bedroom and walked down the hall. On the floor of the closet she found her briefcase, and as she lifted it her glance fell on another piece of luggage right next to it. A black duffel bag.

Lisa's bag. The one she'd forgotten to take with her on the day she'd left.

Maureen picked it up and carried it along with her briefcase back to the bedroom. The briefcase went directly into her carry-on, but she spent the next few minutes sitting on the bed with the duffel on her lap, trying to decide if what she was about to do was in any way unethical.

She could tell by the bag's appearance and weight that there was very little inside. Could the little that was there be of any use to the police? Or to Brody?

What was she thinking? Hadn't the past few hours taught her anything at all? She might be the best forensic artist around, but she was a lousy detective. She ought to just turn the bag over to police and get on that plane to California.

But some habits were harder to break than others. With a shrug she zipped open the bag and reached inside.

If she'd hoped to find a clue as to whom Lisa had met with on Wednesday afternoon, she was disappointed. All that the bag contained was a few pieces of clothing, a small leatherette album of old photographs and a rubber-banded packet of letters.

Maureen leafed through the album. There were about twenty pictures, cracked and crumbling under their brittle plastic overlays. Most of them were posed snapshots of a thin, but well cared for little girl, identifiable as Lisa from around six years of age until what appeared to be her late teens. The others were candid photos of a middle-aged man and woman taken in front of a nineteen-fifties ranch style house. Both the house and the couple seemed faded and worn.

Maureen glanced at the return address in the upper left-hand corner of the topmost envelope in the packet. It read —

Gance
1420 West Road
Garden Park, California.

Gance. Lisa's foster parents. The Granite Run police had already been in touch with them. Maureen wondered how they'd taken the news of Lisa's death. Good old Lucy and Chuck, Lisa had called them, and despite the sarcastic way in which she'd described them, the fact that she'd kept the album indicated she'd felt some affection and gratitude toward these people.

The letters had been sent to an address in Los Angeles, not to Granite Run. After a quick reading Maureen concluded that they were all at least six months old, and there was nothing in them that would be of any use to the local authorities.

But the letters and the photographs might still mean a great deal to Lucy and Chuck Gance.

Garden Park, California, Maureen thought. *I wonder how far that is from San Brava?*

*   *   *

Brody's transfer from a Granite Run holding cell to the Delaware County Jail took most of Saturday morning and afternoon. Brody walked through the admission procedures in a disbelieving daze, clinging to his lawyer's departing words as if they were a rope thrown to a drowning man.

Justice, Hayes Wicklow had assured Brody, was not blind.

It was not blind in Delaware County, Pennsylvania.

It was not blind in the United States of America.

It was not blind anywhere in the world.

So Brody could safely discount some of what Clay Stanton had threatened would be his incarceration experience. His mattress might smell, his toilet might be scummy, but he'd be spared a cellmate, friendly or otherwise.

The state of Pennsylvania had no plans to throw its affluent and well-connected arrestee in with the general prison population. The authorities would see to it that Brody Parrish took his meals in the privacy of his cell and his exercise after his fellow inmates had taken theirs.

That small comfort carried him through a body search and the confiscation of his clothes. But it deserted him when, dressed in a yellow prison uniform, he finally stepped across the threshold of a ten by six windowless room with three concrete walls and a double set of doors.

Once Brody was inside, the guard who'd brought him slammed an iron grate across the entrance. Brody shuddered and looked around. There wasn't much to see. A stainless steel sink and toilet in one corner, a metal rack jutting out from the opposite wall, topped by a thin mattress and bedding.

"Now, don't go trying anything funny, or I'll have to take away your sheets and blanket," the guard said from the other side of the bars. "Mattress ticking can be kind of hard on the skin."

Brody turned and stared at him. He was a tall black man, with the neck and shoulders of a professional linebacker and a huge pock marked face. But his voice had been kind.

"Funny?" Brody repeated.

"Like trying to off yourself." The man shrugged. "It doesn't appear to me that's your style, but it's hard to tell with you virgins."

Brody cringed. "What's your name?"

"Leo," the guard replied.

"How long have you been a prison guard, Leo?"

"Too long."

"Well, you don't have to worry about me offing myself."

The other man's smile seemed almost sad. "That's what they all say." He shook his head. "I'll be back in a few minutes with your grub." With that he dragged a second door, a solid steel contraption with a square of glass at eye level, across the entrance. His dark face peered at Brody through the glass for a moment and then disappeared.

Brody walked over to the bed and sat down, staring into space. So far the day had felt like a nightmare. Any minute he expected to wake up and be back in Riverbend.

But the minutes dragged on and the nightmare didn't end. He took a deep breath to clear his head and immediately gagged. The place reeked of disinfectant. They must hose down the cells with the stuff every time they brought in a new inmate.

True to his word, Leo was back before Brody had time to panic. He handed Brody a tray through an opening in the bars, and then stood back and watched while Brody returned to his cot and proceeded to pick at the pathetic excuse for beef stew in front of him.

Brody glanced up from his metal plate. "I'd have a hard time killing myself with this spoon, Leo. Don't you have other inmates to look after?"

"You checked in a little late. The other tenants already ate. I have time to deliver a little jail house advice if you're inclined to listen."

"I'm not going anywhere, Leo."

"Maybe not tonight. But I know who you are, Mr. Parrish. More important, I know your lawyer. He's a shark. You can lay odds he's driving everyone in the DA's office crazy trying to set up an emergency bail hearing for tomorrow. I figure you'll be out of here sometime late in the afternoon."

Brody eyed the confines of his cell. "I sure as hell hope you're right."

"Listen up, man. O. J. Simpson would have gotten bail if he hadn't taken off in that Bronco. You played it smart when you turned yourself in. So take it easy, tonight, hear? Don't go nuts. By this time tomorrow you'll be waving this place bye-bye."

He collected Brody's tray with its half-eaten contents and reached into his back pocket. "Here, I brought you some reading material. Body Builder and Popular Mechanics." He grinned at Brody as he passed the magazines through the bars. "Not your usual speed I guess, but hey, they'll help pass the time till we turn off the lights at nine o'clock."

Brody thanked him for the magazines and advice.

"Stay cool, you hear?" Leo said as he banged the heavy steel door closed again.

Brody took Leo's advice and dutifully leafed through the magazines a couple of times, but if anyone one had asked he couldn't have repeated a line of what he'd read. When the lights finally went out he shoved them and his shoes under the rack, and crawled between the sheets without taking off the rest of his clothes.

For a short time it was a relief not to have to see his depressing surroundings. But then the darkness and the silence began to close in on him and he started to sweat. His pulse hammered in his ears and he had difficulty breathing.

He felt like he was inside a coffin.

This was what Leo had been warning him about. A panic attack. *Stay cool, man.*

Think, Brody ordered himself. Think about some place else. Any place else. Where had he slept last night? In the Granite Run Police Station. It had been nothing to rave about, but at least there'd been a window high up in one wall. But a cell was a cell. Where had he slept before that?

It had been in Maureen's champagne-colored condo. In her room, on her bed . No. Better to forget about Maureen. That was over and done with. She didn't want to have anything more to do with him.

Where before that? Ah, Christ, it had been in his apartment, her bright hair spread across his pillow. Her breath in his mouth.

And before that, in the little guest room at Riverbend, her face so earnest when she told him about being in Brandywine Park the day he'd "rescued" Jeannie.

God, he missed Maureen. It was amazing how quickly you could get used to someone. How soon she could become your touchstone, your anchor. He'd actually felt he could come through this situation unscathed as long as Maureen were with him.

Of course it had all been a sham. She'd pumped him about Jeannie and Victoria and funneled the information back to Stanton. Not that Brody could really blame her. After all, it was part of her job.

But while it lasted it had been sweet.

Her hair on his pillow. Her breath in his mouth.

The tightness in Brody's chest began to ease. Over or not, thinking about her, remembering, helped.

It had been sweet. So sweet...

*   *   *

"Garden Park is seventy miles south of here, straight down the 405 Freeway," Santa Brava's Police Chief replied in answer to Maureen's question the next morning. "It should take you an hour, maybe an hour and a half, to get there, depending on the traffic. Which, this being Sunday, may be pretty awful."

Maureen smiled. "I'm heading back to Philadelphia on the red-eye tonight, so I have plenty of time. But I better call ahead just to be sure the people I want to see are going to be home. May I use the phone in your office?"

"Ms. Lowe, San Brava owes you more than a telephone call. When I left that message on your machine Friday morning I didn't think there was a chance you would be able to make it out here so soon."

"I'm a policeman's daughter, Chief. If I'd known the details of this case I would have been here before this."

"Well, I'm going to have copies of your sketch run off right away and see to it they're distributed immediately." He reached for Maureen's hand. "It's going to catch our cop killer for us. You'll hear from me personally when we have the bastard in custody."

It took four or five rings before the telephone at the Gance residence was picked up. Maureen heard a child's laughter in the background, and then a gruff male voice came on the line.

"Gance. What can I do for you?"

"Mr. Gance, my name is Maureen Lowe. I'm here in California on business, but I live in Philadelphia and I knew Lisa Adams."

"So?"

Maureen flinched. Maybe this had been a mistake. "Well, I, ah, didn't know her well, but she did stay with me for a few days, and she left behind something I think you and your wife might like to have. Would it be possible for me to bring it by your place this afternoon?"

Chuck Gance sighed heavily. "I dunno. Maybe it would be better if you just tossed...oh, shit, come ahead. Lucy will want it, whatever it is."

Lucy would want it, not we would want it, Maureen mused as she maneuvered her rental car through the heavy traffic, heading south on the 405 Freeway. She glanced out the side window at the trees and foliage lining the road. It was getting harder to tell one state highway from another. The only thing that distinguished them were the trees and plants that grew alongside. In Philadelphia, it was maples and sycamores. In Southern California, it was palm and eucalyptus, along with beds of ivy and African daisies.

But there was very little greenery or flowers growing along Garden Park's West Road. The street consisted of two rows of almost identical pastel colored rectangles topped by dirty white, crushed rock roofs that had seen better days. In front of each house was a square of dry, yellowing grass enclosed by a chain link fence.

When Maureen got out of the car and approached 1420 the first thing that caught her eye was the figure of a tall, rangy looking man in jeans tossing a ball back and forth with two young boys. Every throw was accompanied by peals of laughter, whether or not it was caught.

For a few seconds Maureen stood by the gate, enjoying the scene, until he became aware of her presence and ambled over.

"The boys are having so much fun," she said. "I hate to interrupt."

He released the gate latch and waved her through. "Ah, they don't mind. They're like puppies. The game is just an excuse to run around and yap."

He was about fifty, Maureen decided, a blue collar Jimmy Stewart, with a wide, shy grin. Not what she'd expected after their brief conversation on the telephone.

He squinted, and wiped a hand on his jeans before holding it out to her. "I'm Chuck Gance. You the lady from Philly? Maureen Lowe, is it?"

One of the boys approached timidly, and stuffed the ball into Gance's palm. This time he heaved it across the yard, much to his little charge's delight. When he turned back to her his expression was serious. "Look, Ms. Lowe, about what I said on the phone. I want you to understand. It's not that I didn't care for Lisa. She was a little wild, but not a bad kid. It was just after she moved out, the people she ran with, the ideas she picked up, the things she said. She hurt my wife real bad."

He walked Maureen to the house and pulled open the screen door. "You go on in. Lucy is expecting you. I better stay out here and keep an eye on these mangy little rug rats."

Maureen found herself standing in the center of a tiny living room in which every available surface was covered with clean, neatly folded laundry. A painfully thin woman waited in a doorway across the room. Her gray streaked auburn hair was plaited into a long tidy braid that hung over one shoulder.

"Excuse the mess," Lucy Gance said. "I did the wash this morning and haven't had a chance to put everything away." Her eye fell on the black duffel bag Maureen held by her side. The other woman blinked nervously. "I hope you don't mind talking in the kitchen. I've got soup on the stove."

Maureen followed the woman into the kitchen. "Not at all. It smells wonderful."

"It's chicken." Lucy stopped by a table littered with colored pencils and loose leaf paper, and ran her fingers through the short golden curls of a toddler seated there, busily filling page after page with pretty, childish scrawls.

"This is Robin. Robin doesn't have much to say, but she loves drawing pictures. Don't you honey?" Lucy winked at Maureen and whispered, "She been with us for a couple of weeks. Her mom says she's autistic but I think a little attention is all she needs."

Maureen placed the duffel bag on the floor and sat down next to the little girl. "I like to draw too, Robin. May I?"

The child gave Maureen a solemn look, and after some thought, handed her a pencil. With a few quick strokes Maureen produced a tree, and Robin's face broke into a smile.

By the sink Lucy began washing and chopping carrots. Over her shoulder she stole a glance at the bag by Maureen's feet. "That belonged to Lisa, didn't it?"

Maureen nodded.

"I bet her little photograph album is inside. It meant a lot to her, that album did. It was the only thing besides the clothes on her back that she had with her when she came to us." Lucy carried the carrots over to a pot on the stove and dropped them in. "She was thirteen. We had her for five years. Longer than any of our other foster kids." Mrs. Gance started to sniffle and turned away. "We got pretty attached to her. She was like, you know, our own."

"I'm so sorry," Maureen offered.

Lucy closed her eyes and took a deep breath. "The cop that called us said they were about to arrest someone for murdering her friend, and maybe he killed Lisa too. Some guy from around there. Brody something or other."

"Parrish," Maureen said.

"Yeah. Whatever." Lucy shrugged and shook her head sadly. "A man. Wouldn't you know. All through high school, and even after she got a job and moved out, you could count on Lisa hooking up with the worst kind of weirdoes and losers. Like that jerk, Ray Neville."

For a second Maureen was tempted to defend Brody. He's not a weirdo or loser, she wanted to cry. He wasn't involved with Lisa. He didn't do it. But one look at Lucy Gance's face was enough to silence her. The woman was caught up in her own private agony, and the kindest thing Maureen could do was to just sit quietly and listen while she talked her way through it.

She picked up a wooden spoon and gave the soup a vicious stir. "It was Ray that really messed up her head. She met him at some kind of support group for adults who'd been adopted or raised in foster homes, and the two of them hit it off right away. So she brings him here to supper one night and, out of the blue, he starts spouting off about how foster parents just take in kids for the money. And believe it or not, Lisa pipes up and says she agrees with him."

Lucy's voice broke and she waved the spoon, taking in the cramped, stuffy kitchen. "Anyone can see that Chuck and me are living high off the hog."

The woman sighed and leaned back against the kitchen counter. "But in a way, you had to feel sorry for the guy. Lisa told me he was put out for adoption on the day he was born, and just before she met him he'd tracked down his birth mom and she wouldn't have anything to do with him. Can you believe that? You could tell he was taking it real hard, but for crying out loud, he was forty years old. Like, get over it. Get a life. Right?"

Robin nudged Maureen's hand, and pointed to a drawing of a house she'd just completed. Maureen reached over and added the figure of a little girl standing in the doorway. Robin clapped her hands, and then put a chimney on the roof.

Lucy rambled on about the night Lisa had brought Ray Neville to supper while Maureen divided her attention between entertaining Robin, and listening to the grieving woman's sad monologue.

"Let me tell you, after a couple of hours of Ray's whining Chuck had enough. He threw them both out, and told Lisa not to come back until she dumped Ray."

Just the way Clay ordered me to stop seeing Brody, Maureen thought. With probably the same results.

Suddenly, the older woman dissolved into tears, long, racking sobs that convulsed her thin body and brought Maureen to her feet.

But Lucy swiped a hand over her mouth and waved Maureen back into her chair. "No. No. I'm, okay. It's just—that was the last time we saw her. Chuck thought what he'd done would bring Lisa to her senses. But I knew she wasn't going to send Ray Neville packing. Not with that movie star face of his. You know the type. Kind of hungry looking, with a lot of long black hair."

Almost automatically, as she listened to Lucy Gance's voice, Maureen's pencil began to move across the sheet of loose leaf paper on the table in front of her. It was, after all, a habit. What she did for a living. Draw, while someone else talked, as Lucy was talking now, describing Ray Neville.

So she shouldn't have been surprised when, after a minute or so, she found herself staring down at a face she'd drawn. A familiar face.

Brody's face. Only something was a little out of kilter, blurred, not quite right.

Lisa, would you take another look at this sketch.

It was Brody's beautifully chiseled features. The eyes were a different shape than Brody's, but it was his penetrating gaze. A "movie star" face.

Only the mouth was drastically different.

Only the mouth.

CHAPTER 16

During most of the drive from Garden Park back to her hotel in Los Angeles, Maureen was on automatic pilot. Nothing around her seemed to register. Not the other cars. Not the freeway signs. Not the trees and foliage growing along the side of the road. Not anything.

Her brain was a centrifuge, whirling unexplainable images and unanswerable questions together so rapidly that it was a miracle she was able to drive at all. Victoria Parrish sitting in the living room at Riverbend, so cool, so self-possessed, so regal. The Gresham painting was being cleaned, she'd assured Maureen.

A lie.

There was no question that Victoria was capable of manipulation and bribery. That was the known part of her history, what Brody had called her "past transgressions." But she had always claimed her actions were motivated by her love for him. Was she now prepared to let him suffer the consequences of her lies? The Parrishes had had only one child—Brody. Another lie? Or a half-truth? Had a younger, more vulnerable Victoria, unwed and afraid, given birth to a child here in California and put the baby up for adoption? And years later when that child, then grown, had contacted her, was it possible she'd refused to see him?

Him. A man who, aside from his mouth and minus that slight Native American cast to Brody's features, looked enough like Brody to be, Maureen shuddered and forced herself to lighten up on the gas pedal, to be his brother.

Looked enough like Brody to fool the casual observer. The bartender at the Crocodile Grill. Lisa? Poor dead Lisa?

But, Lisa hadn't been a casual observer. She'd witnessed Jeannie Starbuck's murder. Or claimed she had. But she'd also known this Ray Neville. They'd been a couple, had left California together.

California. Hadn't Bruce Cahill supposedly represented a California based charity? Why hadn't anyone thought to ask what Cahill looked like? Was he tall? Dark-haired? Did he have a mouth as soft and sensual as a woman's?

Maureen shook her head. God, this felt just like the nightmare she had her first night on the case. Faces changing, shifting, people not what they seemed, nothing certain, dependable. All supposition and guesses.

Well, there was one thing she could be sure about. She had to talk to Hayes as soon as possible. But could she make him understand when she was so confused herself? Especially when she'd have to resort to the damn telephone again to get in touch with him. But what choice did she have? As much as she'd like to deliver the news in person it couldn't wait until she got back to Philadelphia tomorrow, and faxes and e-mail were out of the question. She couldn't depend on someone turning on a computer or picking up a fax. Hayes had to be at the other end of the line. No one else.

There was too much at stake to take chances. The information she had was explosive. It might be enough to keep Brody from spending another night behind bars. Enough to keep him from being arraigned in the morning.

It might even be enough to exonerate him completely.

The importance of that thought, and therefore of her getting back to the hotel in one piece, made her sit up straighter and concentrate on the road ahead. A short time later she was relieved to find herself pulling up to the Bonaventure and finally delivering the car into the parking attendant's eager hands.

Once in her room she sat down at the desk and checked the clock beside the telephone. Two-fifteen. Five-fifteen in Philadelphia. If Hayes were going to be able to do anything for Brody today there was no time to lose.

She picked up the phone, dialed Hayes' number and waited impatiently for his service to come on the line.

After what seemed an eternity a nasal female voice answered.

"I know Mr. Wicklow isn't in his office," Maureen said. "But it's urgent that I speak to him immediately. Can you reach him?"

"What is your name, please?"

Maureen identified herself and the voice became a little more animated. "Oh, hi, Ms. Lowe, Mr. Wicklow has been trying to get in touch with you."

Maureen groaned. When she'd left Philadelphia she had wanted to hide, to get as far away from Brody and anybody or anything connected with him as fast she could. "I know. I neglected to leave a forwarding number or address. But none of that matters now. Just put me in touch with Mr. Wicklow."

"I'm sorry. He's unavailable at the moment. He's in conference with Judge Richmond and doesn't want to be disturbed."

Richmond! That was the name of the judge Hayes had been trying to reach to set bail for Brody. And here she was sitting in a hotel room three thousand miles away with information that could be the deciding factor in whether or not bail was granted.

"Can't you activate Mr. Wicklow's pager?" Maureen persisted.

"He's turned it off. This is a very important conference. All I can do is promise to give him your message just as soon as he calls in."

"Make sure he understands it's important. Urgent." Maureen gave the other woman her room number and hung up.

For a few seconds she sat at the desk, staring at the phone, willing it to ring. Then it dawned on her that a call from Hayes would mean that the bail conference was over and a decision already made.

But even without her input, surely Judge Richmond would grant bail. Apart from the murder charge Brody had a clean record, and with his financial resources he could meet any amount imposed. The only things that might stand in his way were fears that he would flee Pennsylvania's jurisdiction. And his mother's bribery attempt.

The bribery attempt was bad news. It was entirely possible that because of it Judge Richmond would deny Brody bail.

Maureen couldn't wait for Hayes to call. She had to get in touch with someone who could reach the judge. But who?

Of course. Paul Marsh. If anyone could interrupt a bail hearing the police chief could. And the judge would listen to him.

This time she dialed the Granite Run Police Station.

"Granite Run Police. Do you have an emergency?"

"I need to speak to Chief Marsh."

"Chief Marsh is unavailable. I'll let you talk to the officer in charge."

"Wait. Who…?"

Maureen heard a familiar voice. "Stanton, here."

Oh, no. Not, Clay! At one time she would have heard her old friend's voice with joy, confident that he would do everything in his power to make things right. He wasn't a saint. She'd known that. He had a temper and a stubborn streak a mile wide, but she would have trusted him with her life. He'd been there for her after her parents' murder. A solid rock to smash her grief and fury against. Maureen closed her eyes and remembered his dear, ruddy face, his gentle concern and affection.

In that moment she made up her mind to take one more chance on him, to wager everything on his innate goodness and sense of fair play.

"Clay, this is Maureen. Is Judge Richmond presiding over a bail conference for Brody?"

"Where are you, Maureen? I've been calling…"

"I'm in California."

"California! What the hell are you doing out there?"

"I'm here on a case. Listen, Clay. There isn't time for me to fill you in on all the particulars. Just get a pen and paper and take down what I'm going to tell you. Then find a way to get the information to Judge Richmond." Maureen took a deep breath, and prayed Clay would come through for her. "This afternoon I went to see Lisa Adams' foster parents and what they told me is so unbelievable, so mind blowing…"

"Maureen, calm down."

Maureen tightened her hold on the receiver. "No, I won't calm down. Lisa was involved with somebody out here who looked enough like Brody to be his double. She met him through an adoption search organization and they left town together a little more than a year ago. Lisa's foster mother described him to me. I drew his picture, and when I showed her the sketch she swore it was a perfect likeness of this…Ray Neville. There are differences. His mouth and something about the eyes, but other than those he was, is, a dead ringer for Brody."

"Adoption search," Stanton muttered under his breath. "Do you have the group's name and number?"

"Yes, I do, but that can wait. Did you hear me, Clay? This guy's mouth was different, but it was the mouth Lisa originally described during my interview with her. The first time she saw the sketch she got all shook up and changed it. She had lost her focus and described the real murderer, her boyfriend, instead of Brody. And there are other things. The PI that Lisa went to for the polygraph? Doesn't his ad in the yellow pages mention something about helping to find natural parents? And wasn't Bruce Cahill supposed to be from California? Couldn't he be...?"

"Maureen, listen to me..."

"No, Clay. Please. Don't try to talk me out of this. I know you despise Brody. I know the rescue wasn't a rescue, but he didn't murder Jeannie Starbuck. You've got to get to the judge."

"Maureen. Slow down. There's been a new development in the case here, too. Victoria Parrish showed up at the station this morning with what sounded like a cock and bull story she'd concocted just to get her son off the hook. According to her, before she met and married Parrish's father she'd lived in, are you ready for this, Los Angeles. She said she had a child out of wedlock, a boy, and gave him up for adoption. Then last year some guy claiming to be her son got in touch with her and..."

"Thank God. Victoria had finally found the courage to tell the truth. She refused to see him," Maureen said.

"Bingo. You gotta understand, after the bribery attempt, no one here took her seriously. Just sorta blew her off. But with what you've just told me, listen, I'll get this stuff to the judge. I swear. I'll leave right now. You've probably assured Parrish his bail. When are you getting back?"

"I have a ticket on the red-eye tonight. It'll put me on the ground in Philadelphia sometime around eight in the morning."

"I'll let Parrish know, Kiddo. If all goes well, maybe you'll find him waiting on your doorstep when you get there."

*   *   *

Unfortunately, Hayes Wicklow wasn't as confident as Leo had been about Brody's chances to make bail.

"I don't want to jerk you around," Wicklow said as he and Brody sat in a Delaware County courtroom, waiting for Judge Richmond to put in an appearance. "It's not a slam dunk. I have a contact in the DA's office. She says they're going for broke on this one."

Brody stared past Wicklow's shoulder, across the room to where the assistant district attorney was seated at the prosecution table. Paul Marsh was at his elbow, whispering into his ear. Aside from them, and Wicklow and Brody, the only others in the courtroom were a dozing bailiff and a female deputy guarding the back door.

Brody recognized the ADA. Carson Geller was his name. They'd gone to the same prep school in Hershey, had crewed together. But now Geller was bent over his notes, he and Marsh both studiously avoiding eye contact with Brody.

Not a good sign.

He groaned. "What's the problem? The money's there. I have roots in the community and no priors."

Wicklow raised an eyebrow. "Well, well, well. What have we here? One night in the hoosegow and you sound like a pro. Fact is, the damn money and those roots you're so proud of are the problem. The media gurus are all over the authorities on how much time elapsed between your known connection to the Starbuck murder and your arrest. The TV people and the tabloids are howling about rich man's justice. They've got the police department and the DA's office running for cover."

Brody slumped in his chair and glared up at the ceiling. Not another night in that cell. Another night, shit. Not getting bail meant weeks, maybe months, waiting for the police to latch onto another suspect or, he swallowed convulsively, for the case against him to come to trial.

"What do they want from me? They've frozen my assets, confiscated my passport. Where the hell do they think I'm going?"

"Look, Brody, get this through your head. The prosecution isn't worried about you slipping through their fingers. You would be under house arrest, wearing an electronic cuff. Their purpose in fighting bail is to stop the news hounds from stirring up the voters any more than they already have by suggesting that if you'd been under lock and key sooner, Lisa Adams might still be alive."

The attorney paused, studied his client's face. "Of course, I'd hoped to counter that assertion by having Maureen here to testify that you were with her when Adams was murdered. But I haven't been able to reach her. I sent an associate over to her condo to check on her whereabouts, but no luck. A neighbor saw her leaving yesterday, with a suitcase. Surmised she was just off on another case, but no one seems to know where. You wouldn't have any idea where, would you?"

Maureen. Gone, Brody thought. An icy emptiness yawned inside him, but he was also relieved. Now he could stop worrying about her. She was safe. Out of reach of the press and whoever it was that had it in for him.

"Forget about Maureen," he said. "She's no longer part of the picture."

"Really?" Wicklow was visibly surprised. Brody braced himself for an argument, but after a moment the lawyer shrugged. "For the time being, I'll concede the point. But if this case ends up in front of a jury we'll discuss it again." He narrowed his eyes. "Has it anything to do with this rescue thing being a hoax?"

Brody cringed. "She told you?"

"No. Stanton. I saw her face when she ran out of the interview room yesterday. You refused to talk about it, so I asked him if he knew what was going on." Wicklow glanced at his watch, then up at the judge's bench. "Richmond is taking his sweet time getting in here. Probably pissed at being dragged back from his fishing trip."

"I thought you said he was on call."

Wicklow snorted. "In Delaware county there's so little crime that being on call is the next best thing to a national holiday." The lawyer's expression grew serious. "Listen, you're about to be on the receiving end of one of my infrequent apologies. What Stanton told me yesterday was pretty sketchy, and I'm sure more than a little one-sided. I know I told you before that your guilt about the rescue was juvenile and irrelevant. But I was wrong. Dead wrong." He put his hand on Brody's arm. "As long as Richmond is going to keep us waiting, why don't you give me your version of what happened."

Brody raked a hand through his hair. "You already know some of it. Jeannie was mad as hell after I dumped her. Came to my office a couple of months ago, demanding money. Said if I didn't give it to her she'd let all of Granite Run know what a setup the rescue had been, and claim I'd been the one responsible."

"Were you?"

"Jesus, no. Jeannie arranged the whole thing. A 'cute meet,' she called it. Claimed it gave a relationship more punch than a plain old introduction."

"Then for Christ sake, why all the angst on your part?"

"Look, I knew the Brandywine like the back of my hand. From the beginning I suspected something wasn't quite kosher about the boat capsizing. But I was seventeen and the praise and adulation that came my way was heady stuff. By the time I had things figured out, the hero nonsense had taken on a life of its' own. I didn't know how to explain it all and not end up looking like a jerk, so I just took the easy way out and let everything slide."

Wicklow nodded. "Understandable. So, after a while the whole incident was forgotten until…?"

Brody grimaced. "I didn't forget. All these years, I've felt like a phony, wondering if I were helping people just to keep up the facade.

Enduring the smirk on Stanton's face whenever we met. When Jeannie showed up, with her threats and demands, I just decided…shove it. I'd had enough. But when I told Victoria, the shit really hit the fan. She went crazy. Said we'd be the laughing stock of Granite Run. Begged me to reconsider, to pay Jeannie. But I told her no dice. I'd made up my mind." Brody dropped his head into his hands. "The next day Victoria had a stroke."

"The next day," Wicklow mused. "Just in time to stop you from telling the world."

Brody looked up, hearing the speculation in the other man's voice. "If you're suggesting she faked the stoke, you're way off base. I might not put it past her, but Dr. Haslip is a straight shooter."

"All right. So the stoke was on the up and up, but you have to admit your mother is a tricky customer. I assume you're not privy to her latest."

Brody shook his head. He knew he wasn't going to like what he was about to hear. God, when would Victoria learn? Hadn't trying to bribe Lisa Adams with the proceeds from the sale of the Gresham painting done enough damage?

"What would be your reaction," Wicklow continued, "if I told you that this morning your mother was buttonholing anyone who would listen and telling them you have a half-brother, a son she gave up for adoption before she married your father, and that he might be responsible for the murders?"

Brody sighed. Victoria was losing her touch. At one time her stories had at least been credible. "It's a crock," he said wearily. "Forget it."

"You sure? Because if there's even a chance she's telling the truth, I can have a man on it immediately."

"Don't waste your time."

Abruptly, a door behind the judge's bench opened and a tall, scowling man wearing a black robe that only partially hid a denim shirt and jeans stepped through.

The dozing bailiff blinked, looked up at the bench and sprang to attention. "The Fifth Circuit Court of Delaware County, Pennsylvania is now in session, Judge Richmond presiding. All rise."

After the flag salute everyone resumed their seats. There was some discreet shuffling of papers while the judge settled himself behind his desk and polished his glasses, every once in awhile glaring down in the direction of the defense table.

"Will you look at the old fart's face," Wicklow muttered, next to

Brody's ear. "Anyone would think he was the one with a hook in his mouth, instead of some poor fish up in Lake Blauvelt. Demanding a hearing this afternoon might not have been the best idea."

Richmond finally appeared ready to proceed. "All right," he said irritably. "Let's get this show on the road. Mr. Geller, what is the Commonwealth asking for?"

Carson Geller almost tripped over his own feet in his haste to stand. "Your honor, the Commonwealth requests that the accused be denied bail in any amount. Tomorrow morning Mr. Parrish is being arraigned on a capital charge. The prosecution understands defense counsel's desire to remove his client from custody before that occurs, but..."

Geller paused in mid-sentence and peered into the back of the courtroom where some sort of commotion had suddenly broken out.

Brody glanced over his shoulder and was surprised to see the deputy with her hands on her hips, engaged in a nose-to-nose confrontation with Clay Stanton.

"What's Stanton doing here," Wicklow hissed. "He ought to know better than to interrupt a hearing this judge is presiding over. Richmond is going to hand him his ass on a silver platter."

Brody shook his head, suddenly resigned to going back to jail. It was going to be hell, but he'd find a way to handle it. He just hoped Leo had aired out the place and laid in a new supply of magazines.

"Naw," Brody groaned. "Stanton is no dope. Ten to one he's got some new, incriminating evidence in his pocket that he can't wait to share. Nothing would please him more than to be the one to nail me."

Just then Stanton caught Brody's eye. Brody found himself doing a double take that would have made a stand-up comedian proud.

Stanton was beaming at him as if they were long lost buddies. Then the old cop did something even more mind-blowing. He flashed Brody a thumbs up signal.

*   *   *

Maureen had been booked to leave Los Angeles at midnight.

But after her conversation with Clay she'd found it impossible to just sit in the hotel room and wait seven hours until the red-eye left. In a matter of minutes she'd packed her bag and taken off for the airport, hoping to get a standby seat on an earlier flight.

Thanks to express car rental return and carry-on luggage, twenty minutes after she raced through the doors at LAX she was on a plane scheduled to land in Philadelphia at midnight, Eastern Standard Time. A full eight hours earlier than she'd told Clay she would arrive.

As the 747 roared down the runway she took a deep breath, settled back into her window seat, and asked herself what the big rush was all about. What did she think she was going to find when she got back?

Brody, waiting for her with outstretched arms?

In the interview room at the Granite Run police station, even before he'd confirmed Clay's suspicions about the rescue, Brody had made it abundantly clear that it was over between them. Did she need to be hit over the head to get the message?

But if Clay described the role she'd played in Brody's release, and suggested she expected him to be at the condo when she returned, Brody would make every effort to be there. He'd feel obligated to see her, to thank her.

Obligated.

Is that what she wanted to be to him? An obligation?

No. She would rather never see him again than to look into his eyes and find, not the passion that had once been there, not the tenderness, but gratitude.

Maureen stared at the Airphone attached to the back of the seat in front of her. The events of the past few days had certainly changed her attitude toward phones. She was now more than ready to admit that they provided services other than convenience, that a phone could be a servant as well as a master. In fact, it could be just the ticket when one wanted to avoid face to face confrontation.

Like now. Call Brody, she told herself. Remind him about what you said that first afternoon at Riverbend. That you felt you owed him and wanted to help him prove his innocence. And now you had. The scales were balanced. Tell him you're getting back earlier than you expected and you're are too tired to see anyone.

Anyone.

She reached for the phone.

At Riverbend Mrs. Hartman answered. Poor Mrs. Parrish was indisposed, the housekeeper said, but Mr. Parrish had called to say he'd been released and was on his way home. Wasn't that wonderful? Would Ms. Lowe like to leave a message?

While jet engines purred outside Maureen delivered the bright, brittle little speech she'd mentally rehearsed.

"Is that all?" Mrs. Hartman asked, her voice curious.

"Oh, yes. Congratulate him for me, Mrs. Hartman. Tell him I said goodbye."

There, she thought as she snapped the receiver back into its niche.

That was easier than she'd expected. Especially since she hadn't had to talk to Brody in person. If she'd heard his voice, even on the phone, she might not have been able to go through with it.

But actually, she was quite proud of the clever way she'd handled things. Brody would be relieved. He'd be cleared of the murder charge and he'd be off the hook. Hadn't she heard him use that phrase when referring to the end of his relationship with Jeannie Starbuck? Off the hook.

With that thought planted firmly in mind she turned toward the window and watched the plane leave the western sunset behind and head into the eastern night.

* * *

He had to laugh. After so many years of frustration and anger, of patience and planning, it was all about to come together. The bitch who'd left him behind, like so much human debris, had been made to dance to his tune.

Now it was time for her to pay the piper. He, not she, would be making the life altering decisions from now on, playing God with other people's lives. Even the name she was so damn proud of was going to be ground into the dust, her strutting whelp put down, or better yet, caged up for the rest of his life.

Either way, he didn't give a damn. The results were what mattered.

He would be all she had left. She would need him at last. And she couldn't play the grande dame with him. Oh, no. He wouldn't put up with any of her airs. He knew her for what she was.

There had only been that one little hitch. Lisa's defection. His dear mother had had a hand in that too. Lisa and Victoria. Two of a kind. Scheming, money-grubbing sluts. But in the end, even that had worked to his advantage. Because now he was free of Lisa. Free of everything that had tied him to the past. Free to finally collect what was owed him. To claim the women who were rightfully his. His mother and Maureen.

Maureen. She was everything the others were not. Everything he deserved. Everything he'd earned. Like Riverbend, his birthright. He could take possession of them now. Nothing and no one stood in his way.

First, Maureen. He couldn't wait any longer.

She had better not disappoint him.

* * *

Maureen tossed her luggage into the Jeep's back seat and wondered why more people didn't take advantage of the airport's long-term parking section. She refused to fuss with super shuttles and taxis. Whenever she got back from one of her frequent out-of-town trips she wanted to be home, in her own car, and in her own place, as quickly as possible. That was one of the reasons the condo's location had been so important to her. It was only twenty minutes from the airport.

She sighed as she paid the attendant and maneuvered down the curving ramp onto Franklin Boulevard. Overnight parking. Super shuttles. Taxis. Any other silly, mundane subjects she could dwell on just to keep from thinking about Brody?

Well, it wasn't working. All during the short drive home she kept reminding herself that she and Brody were finished. That it was over and she didn't expect to find him waiting for her.

But the second she got out of the car and saw him, she knew that all along she'd harbored the secret hope that he couldn't stay away.

And there he was, in the condo's lighted vestibule, leaning against the wall that held the building's mailboxes and intercoms. His back was to her, but that tall, elegant figure in the oversized trench coat couldn't be anyone else.

And she was so instantly, so deliriously happy, that she made up her mind not to play it cool. She slung her purse over her shoulder, dashed across the street and pushed the glass entry door open with both hands.

"Brody," she cried, reaching out, wrapping her arms around his waist, laying her cheek against his back.

He turned in her arms and smiled down at her.

His body, his face.

But not him.

CHAPTER 17

With one arm Ray Neville held Maureen as tenderly as a lover, and with his free hand pressed a knife against her rib cage, just under her left breast.

"Don't make a sound, my sweet," he crooned. "I don't want to hurt you."

Maureen swallowed a sob. This man's voice was nothing like Brody's. It didn't issue from his firm, generous mouth. Ray Neville's lips were fuller, pouty. Almost like a woman's. Almost like a child's.

He touched them to her neck, and the gorge rose in her throat, threatening to choke her.

"Call the elevator," he murmured close to her ear. "We're going upstairs."

When she didn't react immediately he applied more pressure to the knife. But she couldn't move. She was rooted to the spot, unable to look away from what she could see of his face. It was as if she needed to catalog the differences between the two men before her mind would allow her body to function.

On close inspection not only his mouth, but his eyes were different than Brody's. Not only in shape, but in color. They lacked Brody's fire and flash. His intelligence. Ray Neville's irises' were like slate, flat and lifeless. Maureen had to force herself to study them, to gauge whether or not he was bent on murder. If he were, she would have to scream and struggle now, to be willing to be hurt, to be cut, rather than go anywhere with him.

What she read in those eyes didn't appear to be murder, but it sickened her just the same. But if she were right about what he had in mind, once upstairs he might let down his guard. She might be able to lay her hands on a weapon. A lamp. A vase. Something, anything, before he...

No. Don't think about it, Maureen commanded herself. *Focus. Stay alert.*

"Call the elevator," he repeated. He smiled and flicked the knife and Maureen heard the fabric of her blouse tear.

Self-preservation took over. Instinctively, she reached for the number pad beside the elevator door, her fingers punching in the code. At this time of night they didn't have long to wait. The metal door slid open and he dragged her inside. There, he braced his back against the rear wall of the tiny compartment and held her in front of him, nuzzling her neck from behind. His breath was hot, moist. Again, revulsion threatened to overwhelm her.

"I missed you this weekend," he whispered as they rose toward the fifth floor. "Where were you? Off on a case? The demand for your services never lets up, does it?"

When she didn't answer he laughed softly. "You didn't know I'd been watching, did you? Ever since the day after you'd so helpfully invited Lisa into your home and your lovely face first appeared on the television screen. What luck that my brother found that face as irresistible as I did. I was able to keep an eye on you both. These past few days we've been a threesome, you, my brother and I. Every time you were with him, I was close by. Here in front of the condo, at Tio Pepe's, at Riverbend. I was there. I was always there."

He let one hand glide over her breast. "But never this close. And tonight there's only the two of us."

Maureen squeezed her eyes shut, and remembered images played across her closed eyelids. The old man fixing his car in front of the condo while she and Brody argued, the patron who'd stared at her at Tio Pepe's as she'd made her way toward Brody's table, the window-shopper across State Street while she and Brody kissed in the lamplight, the startled sparrows suddenly flying up from the tall grass beside the Brandywine.

But wait. He'd asked where she'd been. He obviously didn't know about Los Angeles. Or Victoria's confession. Or Brody's probable release.

Ray Neville's being here wasn't an act of desperation or panic.

He'd felt free to come because he thought Brody was safely out of the way, in prison. Perhaps she might still be able to reason with him, to talk him out of out of doing what he'd come to do.

His hand drifted lower and she shuddered. Forget reasoning with him. She couldn't waste time on pipe dreams. She needed a weapon.

When the elevator door opened he grabbed her around the waist and pulled her out into the corridor. In tandem, they started down the hall. Please let us run into one of the neighbors, she prayed, mentally cursing the privacy she'd once valued so highly.

Someone. Anyone. Please.

He read her mind. "I know what you're hoping, Maureen. For one of your neighbors to see or hear us. But it's awfully late, and even if we were to wake some nosy old biddy, she'd most likely decide you were returning from an evening on the town with a gentleman friend in tow."

He came to a stop in front of Maureen's door. "Ah, here we are now, and with no interruptions."

How had he known which condo belonged to her?

"Keys," he demanded.

Keys! She plunged her hand into her purse, grasped the keys and pulled them out. With them she might be able to gouge his eyes or throat and then…

But he was too fast for her. He ripped them from her hand, opened the door, and shoved her inside. She stumbled toward the kitchen, but he caught her before she could get there, and dragged her into the living room.

"Did my brother enjoy himself here, Maureen?" he asked. "You see, I was down in the street looking up at your windows the night he came to you after being questioned by the Granite Run police. Such a long way to come for comfort. But I'm sure you were worth it." His pretty mouth leered. "It was easy to visualize what was happening here that night. Because I'd been here myself. Lisa and I had breakfast in this room while you were out running the first morning she stayed with you."

The coffee cups in the sink. Maureen hadn't been mistaken about them. There had been two. So that's how he'd known which condo was hers.

She scanned the room, looking for anything she could reach. In the meantime, she needed to distract him. Talk to him, she ordered herself. Obviously, he wanted to talk. He hadn't shut up since he'd allowed her to see his face down in the vestibule.

PICTURE OF GUILT

She cleared her throat. "I don't know what to call you," she lied. "You haven't told me your name."

"Oh, yes. I want to hear you say my name the way you said his down by the river. Like a sigh. My name is Ray. Say my name, my sweet."

"Ray." Maureen forced her lips to form the word, investing it with as much feeling as she could muster, and then watched him vibrate like a struck piano wire.

"You were the one who sent Lisa to the private investigator, weren't you, Ray?"

"Of course," he crowed. "She was too stupid to have thought of the polygraph herself. I'd already had some dealings with Messenger. A group called 'Find' had used computers to trace my mother to Granite Run. They hired Messenger to take it from there. He had a name and address for "Find" in a matter of days. They passed it on to me, along with a warning that my mother didn't want to see me." Neville shook his head and snickered. "Oh, but I wanted to see her. So I persuaded Lisa to accompany me to Granite Run. She'd been ready to do anything I asked. Anything. What I hadn't foreseen was that my mother and Lisa were two of a kind. Once she and Victoria got their heads together she was as ready as the old lady had been to run off and leave me."

"So you killed her?"

"Yes, but not with this knife. With my bare hands. And believe me, her death was much more satisfying than Jeannie Starbuck's had been. Poor Jeannie was a means to an end. Lisa was being punished. For desertion. Hers, and my mother's."

"But what is Brody being punished for?"

"For being Victoria's son. For taking my place." He eased Maureen down on the couch and with the knife at her throat he shrugged out of his coat. "For being a blind, self-absorbed fool. I sat across the desk from him in the library at Riverbend and he didn't have a clue. Never really saw me. A fictitious name, a little chalk brushed into the hair and I was just another client. A nobody. A cipher. More food for his overblown ego. Well, now that he's out of the way I'm going to take what's rightfully mine. His place in my mother's life. His place in yours."

Maureen shrank away from him. It was just as she'd feared. He meant to rape her. Of course, he wouldn't call it that. He was delusional. He'd call it making love. But whatever he called it, she wasn't going to be able to endure it. Not even to save her life. She had

208

to think. To think...

He slipped the flat of the blade under her chin and forced her to look up at him. "Don't be frightened. I'm more patient than my brother. I want more than your body. I want what I saw in your eyes when you were in his arms. Desire. Need. Ask me to make love to you, Maureen. Beg me to. Then you'll no longer be his. You'll be mine. And you'll never leave me, the way Victoria and Lisa did. You'll be faithful to me."

He lowered himself onto the couch and picked up Maureen's hand. "Tell me what you and he did first. That's how we'll begin. Tell me. Did he kiss you?" With the point of the knife Neville toyed with the buttons of Maureen's blouse, his voice soft and whining. "Did he kiss you here? Tell me, quickly. I'm hungry for you. I've waited long enough."

Hungry, Maureen thought wildly. Food! "We had dinner," she stammered.

He blinked. "You what?"

"I prepared a meal for him."

He stared down at her and then suddenly laughed. "Oh, that's perfect. So maternal. So womanly. Yes, that's how we'll start. With you feeding me."

He pulled her to her feet and urged her toward the kitchen. "Make me what you made for him. I couldn't believe my eyes when I saw him waiting for you downstairs the morning after that television piece about you. But I suppose it's only reasonable that brothers might share a taste in women. Perhaps it extends to food as well. I'll watch you cook. Anticipation will make what follows all the more special."

Yes, Maureen thought, come into my kitchen, where there are drawers and cabinets full of potential weapons. Where there are pots and scalding water and...

They both jumped when the intercom sounded. Three quick buzzes, followed by a moment of silence.

Ray dragged Maureen back against his chest. She could feel the edge of the blade pressing into her spine. *Whoever you are, don't go away*, she prayed.

Then came three more buzzes. Close together. Impatient.

Then, nothing.

*   *   *

She wasn't answering the intercom.

Brody left the condo's vestibule, crossed the street to where

Maureen had parked her Jeep and ran his hand over the hood. The damn thing was still warm. He bent and looked through the window. There was a piece of luggage, small enough to carry, in the back seat. Why hadn't she taken it with her?

He glanced over his shoulder at her fifth floor windows. Lights. Dim, but definitely lights.

She was home, and awake. Why the hell didn't she answer?

Why the hell do you think, you dumb bastard. She figures its you, and she doesn't want to see you. How clear does she have to make it? You're not the hero she thought you were, so kiss off. Get lost.

When Mrs. Hartman had given him Maureen's message he'd made up his mind to do just what she'd asked. Leave her alone. It was what she wanted, and who could blame her? She'd put everything on the line for him. Stanton's friendship. Her professional reputation. Her personal safety. Herself.

And what had she gotten in return?

Sex, lies and danger.

Not to mention distrust. Ha! Wasn't that a joke? He had distrusted her.

Oh, but he needed her. Needed to fill his hands and mouth with her. Needed to lose himself in her. He was never going to make it through this night without her. It had been bad enough Wednesday, when he'd come here, looking for escape, angry and confused about what was happening to him. Him, Brody Parrish, chief high mucky-muck of Granite Run.

But now he didn't even have his anger to sustain him, and knowing what was actually going on was turning out to be a hell of a lot worse than being confused. Knowing what his mother had told him. What Stanton and Wicklow had told him. He had a brother. A half-brother who hated him enough to want to see him ruined. Enough to kill two women just to bring him down.

Two women dead and Ray Neville was still free. Still out there somewhere.

And Maureen wasn't answering the intercom.

Pulse racing, Brody sprinted over to his Jaguar, tore open the door, grabbed his car phone and called the police.

He engaged in a short, terse conversation with a Philadelphia police dispatcher and then bolted back to the condo vestibule. There, he pulled the key Maureen had given him on the day he was arrested out of his pocket, and punched in the code for the elevator.

At her front door he hesitated momentarily. Did he really suspect that there was someone in there with her? Or was he just using this as an excuse to get past the barriers she'd thrown up between them?

Suddenly, from the other side of the door came the sound of scuffling feet, a crash, and an unmistakable grunt of pain.

Brody's caution evaporated. He shoved the key into the lock and seconds later he was standing in Maureen's doorway peering down the hall at two figures struggling at the entrance to the kitchen.

One was Maureen. The other was, had to be, Ray Neville.

Brody's gaze locked with his half-brother's, and in that instant it seemed that the three of them were frozen in place, caught in a children's game of statues. Brody felt momentarily disoriented, as if he had just turned a corner and come face to face with a fun house mirror.

The door slammed closed behind him, breaking the spell.

Maureen moved first, taking advantage of Neville's surprise, tearing free of his grasp and whirling away from him. He lurched after her, and in the florescent light streaming in from the kitchen, cold steel gleamed in his hand and suddenly a rosette of blood bloomed on Maureen's breast.

Brody went crazy. He hurtled down the hall, past her, and drove his head into Neville's chest, knocking him into the wall and the knife out of his hand. It skidded across the polished hardwood and into the far end of the living room.

Adrenaline and instinct fueled Brody's fury. He held a wheezing Neville by the throat and pounded his fist into the other man's ribs, only stopping when he felt a bone snap under one of his blows. Groaning, Ray sagged toward the floor, wrapping his arms around Brody's legs. The two fell together in a heap.

Caught off balance Brody hit the floor heavily, striking his head on an end table as the two men rolled into the living room. When his brain cleared Ray was straddling him, reaching for his neck. Brody locked his hands around Neville's wrists and the two men thrashed back and forth, neither able to gain an advantage, while the sound of approaching police sirens filled the night.

Suddenly Brody saw Maureen streaking toward the sliding glass door that led out to the balcony. Good girl, he thought, just as Neville brought his knee up between Brody's legs. The pain loosened his hold on the other man and as Brody lay on the floor groaning, Ray jumped up and was after Maureen, catching her by the hair as she tugged the balcony door open.

He spun her against the wall, and the sound she made when she hit had Brody on his feet and moving before she'd crumpled to the floor.

Ray snatched the knife from where it had landed and was waiting for Brody, his eyes blazing. But Brody was beyond caution. This wasn't his half-brother. This wasn't a threat to his life and reputation. This was someone who'd hurt Maureen, and he was going to pay. Once again he rushed Neville, slamming into him with a force that carried both men out onto the balcony.

There, to the accompaniment of police radio static and bullhorns they grappled under the stars. Snarling, grunting, they reeled from one end of the balcony to the other, like a pair of drunken dancers, the knife crushed between them. In the end it was all the years of battling the currents around Riverbend that enabled Brody to shoulder free and shove the other man away.

Brody collapsed against the wrought iron railing, fighting for breath. But Neville still had the knife. With a triumphant cry and an upraised arm, he lunged.

In that instant Brody saw hatred in a face so like his own that he was momentarily stunned. Then, exhausted, expecting any moment to feel the blade slice into his neck, he flung himself sideways, as the momentum of Ray Neville's thrust carried him over the railing and down into the street below.

*   *   *

Maureen pressed her back against the wall and slowly inched her way up, until she was standing, dazed and unsteady, but on her feet.

It had taken every ounce of her strength to get this far, and her head was throbbing, but she had to do something to stop the harsh noise from below, the garish red and blue lights that bounced around the room making her stomach heave and scrambling her thoughts.

The commotion was coming from outside, from the balcony and the street. If it didn't stop soon she was going to be ill.

She lurched in the direction of the door, and then she saw him. Brody, shoulders hunched, standing behind the balcony railing, looking down into the street. She'd been wrong down in the vestibule, but this time she was certain it was Brody. Not the other one. Not Ray Neville.

Neville! Where was he hiding? Where was the knife? Brody had to be careful, had to watch out.

"Brody."

He heard her and turned. She stumbled through the door and reached out to him.

212

"No! Stay back. Don't look," he cried, and pushed her away, off the balcony and back into the condo.

She staggered, but didn't fall. Just stood there, confused and shaking, until he came after her, gathered her into his arms, pressed his lips to the dull ache on the side of her face, touched his fingers to the dark, wet blood staining her clothes.

"I should have taken better care of you," he said fiercely as the police began pounding on the door.

EPILOGUE

Maureen's injuries turned out to be ugly but superficial, requiring little more than a few stitches, some gauze and a couple of aspirin. Upon her release from the hospital emergency room she was asked if she felt up to giving an immediate statement to someone from the District Attorney's office. She did, and both Clay and Paul Marsh made it a point to be present, looking very protective and somewhat uncomfortable in their new roles as allies.

Being the one interviewed instead of the one conducting the interview was a strange experience. What goes around comes around, Maureen thought. She couldn't help wondering if the assistant DA considered her a victim or a witness. Probably a combination of both, she finally decided.

After it was over Clay and Marsh complimented her on how well she'd handled herself. They'd obviously been worried about her having some sort of delayed stress reaction to what she'd been through. But actually, it had been a relief to talk about it. A catharsis.

She'd have to remember that the next time she worked.

It took the rest of a week for Brody to be completely cleared of Jeannie Starbuck's and Lisa Adams' murders. During that time Ray Neville's background was thoroughly checked and his scheme to destroy the Parrishes pieced together to the satisfaction of the authorities.

After all the ghoulish publicity Neville's adoptive parents in California decided not to claim his body. So Victoria Parrish's first born was buried in Granite Run. It occurred to Maureen that that would have pleased Neville no end.

Hayes Wicklow showed up at the condo on the day of the funeral. Together, he and Maureen watched a brief film clip of the service on the Noon News. Brief, because the story was already getting a little long in the tooth. For a while the public had been mesmerized by the soap opera aspects of the case, but interest was beginning to wane. Across the Atlantic another royal scandal brewed, ready to usurp the headlines.

Maureen couldn't tear her eyes from the television screen, but the voice-over commentary that accompanied the film clip was lost on her. All she could focus on was Brody's ravaged face. Even viewed through the cold, distancing medium of television, the sight broke her heart. He and Victoria had been caught by the camera just as they turned away from the gravesight. Maureen was shocked by Mrs. Parrish's appearance. She looked ten years older than the last time Maureen had seen her.

"I thought the burial was private," she said.

"Telephoto lens," Hayes growled. "Some bastard hiding behind a tree."

When the grim images faded they were replaced by coverage of other disasters. Floods in the East. Fires in the West. Tornadoes in between. Hayes picked up the remote and switched off the set. He reached across the sofa cushions and touched Maureen's hand.

She turned and looked at him. "How is Victoria holding up?"

He shrugged. "She's taking it hard, but she's a tough old broad. A survivor if I ever met one. She'll get past it eventually. And even though Brody's moved out of Riverbend, he's being unbelievably attentive. In my opinion, it's more than she deserves considering she waited for him to be arrested before summoning up the courage to tell the truth. If I were Brody..." He peered at Maureen for a moment, sighed and allowed himself a self-deprecating little chuckle. "But then, I'm not Brody, am I?"

"He couldn't have asked for a better lawyer or friend, Hayes."

"Yeah." He raised an eyebrow. "Did you happen to catch my press conference yesterday?" Lately, Hayes had become something of a media darling, acting as Brody's spokesman, telling his story to a rapt audience of television and print reporters, explaining the nuances of the rescue fiasco and all the sordid details of Ray Neville's mad, vengeance-driven plan to bring his mother and half-brother to their knees. And at Maureen's request, downplaying her role in the whole affair.

Maureen smiled. "You hit all the right notes. You did us proud."

He looked pleased. "Well, it doesn't hurt a defense lawyer to get his mug out in front of the public every once in a while. And it was important to Brody that his friends in Granite Run understand he never meant to deceive them. Important to him that you understand."

"I do. Tell him that for me the next time you see him."

Hayes raised an eyebrow. "He hasn't stopped by? Hasn't called?"

"No."

For the rest of their visit he was unusually quiet, but as he was about to leave he took her hand. "Give him time. He'll call, Maureen. He has a lot on his plate right now. But just in case he doesn't, remember I'm on the sidelines, waiting for the damn fool to drop the ball."

Then he kissed her. Tenderly. On the forehead.

The next evening, probably because Hayes had lit a fire under him, Brody telephoned.

It was a few minutes past eight and when Maureen heard his voice she carried the phone over to the couch. Considering what was about to happen she thought it best to sit down.

"Are you all right?" he asked. "I spoke to your doctor and he said you're—"

"Doing fine, Brody. The proverbial flesh wound."

"And the bruises?"

"Fading." At least, those on the side of her face. The bruises on her heart were another matter entirely.

"Didn't some of your furniture get smashed."

Maureen bit her lip. Oh, Brody. Not small talk. Please. "It's been replaced. Everything is as good as new," she said brightly. Just the way it had been a little more than two weeks go, before he'd arrived on the scene. House Beautifully neat. Artistically stark. Empty.

He cleared his throat, and then and there Maureen decided to make it easy for him. Short and sweet. Surgical. Like an amputation.

"Brody, I think it would be best if we didn't see or talk to each other for a while. I know it was my fault as much as yours, but the whole sex thing got a little out of hand. A case of too much, too soon. Of—"

"No," he cut in. "None of it was your fault. I rushed you into things before you were ready. I don't know what I would have done without your help, but I'll never forgive myself for involving you in the first place. For placing you in harm's way."

"Nonsense. You saved my life. We saved each other's lives. We're even, Brody. Quits."

There was a pause. "I suppose you're right. Maybe in a couple of weeks, we can get together. After we've had time to sort out our feelings and think things through. Rationally."

"And after we've seen other people," Maureen added.

Another, longer pause. "Well," he said, "I'll call you."

Maureen switched off the receiver, dropped her head back against the couch cushions, and proceeded to torture herself with memories of his face. Brody Parrish frowning. Brody Parrish smiling. When he let himself, he had a world class grin, but it had been those fleeting, here and then gone smiles of his she'd loved from the beginning.

Here, and then gone.

The knocking on the door started about a quarter of an hour later. It was most likely a neighbor, Maureen thought, but she was more cautious than she'd once been. "Who is it?" she asked.

"Maureen, it's me. Brody."

Of course it was. Pulse pounding, she opened the door. They stood there for a long moment, staring into each other's eyes. Just as they had on the day Maureen had first gone to Riverbend. She finally found her voice. "How did you get...," she began.

"Get up here?" He waved a crumpled piece of paper in front of her face, then returned it to the pocket of his shirt. "How do you think I got up here the other night? You gave me the elevator code the day I was arrested. Remember?"

Remember? She hadn't been able to forget a single second of what had passed between them. "Yes, I do, but what I started to say was, how did you get here so fast?"

He looked sheepish. "I called from the Jaguar. It wasn't that far away." His lips twitched. "Just parked across the street."

Maureen arched an eyebrow. "Then, what took you so long?"

He braced his forearms on either side of the doorjamb and leaned toward her. "I needed time to think about a couple of things. Like that 'seeing other people' bit you tried to slip by me. About what it would feel like to be with another woman. To know you might be with another man."

"And what conclusion did you reach?"

And there it was again. Brody's smile. Brief. Bright. But hesitant.

Not quite as confident as before.

"I concluded, dammit, that I deserve more than a two week trial. I think I'm in love with you, Maureen, but I'm not going to beg. If you don't want this to happen, you better close the door in my face right now."

Reminding her of their first night together was pretty sly, but Maureen did some quick thinking of her own. About her growing appreciation for telephone communication. About the silver silk nightgown that had been draped across the foot of her bed for the past week.

She might just as well admit to herself that Pete Hauser had been right when he'd suggested she'd finally made a place in her life for someone. It would be a shame not to fill it. Especially when the perfect material was so close at hand.

This time he wouldn't have to be sure enough for both of them. This time she welcomed him with open arms.

"Come on in, Brody." she said.

HELEN HADDAD

Helen Haddad was born in New York and graduated from that city's prestigious School of Art and Design. Early in her marriage she and her husband moved to Southern California where she attended California State University at Fullerton and worked for many years in the Los Angeles County Library System before leaving to write full time.

She is a member of Mystery Writers of America, EPIC, the Orange County Chapter of Romance Writers of America and Sisters in Crime. Helen can usually be found, surrounded by her wonderfully supportive family, in her hillside home in La Habra Heights, where she lives, loves, and writes.

Picture of Guilt is her first published novel.

Amber Quill Press, LLC
The Gold Standard In Publishing

Quality Books
In Both Print and Electronic Formats

ACTION/ADVENTURE	SUSPENSE/THRILLER
SCIENCE FICTION	ROMANCE
MAINSTREAM	MYSTERY
PARANORMAL	FANTASY
HISTORICAL	HORROR
YOUNG ADULT	WESTERN

AMBER QUILL PRESS, LLC
http://www.amberquill.com